FAR CRY

A TALBOTT'S COVE NOVEL

KATE CANTERBARY

Editing provided by Julia Ganis of Julia Edits.

Proofreading provided by Marla Esposito of Proofing Style.

Cover design provided by Lori Jackson of Lori Jackson Designs.

Cover Photography by Wander Aguiar.

❀ Created with Vellum

ABOUT FAR CRY

Brooke Markham needs a man. A real good man.

But she's not looking for a keeper. She's too busy kicking ass, running an empire, and caring for her ailing father to spend time with men who want annoying things like relationships and commitment and…conversation.

Brooke knows what she wants and it's not a future with the growly barkeep.

JJ Harniczek needs money. A whole lot of money.

He's determined to launch his distillery, expand his tavern, and put Talbott's Cove on the foodie tourism map. But there's no way he's asking Brooke for a dime. Not before he takes her to bed and definitely not after.

JJ knows where he's headed and the blonde bombshell isn't about to change that.

Not until she changes his entire world.

For angry women.

CHAPTER ONE

BROOKE

*Deferred Revenue: liability arising upon the prepayment
for goods and services yet to be delivered.*

September

I DIDN'T THINK I'd see the day it happened. I didn't think I'd cross this line.

But here I was, standing on my deck in the middle of a weekday, wearing the short kimono robe I'd lifted from a roommate years ago and wondering how my life was reduced to this. My hair was wet, my feet were bare. My thirty-fourth birthday lurked on the other side of today's sunset and I couldn't remember the last time I sat down to eat a meal.

And I'd jackhammered my orgasm right out of existence.

I never would've believed such a thing was possible if I hadn't spent the morning plowing through my toy box only to discover those toys weren't getting me where I needed to go. *Again.* The floor of my bedroom was littered with vibrators, some of them still buzzing away.

I'd hoped a shower would check some boxes on both the hygiene and gratification fronts. I was as clean as any person could be after aiming a steady blast of water at her clit until her hand cramped and her fingers went numb.

Clean and wet and crawling out of my skin.

By my math, it added up.

My best friend was living with her own personal Ken doll, bound to get engaged any day now, and she repeatedly rejected my suggestions of forming a sister-wife arrangement.

My job was a remote game of Battleship that involved shifting mind-blowing sums of money around the globe with the dual purposes of making more money and upstaging every banker boy who'd called me Blondie rather than Brooke.

My father was suffering from frontotemporal dementia and couldn't remember how to use a fork.

My mother was six years gone (icy driveway, lights out) and I couldn't remember the last time I'd spoken to her before she died.

I hadn't had sex—the kind that rearranged organs, made ears ring, and required a recovery protocol—since coming home two years ago to this tiny seaside village that looked like a postcard from coastal Maine and felt like a prison sentence against progress.

And I was trying to get off in my childhood bedroom,

the one still decorated in cloyingly virginal shades of rose pink and mint green.

Even the best vibrators were no match for all that.

It wasn't an issue of taking matters into my own hands. My hands were managing this matter—until I'd desensitized the shit out of my clit. Nothing worked for me anymore.

That wasn't a fair statement. I couldn't say nothing worked when I hadn't tried *everything*. As far as buzzy buddies went, I had one in every shape, size, and horse-power. I was game for fingers, showerheads, and a rainbow of porn—but only the respectful, tasteful, femi-nist stuff.

If I could do it alone in my bedroom of childhood innocence, I'd done it.

With the small exception of good old-fashioned sex with another person.

I wasn't one for abstinence. Aside from my present drought, I hadn't gone more than a few weeks without since I was seventeen or eighteen. If I'd wanted to have sex, there was always a dick available for the catching. And that dick accounted for nearly half of my life.

It was no wonder the mechanical options failed me.

But catching some dick in Talbott's Cove, Maine was fundamentally different than doing it in my true home-town of New York City, an island designed for casual sex. Think about it: young people flocked there with the hopes of making it big, only to discover the real world was boring, cruel, and unfulfilling. Alcohol and drugs—legal and otherwise—were as common as coffee and bagels. Cabs and car services ran nonstop, making late-night visits easy and early morning escapes discreet. You had to put a concerted effort into *not* having sex under those conditions.

The most dangerous consequence of casual sex in the city was running into that person at a bar—worse, a bodega without the cushion of loud music and liquor—and making the snap decision whether to ignore or acknowledge. That was it. An awkward moment. New York City was beautifully efficient in its ability to absorb good and bad and everything in between, and spit out overripened cynicism.

Talbott's Cove offered no such mechanism.

There was no illusion of privacy here. Everything happened out in the open, even that which occurred behind closed doors. Lies festered and secrets didn't keep. Not when your neighbors lived in your back pocket and personal business was subject to public purview.

It wouldn't surprise me to find the demise of my orgasm in this week's edition of the Talbott's Cove newspaper and that was the exact reason I hadn't hoisted my dick-catching net and headed off to the area's man forest.

I didn't need to run into my second grade teacher and the high school softball coach while they discussed my sex life over honey-dipped crullers and coffee tomorrow morning at DiLorenzo's Diner. I didn't need my mother's friends sharing shock and horror at my wanton ways at their next bridge game. There was more than enough on my plate right now, and putting out small town slut-shamey fires wasn't the side dish I was willing to order, even if I didn't know how to experience shame much in the way some people didn't notice their bad breath.

But some things were worth an extra helping of local drama. "Fuck it," I murmured. "I need to find myself a man."

Before I could go hunting, I had to make my way inside, throw on some clothes, and run a comb through my hair. Instead of doing any of those things, I searched my bedroom for the phone I'd abandoned in the pocket of yesterday's shorts. Keeping track of mobile devices wasn't an aptitude of mine. In New York, I'd hired an assistant with the singular responsibility of holding my phone. In Talbott's Cove, I had no such luxury. If it wasn't in my pocket or tucked under the band of my bra, I was hopeless. But I'd vowed to do better following recent events.

Over the summer, one of Dad's home health aides texted me while I was on a video conference call with investors on four continents. She reminded me she had a personal thing and was due to leave early and other details I should've known in advance but didn't. That left me pitching my investors with my phone switched to silent and set facedown while Dad went unsupervised —*for two hours*. Since dementia functioned like a goody bag of jigsaw puzzle thoughts, Dad managed to get out of the house, leave the property, and walk his bathrobed ass two miles down the coastal highway while I closed a deal worth more than the state of Maine's annual operating budget.

Since I'd earned a sweet seven figures that day—and it was obviously the right thing to do—I doubled Dad's staffing and committed to keeping my phone visible at all times. I succeeded on the visibility front for a little while. Last month, I forgot my phone downstairs, and when I went looking for it I found my father using it as a sounding block for his gavel. He remembered all of his fifty-two years on bench but not that he had a daughter. Dementia was fun like that.

He'd cracked the screen to shards, but he had a lot of fun playing courtroom. Since there was no salvaging the device, I taped up the glass and let him keep it. His happiest, most calm moments always involved presiding over his courtroom.

As if those reasons weren't enough to keep me connected, Annette Cortassi, my best friend and this town's only redeeming quality, messaged me throughout the day. Usually between customers at the bookstore she owned in the harborside village. Today was no exception.

Annette: Did you ever watch that Netflix comedy special I told you about? The one where I strained a muscle laughing and couldn't pull a shirt over my head for a week because my side hurt so much?

Annette: I swear, it was worth the pain.

Annette: I'm going to assume by the delay in your response that you're either buying a country or dealing with some shit. Let me know when you're free and/or if I can help.

Annette: I can't do anything with buying countries, but...

Brooke: So long as I'm here, I'm not free.

Annette: Oh, would you shut up?

Brooke: You're more capable than you think. You could run a small country, no problem.

Annette: I'm going to stick to running a small bookstore. That's challenge enough for me.

Brooke: I don't buy countries. That's not what hedge fund management is about.

Annette: You say that, but it doesn't clarify your job to me at all.

Brooke: I oversee the investment and strategy of macro and long/short hedge funds with the objective of minimizing risk and maximizing profits.

Annette: Nope, that doesn't help either.

Brooke: People give me lots of money and I decide where to put that money to turn it into more money, and for my trouble, I keep a lot of that money.

Annette: That's a little better.

Annette: Let's talk about you now, Miss Brooke.

Brooke: We are talking about me. This entire conversation has been about me.

Annette: Any chance you're excited about your birthday weekend?

Brooke: That really depends on whether I have to acknowledge that I'm older.

Annette: You do not.

Annette: Once you hit 30, you don't have to acknowledge each individual year. You're a woman in your 30s and everyone knows better than to ask for specifics.

Brooke: It's not that I have an issue with this year. I just don't like the look of 34. It's obnoxious. I mean, 32 was cute. That was a cute year. Everyone is cool with 32. But 34 is that awkward phase after the early 30s and sliding into the mid 30s. It's not cute anymore. It's a nightly serum regimen and a living will.

Annette: I remember being young and my parents throwing a 40th birthday party for one of my uncles. It was over-the-hill themed. All black. A tombstone cake.

Annette: And here I am, 34 now, wondering what the fuck that was about.

Brooke: I could be wrong, but I think you'd light things on fire if anyone threw you an over-the-hill party, ever. Even if you were 95.

Annette: You're right. I would burn it down.

Brooke: I'd help.

Annette: But I don't mind gaining some pearls of wisdom as I age.

Brooke: Those pearls of wisdom are from me. They have nothing to do with age. It's who you know.

Annette: And aren't I lucky to know you?

Brooke: The best thing about being over 30 is blow jobs.

Annette: I'm going to need you to unbox that one, honey.

Brooke: No blow jobs after 30.

Annette: …okay. I'm trying to follow you, but I'm not sure I am.

Brooke: I haven't given a blow job since I was 29.

Annette: I gather you're pleased with this?

Brooke: Don't pretend you like the feel of fuzzy balls on your chin or having that dick taste in your throat.

Annette: I'll say this. I enjoy reciprocity.

Brooke: Oh my god, stop it.

Annette: Stop what? It's only fair.

Brooke: And what do you do, darling deep throat, with all the jizz? Because that's a riddle I've never solved.

Annette: Are you asking me this literally or…?

Brooke: Swallowing isn't an option. I can't. I won't. That

means I have to duck out of the way before he goes off
like the Bellagio fountains or offer up my skin for the
Jackson Pollock treatment. And you know what happens
after that? On the off chance he's a considerate guy, I get
to wait with a puddle of human fluids on my chest while
he finishes with the convulsions and heavy breathing to
fetch a washcloth. Entire minutes of my life go by while
I'm marinating like tonight's pork loin.

Annette: You're so special.

Brooke: You go right ahead and enjoy your reciprocity.

Annette: I'll ask one more time. Are you ready for your
birthday weekend? Because I have plans, lady. PLANS.

Brooke: If you're asking whether I'm ready to dance like
I'm working hard for the money, then yes.

Brooke: I reserve the right to slap you if there's cake and
singing involved.

Annette: So…that means we won't be going to that place
we like, the one that isn't a karaoke bar but they still have
the equipment and they always let us go to town on
Britney and Christina songs?

Brooke: I did not say that. I don't want anyone singing
AT me. There is a difference.

Annette: Mmhmm and the cake? I was under the impression you required a yellow cake with chocolate buttercream frosting, but it sounds like that's canceled too?

Brooke: I don't mind cake. I just don't want someone to
walk up with a cake and put it in front of me while
everyone stares.

Brooke: That shit is fucking awkward.

Annette: Right, right, right. Let me see if I have this
straight. You want singing, but not at you. You want cake,

but you don't want anyone presenting it to you. Is that correct?

Brooke: Mostly.

Annette: Ah. All right. I'll see what I can do about meeting these specifications, then.

Brooke: You're implying that I'm super high maintenance and I'd like to point out that while it's true, it's also very strange that modern tradition requires people to sit in front of flaming baked goods while others sing.

Annette: Sure, honey. Whatever you want. I'll just hide the cake and leave you to find it alone, without anyone watching or singing.

Brooke: Now you're just being absurd.

Annette: I'm absurd. Sure.

Brooke: I never should've told you my birth date.

Annette: Yes, you should have. You just don't want to be the center of attention in ways you can't control.

Brooke: Well…shit.

Brooke: I don't know how much of Annette Unfucks My Life I can handle today.

Annette: It's what you get. You unfucked my life.

Brooke: Did not!

Annette: I distinctly recall a conversation where you YELLED at me IN PUBLIC about how I am to proceed when there is a cock in my hand. I call that unfucking my life.

Brooke: You needed permission to have sex. I need…a field of lavender and sage, a wheelbarrow of crystals, a shaman, a priest, a psychiatrist, Marie Kondo, Cesar Millan, and Jillian Michaels.

Brooke: And some good dick. You don't even understand

how much dick I need. The wheelbarrow I really need is a wheelbarrow of dicks. It's at crisis levels.

Annette: I understand the sage, lavender, crystals, and dick, but why do you need a dog whisperer? You don't have a dog.

Brooke: Cesar Millan just seems like the kind of guy who takes one look at you and tells you how to solve all your problems. Dog or otherwise.

Annette: And Jillian Michaels?

Brooke: She'd yell at me.

Annette: Isn't her thing yelling at people while they exercise? You don't exercise. At all.

Brooke: Yeah, but I'm sure she'd yell at me about anything I need for the right price.

Annette: And why do you need someone yelling at you?

Brooke: Same reason I need crystals and lavender. My life is a hot mess and I'm irrationally concerned about cakes and singing.

Annette: Mmhmm. Okay. And Marie Kondo?

Brooke: This house is full of stuff. It drives me bananas. For once, I'd like to open a closet and find it empty. One less pile of shit for me to deal with.

Annette: She's going to make you touch all the stuff and decide if it brings you joy.

Brooke: I'd really prefer she make those decisions for me.

Annette: Not how it works.

Brooke: All I want is one full day where I don't have to make the decisions or deal with the problems.

Annette: And you'll have it. Birthday weekend, my darling. No decisions, no problems.

Brooke: Will you be arranging the man meat as well?

Annette: Excuse me, what?

Brooke: That's what I thought.

Annette: What are we talking about?

Brooke: I need to get laid. Like, immediately.

Annette: Brush your hair and go to the Galley. It's apple, pumpkin, and leaf peeping season. I bet there are some tourists in town.

Brooke: The Galley? Really? Isn't that a little too close for comfort?

Annette: Allow me to stress this point one more time—pick up a tourist, not a townie.

Brooke: Yeah yeah I get that. But townies hang out there. Lincoln's ass print is permanently carved into his seat at the bar.

Annette: So what?

Brooke: So…one does not simply initiate a one-night stand with a Greek chorus of locals watching.

Annette: One is more concerned with neighborly gossip than self-care.

Brooke: We're calling hookups self-care now?

Annette: You need to take some time for yourself. You know what they say about oxygen masks.

Brooke: The bag might not inflate, but air is flowing?

Annette: Yours first, everyone else second.

Brooke: You're sure about the Galley?

Annette: Believe me. You'll find someone there.

Brooke: If I don't, can I borrow Jackson?

Annette: I'll share just about anything else with you, but not him.

Brooke: It would make things so much easier…

Annette: I know you think so, yes.

CHAPTER TWO

BROOKE

Derivative: a financial contract whose value is determined by the fluctuations in the value of underlying assets often used as an instrument to hedge risk.

"DON'T EVEN THINK ABOUT IT."

I stopped drumming my fingertips on my lips at the sound of his voice behind me. Rolled my eyes. Thought about throwing an elbow in his direction. "Think about what, exactly?"

Still concealed over my shoulder, he replied, "Whatever the hell you're cooking up, don't do it. Stop cooking. Give it up and get the hell outta my tavern."

I turned my head, but this dim corner of the Galley between the now-empty pay phone nook and restrooms didn't reveal more than JJ Harniczek's silhouette. Dark jeans, dark shirt, dark boots, dark mood. "You won't sell much beer with an attitude like that."

"I don't have the patience for games tonight, Bam Bam."

That goddamn nickname. It was my mother's fault. She was nearly six years gone, but I still blamed her for this shit. She'd been fanatical about initials. If there was a bare inch of fabric, metal, or glass, she wouldn't rest until it got a serving of initials. I could've lived with this fanaticism, but my name was Brooke-Ashley Markham and she had B.A.M. embroidered on my backpack, lunch box, scarves, mittens, socks, sweaters, everything. There was no escaping it, and even in first grade, JJ knew a tease-worthy nickname when he saw one.

I believed in karma and I knew it was real because JJ had been gifted the equally troublesome name of Jedediah Judson Harniczek. The torment flowed both ways. "I'm not playing games, Jed."

"You're at my tavern without your sidekick and you're hidden away back here, watching my customers like a jaguar licking its chops before an ambush. I'd say you're playing something." He stepped into the light, turned to face me. "And I'm not interested in having it tonight."

I gave him the *I'm just a sweet, innocent girl and I don't know what you mean* pout as I blinked up at him. He was tall and solid with a beard that meant business, only an ax short of achieving full lumberjack status. If you liked that sort of thing.

"Annette is home with Jackson and I had a"—I paused, searching for the right word to adequately describe my experience with involuntary edging—"frustrating day, one might say. I just want to have a drink and unwind like everyone else."

He crossed his thick arms. Scowled, blinked. "I seriously doubt that."

"Doubt all you want, but you're making me a drink.
I'm sure you can manage a vodka gimlet with extra lime."
I tipped my chin toward the bar. "I'll be over there.
Thanks in advance, Jed."

I breezed past him and settled on a stool at the far end
of the bar, a prime position. From here, I could scope out
everyone seated around the three-sided bar without being
obvious or drawing attention to myself. If I sat somewhere in the middle, I'd have to lean forward to check out
the people on either side of me and I'd lose a good view
of those seated at tables and in booths. There was no
greater mark of an amateur dick hunter than getting
caught in the process of assessing the territory. Eyeballing
men required perfecting the air of disinterested disaffec-
tion—be bored and ignore everything around you.

As much as I hated to admit it, Annette was right
about the Galley. There were a number of new faces here,
and the locals were busy watching some sportsball game
on the big-screen television suspended from the ceiling. I
could've stripped to my skin and offered lap dances to
anyone interested without snapping the loyalists out of
their sportsball trance.

Come to think of it, that wasn't an awful idea. It was a
quick method of assessing the *responsiveness* of this
crowd.

"One vodka gimlet. Extra lime." JJ plunked a glass in
front of me. He rocked back on his heels and spread his
arms out wide, planting his hands on the edge of the bar
top as if he was doing his best to keep from strangling

me. He was never more than a couple of steps away from second-degree murder. "Drink up and go."

I knew that look well. Our interactions were fitting for people who'd known and teased each other since babyhood, shared one strange—and never spoken of since—kiss and some light groping the night after our high school graduation, and now found ourselves in the same small town we'd vowed to leave behind us forever.

With my gaze locked on JJ, I reached for the napkin dispenser stationed two seats to my left. One by one, I pulled out ten napkins. My collection formed a small paper plateau, a landform that seemed to anger the barkeep as it grew, if his quiet snarls were any indication. Once my supplies were in place, I made a show of mopping up the clear liquid that'd sloshed over the rim, down the glass, and all over my section of the bar. I was dainty about it too, using only the corner of a napkin as I tidied his mess.

And it worked.

"Fucking hell, Brooke, give me that." He gathered the used napkins in one hand, the glass in another. Without breaking his stare, he pitched the napkins into the waste bin and dumped the drink into the sink. "What do you think you're doing?"

I gestured to the empty—but still damp—space before me. "I was attempting to enjoy my gimlet until you ripped it away from me. Honestly, Jed. It was rather rude." He responded with a smirk that only highlighted the splattering of freckles across his face. Some were faint angel kisses, others were as dark as his hair. "May I have another?"

He nodded at the damp, empty space. "I'm short-staffed. I have pressing issues to handle. I don't have time for your games tonight—"

"Get a grip, Jed," I snapped. I drove my hand through my hair and sucked in a breath. "I'm not going to whip the townspeople into a fury and convince them to haul off and kill the beast. This obsession with my games, as you call them, is unhealthy. I take a lot of joy in busting your balls but if my presence in your tavern is truly disruptive to business, please escort me off the premises. Otherwise, I'd like a vodka gimlet, nice and limey, and a couple of moments where you aren't harassing me about my intentions. I realize I don't possess your barkeeping wisdom, but I cannot see how a nice lady enjoying a cocktail could incite the type of mayhem you're suggesting. But go ahead. Explain it to me."

JJ regarded me for a second, the hard gaze of his hazel eyes giving nothing away. At first glance, they appeared brown, but I knew they were hazel. He worked his jaw, rocked back on his heels, dropped his hands to his lean hips. He seemed poised to say something, but instead, he turned and retreated to the opposite end of the bar.

I stared at the strong, broad line of his shoulders. The dark, unruly hair gathered with a band at the nape of his neck. The jeans skimming his taut backside. It made for a pleasant, if not problematic, picture.

"Ah, the pleasures of small town living," I called after him. "I'd pay three times as much for a bartender to chastise me in Manhattan. Then again, the only time a bartender would chastise me in Manhattan was if I asked for a side of ice with my cabernet."

He didn't respond and I was content with forfeit by way of silence. It gave me an opportunity to evaluate my options. There were a handful of fresh faces, but the pickings were slim. Strategy was essential. The Galley was theatre in the round, wide and open for everyone to observe. I couldn't flutter around, visiting every guy with clean fingernails and no wedding ring like a hookup hummingbird. I needed an airtight plan of attack before my ass left this stool because I wasn't taking aim for a second shot.

That left me eyeing a late thirtysomething man who seemed promising on looks alone. No rings, no grubby fingernails, and no one seated beside him. Other out-of-towners were scattered around him, a stool or two separating them. This one was working the "dress shirt with an open collar" angle to his advantage, even if the shirt wasn't appropriately fitted. His hairline was a pair of cul-de-sacs and his brows needed a trim. But his hands were big, wrapping around his pint glass like it was a pixie stick, and that counted for something.

All things considered, my target was remarkably average. In these situations—and my entire life was composed of these situations—I always went for the average guy. The gorgeous ones knew they were hot shit and fucked like they were doing you a favor. While I was in desperate need of that exact type of favor, I wasn't interested in communicating it to anyone but myself.

A few minutes later, JJ set a fresh drink in front of me. He didn't speak, didn't look at me, didn't slow down for more than the delivery. "Thank you," I called to him.

His back to me, he lifted a hand in acknowledgment.

This was how we did it: name-calling, senseless bickering, and low-key ultimatums followed by a cease-fire. He was going to his corner, I was staying in mine, all was well in Talbott's Cove.

I sipped my drink until the ice melted to the point of diluting the liquor, all while JJ pretended to ignore me. It was amusing of him to think I could miss those side-eye glances.

He circled back in my direction, busy organizing and polishing everything behind the bar as he went. When he edged toward me, his focus stayed on his work. I stayed focused on my work too. The work of poaching a man for the night.

Without glancing toward me, JJ asked, "Did you eat? Tonight?"

I swirled my glass, shook my head. "I don't think so."

His brows shot up. "How do you not know?"

"I don't know," I answered. "I don't keep track of these things."

"For fuck's sake, Brooke." Grumbling the whole way, he bent down, reached into a cupboard, and retrieved a small bowl. He set it on the bar and motioned for me to take it. "Eat."

I tipped the bowl toward me. Pretzels. "Thank you, no. I have no idea where this has been and who it's been with and I'm sure you know how people are about restrooms and hand washing and such."

He snatched the bowl away, dumped it in the waste bin, and set a fresh refill in front of me. He drilled his finger on the shiny hardwood surface. "Eat."

With an eye on my slowly balding target, I shook my head. "I don't like pretzels."

Again, he muttered, "For fuck's sake, Brooke."

My guy glanced at his watch and that was my cue. I leaned over the bar top, snatched a cocktail napkin and pen, and scribbled my phone number.

"No fucking way." JJ reached for a dish towel. "I warned you, Brooke. No games."

"Stay out of it, Jedediah," I replied under my breath.

"My bar, my business," he snapped, wrapping the towel around his palm.

"Why can't your business be stocking more than one shiraz? That would be smart business. Interfering with my Thursday evening is not."

I hopped down from my seat and made my way to the opposite end of the bar, my gaze steady on the visitor. I slipped between him and the empty seat to his right. No one looked good climbing up onto a stool, and standing at this angle allowed me a swift exit. It also gave him a clear view of my cleavage, not that there was much to see.

"Hi. I couldn't help but notice you," I said, brushing my palm over his forearm. "Visiting from out of town?"

From the corner of my eye, I saw JJ toss his towel to the floor. He pushed through the storeroom door with force, leaving it to slam shut behind him.

"Yeah, up from Manchester," the tourist replied. "New Hampshire."

"All by yourself?" I cooed. "You must love those autumn leaves. Or is it pumpkins you're after? Maybe apples?"

"Mostly leaves, but I think we're stopping at a

pumpkin patch too." He dipped his head, laughed. "I'm meeting up with my—uh, a group of people. They left for dinner before I arrived, so I have some time on my hands."

JJ didn't last long in the storeroom. He returned with a case of wine and dropped it on the bar with enough force to rattle glasses and draw the attention of everyone seated there.

"Listen," I said, reclaiming the visitor's attention and forcing my lips into a flirty smile-pout. "I think you're really hot and I'd like to get to know you better."

"I'm really—me? Yeah?" he asked. "Okay. Yeah. I'm—"

I pressed my finger to his lips and dropped the napkin on the surface in front of him. Patted it twice. "Shh. Tell me later."

I stepped away from the tourist—and JJ—and sailed out of the bar without a backward glance.

Shot fired.

CHAPTER THREE

JJ

Fungibility: the ability to interchange one asset with another, similar asset.

I STARED at the door for a solid minute.

Staring was safer than running through it, ripping it off its hinges, or throwing bottles of liquor at it. Those were the only options as I saw them.

Motherfucking Brooke Markham.

From behind me, I heard, "You saw that, right? That really happened?"

There were a lot of things I didn't have tonight. Not enough staff to cover the dining room and bar.

Another man said, "If I hadn't seen it with my own two eyes, I wouldn't believe it."

Not enough time to hammer out updated financial projections before meeting with my business partner tomorrow morning.

He asked, "Do you think it's legit? If I text this number, am I gonna find out it's the local pizza place?"

Not enough tolerance for out-of-towners here for an authentic autumn weekend in Maine. Especially the ones who took off their wedding rings while ordering a Moscow mule.

Other man replied, "A certified dime piece was sitting in your lap. Even if it is a pizza place, you're still winning."

And not even an ounce of patience for Brooke Markham and her bullshit.

He said, "I'm gonna text her. Can't pass up an opportunity like this one."

Something inside my head snapped. Whether it was the muscle keeping bad choices from overruling good sense or my tenuous hold on everything I'd tried to keep in check, the seal was broken.

I gave the door one last scowl before turning and snatching the napkin out of that asshole's hand. "Not a chance in hell."

For a second, he had the decency to look guilty. But assholes bounced back quick and this one was no exception. "Does this involve you?"

From the other end of the bar, two of my regulars, Bobbie Lincoln and Rhys Neville, shifted away from the televised baseball game. Their concerned expressions seemed to ask whether I needed assistance. I shook my head. I had this well in hand.

"Yeah, it involves me." *More than you'll ever know.* "Get the fuck out of here."

THE MAIN DOOR banged open five minutes before midnight and I knew it was Brooke before glancing up from the evening's receipts. No one flung a door quite like Ms. Markham.

I knew she'd come back. A masochistic part of me had spent the past four hours craving it. There was no other explanation for me leaving the door unlocked long after my last customer settled up for the night. But this knowledge was more than a basic understanding of her operating system. The air changed when she was around. It was charged, unpredictable, almost dangerous. No, *always* dangerous. There was no trusting this woman.

"You gonna fix those hinges for me?" I gestured toward the threshold with a roll of quarters. "Because I can see from here they're loose from the rough treatment you're giving them."

"Get me a screwdriver." She stomped across the empty tavern, her long blonde hair spilling over her shoulders and anger rising around her like a bank of coastal fog. If I knew anything about Brooke—and fog—I knew I wouldn't be able to see the hand in front of my face real soon. "I'll tighten them right up after you and I have a little talk."

I returned to my receipts. "Sorry, sweetheart, closed for the night."

She slipped onto her usual stool, the one near the end with a sniper's view of the tavern. "Would you care to explain to me what the fuck happened here, Jed?"

"Gonna need you to be more specific, sweetheart."

Brooke paused, laced her fingers together on the bar top. "I came in here earlier."

"That you did." I nodded as I shuffled the cash again. I couldn't even count when she stared at me like that. "Left without paying too."

"Put it on my tab."

"Last I checked, you haven't opened a tab." I shoved everything into a bank bag and finally shifted to face her. A feral smirk pulled at her lips and her brilliant blue eyes sparkled. I'd never seen anything more beautiful—or infuriating—than the wrath she kept simmering beneath the surface.

And it was a goddamn problem. Of course it was. Pissing her off made my damn day, but moments like these, when it was me and Brooke and all that fog rolling around us, made for a different kind of day.

"Then let me open one right now." She drew her narrow shoulders in, lowered her lashes, and peered up at me. I wanted to believe that move was pure and unpracticed, although Brooke got everything she wanted not because she deserved it but because she knew how to demand it. "I think you know I'm good for it."

So fucking dangerous.

I ran my palm over my head, tugged the hair knotted at the base of my skull. "Like I told you earlier, I don't have time for this." Didn't have the time, the mental fortitude, the goddamn strength. "Get to the point or get the hell outta here."

Every ounce of sweet drained from her. In its place was rock salt in the shape of an obnoxiously lovely woman. "What happened with"—she pointed to the empty stool where the stuffed shirt from Manchester had sat—"that one?"

I went in search of something to do—or break. Ice was the only thing I could shatter without creating more work for myself. I pushed back the top on the chill chest, speared the metal scoop inside. "Why the sudden interest in visitors to the Cove?"

I heard her snicker over the tumble of ice cubes. It was a halting breath that twisted into a brittle laugh. That rough, unsatisfied sound tightened my shoulders and locked my jaw. I wished I hadn't heard it because that reaction told me everything I needed to know about her in this moment. For starters, she didn't give a shit about the guy she'd tried to pick up for the night. Not surprisingly. Second, the *who* was far less relevant than the *what*. Finally—and this was the most important one—she was damn close to combusting. The only question was whether she wanted someone to light her up. Not the way that Manchester asshole would've done it, if he'd managed to fumble his way to that point. But really set her on fire. Make her burn—and glow.

"My interest in visitors is none of your business," she answered. "Since you've inserted yourself into my business, I'd like to know what you did with the gentleman I met earlier."

"'Met' is a rather civilized way of describing it, don't you think?" I snapped the chill chest shut, looked around, shrugged. "My tavern isn't your hookup pool."

She cast her gaze from one end of the empty bar to the other. "I wouldn't call it much of a pool."

"Why can't you use Tinder like everyone else? Come

on, sweetheart. Get yourself some apps and get the hell outta here."

"I hate apps," she replied.

"And I hate cilantro, but you don't see me passing on the tacos, do you?"

"No, I mean I *hate* apps," she said, holding up her phone. "I hate them so much that I don't have any." I snatched the device away from her and peered at the screen. "Look. No social media. No news or weather. No food delivery."

"The only delivery around here is DiLorenzo's and it's only when Denny gets tired of washing dishes and needs some walking-around money."

She sliced her hands through the air. "Irrelevant. I didn't have delivery apps when I lived in New York."

I hit her with a glare. "If you really wanted something, you'd download an app for it."

"And that's where you're wrong, Jed. If I really wanted something, I'd go out and get it." She waved her hands. "That's what I was attempting to do earlier."

I set her phone on the bar top. "You have the newest iPhone and you use it for what? Phone calls? Texting Annette?"

She tilted her head, schooling me with an expression that said I should know better than to pick at her spoiled little rich girl status. "Not that I owe you any kind of explanation, but until recently, when my previous phone met with an unlikely end, I had one of the earliest models." She pursed her lips. I looked away to keep from staring at her there. "And yes, Jed, I use it to make phone calls and text my bloodless sister."

I blew out a breath as I reached for a towel. All the glassware was dry, but goddamn, I needed something to keep my hands busy. "You come out with a lot of strange shit, Bam Bam, but that's the strangest."

"It's so great that you have opinions," she mused. "Even better that I don't give a single fuck what you think." She leaned forward, folded her arms on the edge of the bar. "Then again, I can't give a single fuck because I don't have any. Literally. I have no fucks because you cockblocked me."

Why I thought I could carry on this conversation without submitting to her like every other object in her orbit was a mystery to me. Whatever it took to stand here without wanting to fist her platinum hair and bite her bow lips and give her the kind of fuck she'd never forget, I didn't have. And I'd looked. Fuck me, I'd *looked*. I'd spent the past two years searching.

"What d'you want from me, Brooke? An apology? You're not getting one. I kicked the guy out because he annoyed me. When you own the joint, you can do that."

"You kicked him out while also cockblocking me," she replied.

"Not that it'd matter to you, but I'm pretty sure he's married."

"'Not that it'd matter to you,'" she repeated. "Your dick isn't big enough to use that tone of voice with me. Check yourself, Jed."

Nothing about her words was particularly infuriating —no more than the rest of this conversation—but they sent me over the edge nonetheless. "Sweetheart, you don't know the first thing about my dick."

Her hair cascaded over her shoulders as she leaned forward. "Oh, I know more than enough."

I twisted the towel around my fist. "Big talk from a girl trying to pick up tourists."

"Funny how it's only a problem when I do it."

I blinked at her. Dropped the towel. Swallowed down the words I wanted to say to her. Rounded the bar. I closed my hand around Brooke's bicep and tugged her off the stool. "Let's go," I murmured.

"And where, may I ask, are we going?"

I gave her only a clenched jaw in response as I yanked her past the bar and into the dim storeroom. This was happening somewhere dark and private—and it *was* happening. I kicked the door shut behind us and marched her toward a wall of empty kegs until her back met the cool metal.

"Excuse you," she said, glaring at my hold on her arm. "What do you think you're doing with your hand on me?"

"We both know you would've ripped my fucking ear off and kicked my balls into my gut by now if you didn't want my hand on you."

"Oh really?" she scoffed. "So, what? I'm *asking for it*?"

"You're asking for something, sweetheart."

I was right about that. She was asking for something. She was fishing.

And I was taking the bait.

I flicked a glance at her eyes, her lips. I hated how much I wanted to taste her. "Tell me what you're looking for."

Her eyes narrowed and her lip curled up in the way it always did when she was drowning in all the contempt and condescension she kept close. It wasn't meant to be hypnotic, but fuck me if I could convince my cock otherwise. "I don't need to tell you anything."

"Need? No. But you want to, Bam Bam." I shuffled closer to her, my lower body settling against hers. "Go ahead. Tell me what you want."

Her breath caught and that small proof she wasn't nearly as contemptuous as she pretended felt like a victory. But she wasn't letting me enjoy the win. Not even for a second.

"It's nothing you'd be able to manage."

I traced the neckline of her sweater, just barely brushing my fingertips over her pale skin as I went. Not a freckle or tan line to be seen. "Try me."

A beat of silence passed between us before I vaulted over a line I swore I'd never approach, much less cross. Not again. I shouldn't have done it. Shouldn't have dragged her back here to begin with—to this room scented with stale beer, and to the moment where everything between us changed—but I never should've bowed my head and closed my lips around the tender skin below her ear. It was a quick taste that turned into a kiss and then a scrape of my teeth less gentle than I'd intended.

But while I was tasting and kissing and biting her neck, Brooke was statue still. She didn't react, didn't move, didn't even breathe. She was dead silent until, "Do that again."

There it was, the single most important reason for staying far away from that line, and it was spoken with her special blend of entitlement and ice that burned the sense out of me.

I pulled back. "No."

Her lips flattened and her brow arched up. "Again."

"That's not how it works here, sweetheart."

She blinked, tipped her head to the side as if she hadn't heard me. "My universe isn't the one where I take orders, Jed."

"And my universe isn't the one where you get what you want simply because you want it." I kicked her ankles apart and pressed myself into the notch between her legs. Her body shuddered against mine in a violent, lingering jerk. A man who hadn't devoted entire years to observing this woman would've blown the whistle and called the game, but I knew we were just getting started. Brooke, the woman constructed from ice and salt and fire, was only warming up with sighs and shudders like these. "Go ahead. You don't like my rules, you're welcome to walk out of here."

She pouted. She whined. Then, "Again—*please*."

And I damn near died.

I pulled myself back from that free fall and brushed my beard over the curve of her neck. "That's it, that's right," I murmured.

She twisted her wrists out of my grip. I expected her to take that freedom and use it to pop me in the eye, but she dragged her palms down my back and curled her fingers around my belt. She used that leverage to pull me closer. *Fucking closer*.

I rocked my hips into the heat between her legs and dragged my lips up the slender column of her neck. She smelled like soap and flowery shampoo and her skin was softer than I'd imagined. Than I'd remembered. It was irritating as hell. I wanted to hate every second so I could discard this desire and move on with my life.

"If this is all you want, sweetheart, you went to an awful lot of trouble for a little necking."

"No one says necking, Jed. They haven't in fifty-seven years."

"Fifty-seven, huh?" She bobbed her head, humming in agreement. "What would you rather I say?"

"Say your mouth is auditioning for me."

I kissed down the line of her jaw, telling her, "I'm not auditioning for a fucking thing. Tell me what you want or go home."

"Mmhmm. Yes."

She sighed as I mapped her skin with my mouth, tipping her head back to grant me greater access. Now that I'd started, I couldn't stop thrusting against her. Couldn't keep myself from nipping and sucking her neck. Couldn't come to the realization this was a terrible idea. Couldn't. Wouldn't. Her grip on my belt tightened and she moaned like I was creating magic and then—

"Good night, Jed."

She slipped out of my arms and away from the kegs, and she marched her fine ass to the door while I stared after her once again.

There was no moving on. Not from this.

CHAPTER FOUR

BROOKE

Short Selling: the practice of borrowing and selling shares of stock based on expectations of declining value only to then repurchase those shares at a lower price to turn a profit.

"THAT WAS NOT THE PLAN," I said to myself for the fifth time since leaving the Galley. "Not the plan *at all*."

I stamped my foot on the sidewalk outside my father's house, but it didn't help. *Nothing* helped. Wasn't that the story of my life right now? No matter what I did, it wasn't getting better. And if I thought I'd been in rough shape earlier today, my current condition could only be expressed by wailing at the moon.

Shoving my fingers through my hair, I glared at the walkway that led to the door that would take me inside. Back to the place where nothing helped, nothing got better, and nothing ever would. I wasn't ready to go in and face that reality.

"Not yet," I murmured, turning away from the house.

Down the hill sat the village of Talbott's Cove, quiet and dark in the crisp September night. Harbor lights cast a golden glow over the water and surrounding homes and businesses.

There'd been a time when I loved being able to see the entire town and everything happening in it from my father's house. It wasn't until I'd returned home after years away that I realized isolation was the price paid for this vantage point.

I was alone, even with round the clock staff and my father and my best friend never more than a text away. I was so damn lonely and overwhelmed and resentful and —and I didn't want to be any of those things tonight.

I turned back toward the village. And I ran.

As I barreled down the hill toward the village, I didn't allow myself to think this through. If I started thinking now, I'd come up with several strong reasons why I should return home, plug into the Asia-Pacific markets, and forget about the feel of JJ Harniczek's hands on my body. And yet, as my shoes slapped the pavement, I allowed myself a pair of thoughts.

One: Running was awful. Why did anyone do this for sport?

Two: Would JJ be home yet or should I stop at the tavern first?

When I reached the town square, the tavern was dark save for a single light over the door. "All right. Onward," I said to the night air. "The things a girl has to do for some dick."

On days when the dementia wind blew a certain way, my father would sit by the bank of windows facing the village and recount the history of this town as he knew it. He was careful to note the exact years each road was constructed and structures that followed, and the reasons for all of it. JJ lived at the end of a narrow, bungalow-lined street set behind the harbor that was built in the mid-eighteen-hundreds. Better roads were needed around the harbor then, and as the lobstering trade took off more local housing was required.

This was the predominant thought in my head as I run-walked down the sidewalk at twelve thirty in the morning. The approximate age and purpose of this road. I had to mentally box that noise up and hide it in a brain closet when I reached JJ's house because dick and Dad's dementia monologues didn't mix.

I'd nearly caught my breath when I knocked on his door, but the bare chest and scowl he greeted me with stole it all over again.

Goddamn. When did he get all that ink and chest hair and muscle?

He raised his arm, braced it on the doorframe. An octopus wrapped itself around his bicep and over his shoulder, and a little round bird with a long beak lived on his flank. "What the hell do you want?"

I glanced down at his jeans. "Take off your pants."

His brows pinched together. "Come again?"

"I'd love to, but I'm going to need you to drop those

jeans first." I ducked under his arm and stepped into his home. "I trust you have a condom or two."

JJ stayed rooted at the threshold while I explored the living room. Dark blue sofa, white walls, hardwood floors. There was art and photos too, but I didn't stop long enough to take them in.

"Two?" he called. "What gave you the idea I want to have sex with you twice? Or even once?"

I wandered into the dining room and circled the table. It was an old, battered, family-style table, and none of the chairs matched. I kind of loved that. A laptop and stack of file folders sat beside a glass of water.

"Your dick was on my thigh like it was drilling for oil thirty minutes ago," I replied. "I don't think I'm the one overselling here."

He pushed the door shut and flipped the locks, but didn't turn around for a long moment. When he did, he leaned back against the slab, his arms folded over his chest. Making me stare at him while he stood there with his tattoos and chest hair on display was the most outrageous thing he'd ever done to me.

"What are you doing here, Brooke?" His voice was low and rough but free of all the hostility he often aimed at me.

"I'm telling you what I want."

He rolled his eyes up to the ceiling. "And what's that, sweetheart?"

I gestured to his jeans. "Off."

Shifting on bare feet, he brought his hands to his belt. The fabric dipped, highlighting a trail of dark fuzz and muscular grooves. Now, that was truly outrageous. "I'm not playing another game with you."

"No games. No bullshit," I said, blinking away from the belt-to-belly button region. "Just you, me, a condom or two."

"Lose the sweater."

I reached for the hem. "Fine." It sailed through the air, landing in front of his feet. "Your turn."

JJ charged across the room and curled both hands around my waist. "Let's get something straight. You tell me what you want, I tell you what to do. You're not the one issuing orders here."

I glanced between us and grinned at the hard bulge trapped behind his fly. "I'm pretty sure I am." I reached up, traced the lines of the octopus strangling his arm. "Here's what's going to happen, Jed. You're going to take me to a room with a bed. Once we get there, you're going to drop these jeans and I'll do the same. When I'm satisfied with the condom situation, you'll fuck me." I smiled up at him. "I prefer to be on top, so that's how we'll do it."

"Yeah. All right. You'll get what you want, sweetheart." A smirk tugged up his lips. "This time."

I blinked. "Excuse you?"

"This way." He squeezed my waist and nudged me backward. When I didn't move, he said, "I don't have all night and like I said, I'm not playing around with you."

"And I told you this isn't a game." He stared at me, his hazel eyes cool and his expression stony. "It's up to you whether you believe me."

I turned with the intention of marching myself down the hall and making him appreciate all the amazing things these jeans did for my ass, but he wrapped his arm around my waist and pressed his chest to my back within two steps.

"You're a lot of work," he murmured, his lips on my neck. "An awful lot of work."

"And you love it."

"Not how I'd describe it."

JJ reached for the light switch when we stepped into his room, but I batted his hand away. It was as if he'd never done this before. "No. No lights, thank you. We don't need them."

"So much work."

He flipped open my button fly and yanked my jeans and underwear down my hips. "That was also unnecessary," I said, righting my panties. "These will stay."

His fingers traced the underwire of my bra while he kissed my neck just like he had at the tavern. It was rude, the way his lips and teeth pulled at my skin. Just…rude. Like it belonged to him and he was well within his rights to bite me simply because it pleased him.

"I don't know what you're used to, sweetheart, but I'm gonna need these off if you want me to fuck you."

"No, you don't. I'll pull them to the side," I answered. "That's all you need."

He barked out a laugh. "You have no fuckin' idea what I need."

If I tried to explain to someone the lengths and hurdles I was going through to get laid, they wouldn't believe me. They'd insist I was exaggerating because there was no one alive who'd prefer to argue about whatever-the-fuck while my shirt was off and I flat-out demanded sex rather than get his cock out. Apparently, I'd stumbled upon the exception to every rule.

"Then take your fucking pants off and show me." I shoved out of his arms and ripped off my jeans. They landed on the other side of the room, one leg snared on a lamp, but neither of us moved to right them. I climbed to the bed and kneeled in the center, hoping to hell he didn't notice that every inch of me was dotted with goose bumps and I was shaking like a virginal leaf. I couldn't explain either reaction, but I knew I needed him to help me fix it right now. "Come on, Jed. Show me what you need."

He stared at me for a moment that stretched long enough to make me wonder whether I'd completely miscalculated, but then he glanced down at his belt. Mumbling to himself, he loosened the buckle, lowered his zipper. He closed his fists around either side of the open placket, pausing and shaking his head before pushing his clothes to the floor.

I knew good dick when I saw it and that was it. The shaking, the goose bumps, they only intensified.

"On top?" JJ produced a condom from a nightstand drawer and ripped it open. "You're sure about that?"

I didn't respond until he'd rolled the condom down his length. "Very sure."

A noise sounded in his throat, like a husky hiss or a growl. "Brooke."

I couldn't stop staring at his cock. I hadn't looked away since it'd appeared. "Mmhmm?"

"Close your mouth, sweetheart, unless that's where you want me putting this."

I glanced up as he joined me on the bed. "Could you talk less? Your cock looks bigger when you're quiet."

JJ twisted his fingers around the side of my panties and jerked me down into his lap. I landed with his face in my cleavage and his other hand on my ass. He closed his teeth around the side of my breast, bit down hard enough to soak my panties. A moan slipped past my lips and a tremor moved down my spine as he rocked against my core.

"If you wanted a taste of my tits, you could've asked."

Another bite, another growl. "Are you taking this bra off? It tastes like fabric softener."

I braced my hands on his shoulders and straddled his lap. I shook my head. "Can't see why I should."

"How about the fact I've barely touched you and there's a decent chance you came from that alone." He drew his index finger along the leg of my panties, slowing to drag his thumb through the wet. "Push these out of the way or whatever the hell you're doing."

I kept one hand on his shoulder and my gaze on his face while I edged my panties to the side. "I sincerely hope you know how to use that thing."

As he thrust inside me and ripped a gasp from my lips, he met my gaze with a smug grin. I would've told him where to shove that grin, but I was stuffed speechless. There was so much dick inside me, I wasn't certain I could properly inhale. I flattened both hands on his chest to hold myself still while I adjusted to him. It was a sharp, stinging reminder that sex toys weren't the same as the real thing. They just weren't.

"What'd I tell you about closing that mouth, sweetheart?"

At least sex toys didn't have an obnoxious comment for everything.

"If you think your dick is getting anywhere near my mouth, we need to get you medical attention because you're suffering from delusions." I rocked forward and back several times as I tried to find a rhythm that didn't feel like it would end with a broken vagina. "Just be quiet and let me get comfortable. I need a minute. Okay?"

All I'd wanted was to resurrect my orgasm and look what it got me. If I was going to crack my vagina in half, I would've thought it'd happen with one of the vibrators that didn't concern itself with anatomical correctness, not the mouthy barkeep.

"Yeah. Okay." JJ tucked my hair behind my ears and held my face in his hands. "There's no rush, Brooke."

He ran his hands down my spine, moving his fingers in slow circles. It helped. I didn't know how, but it did. As the seconds ticked by, he started rolling his hips in tiny waves that matched the soothing pressure on my back. With each rise and fall, my body relaxed—and tightened.

"That's good, that's good." I dragged my tongue over my lips as I sank all the way down on his cock and moved with him. "Yeah, good, that's—*yes*."

He smiled up at me, nodding. "This is what you want?"

I didn't answer. I was busy finding my way, learning his body. And answering while impaled on someone's rolling-pin cock usually meant showing some vulnerability. I wasn't here for that.

"Brooke." He closed his eyes, turned his head to the side. Murmured and moaned into the pillow. "Fuck, Brooke. What am I allowed to do?"

This would've been better if we didn't talk. I wasn't here for that either. I needed to remind my body what sex was all about, realign my orgasm settings, and get back to my life. I would've been able to do all of that if JJ didn't insist on reminding me it was *his* dick I was riding.

"What is it you want to know, Jed? And what kind of question is that?"

He moved his hands from the small of my back and yanked my ass cheeks apart, forcing himself deeper inside me and ripping a gasp from my lips. This was officially more than I'd bargained for.

"I want to know what I'm allowed to do," he gritted out as he dragged a pair of fingers to my clit. "Am I allowed to touch you here?" With his other hand, he brushed his knuckles down my backside. "What about here? Can I have this?"

I stared down at him, blinking. His jaw was locked and the tendons in his neck pulled taut. Under my hands, his chest and shoulders felt like granite.

He abandoned my ass to cup a breast. "What about here? Can I suck you, pinch you, bite you?"

"You've already bitten me." It wasn't the cleverest thing I'd ever said, but it was the only response I could manage.

He started moving his hips faster. Harder. He held me like he didn't care if I broke. "And you seemed to enjoy it."

"*Enjoy* seems like a strong endorsement," I replied. I

shifted my hands to the mattress, not wanting to rely on him to stay steady. "More like a means to an end."

JJ speared up and stayed buried inside me for a beat. A noise rattled out of me, some kind of gasp or cry. "Is that all you want?" His fingers circled my nipple and clit at the same time, and that cry kept breaking free. "An end?"

"It would be preferable, yes."

"And that's it? That's all you want?"

I rolled my eyes as best I could when stuffed three ways to Sunday and going cross-eyed from the clit-and-nip program. "Yeah, Jed. That's all I want."

He closed his fingers around my nipple, pinched hard. "And you usually get what you want."

A laugh shot out of me. "It's nice to think that, but no." I almost continued, almost added that I hadn't gotten what I wanted in such a long time. But that kind of statement invited questions I wasn't interested in answering. Definitely not while his balls slapped my ass.

"Then get what you need." He punctuated each word with a pinch. "Go ahead, sweetheart. Get it."

I didn't comprehend his command at first, but then he brought his hands to my hips and shuttled my body over him. He wanted me to get what I needed—from him. "Keep doing that," I said, rocking against him. "*Keeeeeep* doing that."

If I'd caught a look at myself in a mirror or window reflection, I was certain I'd hate the visual of him bouncing me on his dick and using me like a fuck doll, but I wasn't looking or caring. I was almost there, *close close close*, and I just needed a little—

"*Fuuuuck*. Brooke. Say something. Anything."

"This would be so much better if you didn't speak." I squeezed my eyes shut and held myself tight as the first bites of pleasure pricked at my cheeks, my lips, my shoulders. "Just shut the fuck up and fuck me."

Thankfully, JJ did exactly that. He hammered into me with no more conversation than the occasional curse or growl. It was quiet and his cock was great and this was what I needed to reclaim my orgasm. I made the completely unnecessary announcement "I'm coming" while my body refused to do anything but bathe in those sensations.

"I know, I know. You're right there," he murmured, his brows drawn tight and his forehead creased. "I can feel it, sweetheart. Keep going."

But there was nowhere to *go*. It popped and fizzed and now, it was over. "Yeah, I don't think that's happening."

Once again, he surged into me, his cock deep enough to nudge my vital organs out of place. This time he stayed there, his grip on my hips tight and his gaze burning my skin. "What do you mean by that, Bam Bam?"

Without giving it much thought, I clenched around him. JJ tossed his head back on a chorus of my name and colorful variations of *Fuck*, and I did it again. That was when it happened. When I tripped his kill switch. He didn't thrash or scream, but he came like a train running a minute behind schedule, all raw power and steam and a flat-out refusal to let me get away with anything.

But I was always getting away with something. Always playing. I couldn't do this unless I played a fuckton of pretend. Right now, I wasn't me and he wasn't

him, and this was acceptable only under those circumstances. Except when he squeezed my waist, threw his
head back, and released a mile-long breath as he pulsed
inside me.

When he finished, I pushed up from his chest. His
hands fell away from my hips and I crawled out of his
lap. "Since this is finished, I should go now," I said. "As
you've mentioned repeatedly, you don't have much time
tonight."

"That's what you wanted?" He eyed me as if he didn't
expect the truth. I wasn't convinced he'd earned the right
to the truth. It wasn't something I shared often.
"That's it?"

I turned in a circle but didn't see my sweater
anywhere. I couldn't remember where I'd left it. "Yeah.
This was good."

He balled the condom in a tissue, shot it into the waste
basket. "Good?"

"That's what I said." And that was honest. It was good
sex. The dick was well above average and the conversation was abysmal, and when factoring in the overall
mechanics, it came out to an overall positive event. There
was an entire corporate belief system about good being
the enemy of great, but that kind of touchy-feely-organi-
zational-behavior bullshit didn't hold much water
with me.

"I don't believe you." He laced his fingers behind his
head and pulled that smug grin again. "I don't think that
was what you wanted and I don't think it was good for
you."

I knelt down to grab one of my shoes from under the

bed. When I stood, I said, "It was fine, but thanks for making this weird in the comments section."

"I'm not making it weird," he replied with a brisk shake of his head.

I gathered my jeans from the lamp and clutched them in my arms. I wasn't going to give him the satisfaction of watching me shimmy into slim-cut jeans while he lay there with his dick lengthening on his belly like a damn periscope. Men were the worst. Thank god I wasn't going to need one again for another two years.

"Then what the hell are you doing, Jed? Because it seems like you're telling me I'm bad in bed and that's strange because I know you enjoyed it just fine. It's also extremely rude, but that's your usual." He swung his legs over the edge of the bed and snagged me around the waist, but I stepped out of his reach. I wasn't doing that again. "Thank you, no. I'm going to find my sweater and go home, and we're never talking about this night ever again."

"Brooke." He pushed off the bed. As much as I wanted to erase these events from memory, the heaviness in his tone rooted me in place. He stopped behind me, his hands settling on my hips. His cock tapped the small of my back. "I'm not telling you you're bad in bed."

"Then what are you telling me?"

He plucked my jeans and shoes from my arms, tossed them to the floor. "You had it your way," he said, his beard scraping my shoulder as he spoke to my skin. "Now, it's my turn."

CHAPTER FIVE

JJ

Elasticity: a measurement of shifts in demand for a product correspondent to price shifts.

IF I WAS GOING to ruin my life, there was no sense in half-assing it.

To be sure, I *was* ruining my life. Even as I kept telling myself this was a one-and-done situation, having sex with Brooke was suicide. I'd never come back from this. Never shake it off. And not because she was a spectacular lay—she was—but because she'd never let me forget how I bent to her will and gave her everything she wanted, even when I knew it was a goddamn mistake.

"Now it's my turn." I dragged my hand up her spine, stopping between her shoulder blades. I stroked her alabaster skin for a second before shoving her facedown onto the bed.

She went with an indignant shriek and, "You better watch yourself, Jed."

I climbed over her and straddled her thighs. Front row seat to the best ass in the state and my complete downfall. "Let me ask you this one more time, Brooke. What am I allowed to do?"

She huffed out the sigh of a woman who'd never been thrown on a bed and didn't want to admit she liked it.

"You're allowed to get the fuck off me," she replied.

I filled my hands with her ass cheeks, kneading and squeezing and separating while Brooke shot her most vicious scowl at me over her shoulder. "For such a mouthy, bratty woman, you're shit at asking for what you want."

"I just asked you to get off me."

I moved my hand between her thighs, but I waited, drawing circles on her leg with my thumb. I waited while her pale, narrow shoulders loosened and a breath whooshed out of her. Waited until she glanced at me from under that long curtain of platinum hair and those pale lashes, and tipped her stubborn chin up in the tiniest unspoken *yes* I'd ever heard.

So, this is how it's going to be.

Finally, I cupped her the way I'd wanted all night. The black panties she insisted on wearing were warm and wet. She pressed the back of her hand to her mouth when I brushed her clit over the fabric. "It's not that hard, sweetheart. You tell me what you want, I give it to you."

"Haven't I told you to shut up? You're the most conversational dick appointment I've ever had," she hissed. "It's a tragedy I don't carry ball gags with me anymore."

I gave her cheeks a harsh squeeze. It took real restraint to keep from tearing off those panties, leaning forward, and licking her. Just to know, once and for all, how Brooke Markham's ass tasted. "Maybe if you answered my fucking questions the first time I asked them, you could get the dick you came for."

"I distinctly recall you telling me you didn't want to have sex with me twice."

"You should take your own advice and shut up." I slipped my fingers under the fabric, inside her. We groaned at the same time. She fisted the bed linens, buried her face in the blankets. Worked damn hard at denying herself as she moved against my hand like she was made for it. "Fucking hell, Brooke. Let me take these goddamn panties off you."

She was panting as she found a rhythm on my fingers. Watching her like this—with my cock hard on the back of her leg and my hand between her thighs and her body writhing on my bed—made it easy to ignore the consequences. The price I'd pay for this.

"Fine," she snapped. "But don't you dare ruin them."

I hooked my free hand around the waistband, edged it down. "How could I ruin your precious underwear?"

"You're approximately two hundred and fifty pounds of lumberjack man," she answered. "I wouldn't put it past you to ruin some fine lingerie."

I couldn't identify anything fine about these panties beyond the delicate script lettering on the waistband reading *Agent Provocateur*. Shifting to my knees, I dragged the overpriced scrap of fabric down her thighs. Once it was free, I chucked it over my shoulder. Fuck her fine lingerie.

Slipping my fingers under the band of her bra, I said, "This too."

"*This*," she muttered, "is hand-sewn lace imported from France. Handle with care."

I flung that French lace clear across the room. I ran my hands up the back of her thighs, now well and truly obsessed with licking this woman. "I'm going to ask you one more time—"

"You've said that at least four times," Brooke interrupted. "Maybe you should save your breath. It's not getting you anywhere."

"Maybe you should answer me."

She folded her arms and rested her head there. She stared in my direction without meeting my eyes. I wasn't positive, but it seemed like she was studying my cock. I had no problem with that, not when her hooded-eye gaze was the most honest thing she could offer.

"Why? Nothing about this needs to be complicated or customized, Jed. It's not like I'm ordering a burrito bowl."

I braced my arms on either side of her, pressed my chest to her back. "Because"—I paused to scoop her hair off her shoulder—"it actually matters to me that you want this."

She lowered her eyes, pursed her lips, stayed silent for a long moment. Then, softly, "I do."

I grabbed her around the waist, jerking her up to her knees. Kept my lips on her back and her shoulders as I slipped my hand between her legs. Without any fancy underwear to slow me down, I was able to touch all of her at once. She jerked and gasped when I traced her clit, her seam, her ass. "You want me to fuck you like this?"

She nodded, hummed. "Yes."

"On your knees?"

She replied with another nod and a high-pitched noise I couldn't decipher. I'd call it a squeak, but this woman didn't squeak. She screeched and screamed and roared, and I wanted to hear all those things from her before the sun came up on this day.

Fisting my shaft, I said, "That wasn't an answer, sweetheart." I dragged the head between her cheeks, through her wet, stopping only to slap her clit. "On your knees, ass in the air, head down?"

It took her a second to find her voice, but when she did, she snapped out an impatient "Yes."

"You're sure about that?" Reaching for the table, I grabbed the other condom and rolled it on. "You know you don't get to call the shots from down there, sweetheart."

"The hell I don't," Brooke replied.

I took hold of her hips and filled her with one thrust. "Go ahead and try."

Jesus Holy Christ, she felt incredible. There was all the usual pussy goodness—hot, wet, tight—but that fire-breathing rage of hers made everything better. I couldn't shake the sense she'd let me fuck her until she couldn't walk right, but then she'd rip one of my kidneys out and keep it as a trophy.

She reached back, grabbed hold of my thigh. "If you don't move in the next zero-point-two seconds, I'm gonna show you what it looks like to call the shots from down here."

I eased out, sucking in a breath as I dragged my length over her folds. "You could do that," I said, staring at the place where her body yielded to mine. "But we both know you didn't come here for that."

Brooke muttered something into the mattress I couldn't understand. She was so damn angry about everything. Most of the time, that poor little rich girl fury clawed at my last nerves, but this was different. I couldn't explain how or why it was different, but I knew this night wasn't like the others. She needed something—or someone—and that need wrapped around the nerves dedicated to this woman in a way that compelled me to give her everything. Even if it meant trashing the life I'd established for myself to meet that need.

She rocked back, claiming the head of my cock. Even that inch of heat was enough to make me dizzy. Enough to start me thinking about the ways I'd take her the next time and the next and all the times after that. And that was only one of the reasons she was ruining my life.

"Is this some kind of art house film where you tell me you're going to fuck me in half and go to a lot of trouble to position me the way you want, but then stare off into space while you wonder where your one true love is tonight?" she asked. "Because that's the way this is unfolding."

I ran my hands over her backside, dug my fingers into her skin, spread her cheeks to get a better look at my cock pushing inside her. I watched as she stretched and opened around me, moving slow to aggravate her and amuse myself. "I'm just making sure you can handle this."

She laughed, causing her muscles to contract around me. For a second, my eyes rolled back in my head. "That's not going to be a problem."

"You sure about that?" I gripped her ass like I meant to mark it, pushed all the way inside her. She responded with a choked cry that shifted into a moan, a hum, and then a hungry, desperate whine. Her hands shifted, scrambling to fist around the blankets. To hold tight. "I don't know, sweetheart. You had a hard time handling me last time and I just lay there, as you requested."

"That's because after high school your dick grew up to be a freak of nature elephantine baseball bat that might actually destroy my uterus. Thanks for warning me about that, by the way."

She shot a withering look at me over her shoulder, but that didn't stop her from working herself on my cock. She was taking what she wanted. Finally. She was gorgeous like this, her face flushed, her hair everywhere. And on her hands and knees for me while I carved fingertip bruises into her ass.

"You're welcome." I brought a hand between her shoulders, pushed her head back down to the mattress. "Hush, now."

"Hush yourself," she yelled into the blankets. "Fuck me like you know how to do it or let me go home to my vibrators."

The mental picture of Brooke spread out on a bed, her knees bent and her hand working between her legs while a battery-powered hum and the sharp spice of her arousal filled the air, was enough to snap my thrusts into an urgent, primal rhythm. "You'd be there right now if that was what you needed, Bam."

I expected a retort, but not the one that came. A high, breathy whimper sounded in the back of her throat and— "I don't know what I need."

I paused, my hand still flat on her back and my cock as deep as she'd take me. I blinked down at her, ran my thumb over the bony ridge of her spine. This was how she did it, how she destroyed me. How I let her.

Leaning down, I licked a trail up her back, along those notches. Rested my forehead there, kissed her once—then again and again. Whispered into her skin, "Then let me show you."

I felt her nodding, felt her cry, "Yes, please," felt her clench around my cock like she never wanted to release me. Then, "For fuck's sake, Jed, *please*."

Once she spoke those words, we stopped having sex. It wasn't about anatomy or friction anymore. This was fucking, fast and frantic, as if we were trying to get away with something we knew was wrong but couldn't help wanting.

She thrashed beneath me, her eyes shut and her mouth open as I hammered into her. The bed creaked, scraped at the floor, pounded against the wall. She cried out; I growled. I flipped her on her back; she wrestled her way into my lap. She swore at me; I swore right back. Sweat clung to my brow, my hair came loose from its knot. We batted away pillows, blankets. The sheets were off, gone. She scratched; I sucked. Nothing was off-limits, and we pushed hard at those boundaries.

We were loud, messy, almost violent. It ended with shouts and roars certain to wake half this town, but I didn't care. I'd wake the whole fucking world to feel Brooke come apart on me again.

Without a doubt, I would. I ruined my life for her and I'd do that again too.

CHAPTER SIX

BROOKE

Break-Even: the level of revenues and expenses at which a project earns zero profit.

THIS WAS A MISTAKE.

The word *mistake* felt inadequate for my current situation. Mistakes were buying bubble bath instead of body wash, or closing a spreadsheet before double-checking it was saved. Mistakes were not running down a hill, through a village, and along a side street at midnight and demanding sex not once but twice from a man who despised me—and doing it on my damn birthday.

But I wasn't prepared to call this a disaster, not even when he locked his arms around my torso and fused his lips to my neck. Knowing Jed, he wasn't cuddling so much as debating whether he wanted to smother me with a pillow or bite my carotid artery open. No, this wasn't a disaster. Those left damages in their wake. The only damages here were the ones to my vagina and I'd invited those.

Not a mistake but not quite a disaster meant this was a problem teetering into crisis territory. I'd breach that threshold if I stayed in this bed—in this man's arms—for more than five minutes. That was the limit, five minutes. Enough time to catch my breath and plan my parting remarks.

"What's wrong?" he asked, his words sleepy. Almost scratchy.

I managed a small shrug in spite of his straitjacket hold on me. "Nothing's wrong."

"No, of course not. Your ass is always tight enough to bounce quarters off it."

"As a matter of fact—"

"Save it, sweetheart. We have argued enough for one night, don't you think?"

Something about that roughly spoken *we* scratched up my spine and sent me scrambling off the bed. "I think this is never happening again," I said as I gathered my things. "And we're never speaking of it either."

JJ propped his head on his hand, watching as I plucked my bra off the curtain rod. "Would you care to explain to me what just happened?"

Stepping into my panties, I said, "This is how it ends, Jed."

He went on lazing in the bed, the sheets gathered at his waist and his head bent as if I was a great curiosity. "Uh huh. Sure, Brooke. If that's what you want."

I gave him my back as I pulled on my bra. "Let me explain a few things to you, Jed."

He barked out a laugh. "No explanations needed. You came here with one thing in mind and you got what you wanted. Now it's over. I got that loud and clear, sweetheart."

I stared at the wall, a bitter smile twisting my lips as his rough, faintly Maine *sweethahht* washed over me. It wasn't meant as an endearment. It wasn't intended to hit me in my hardest, toughest spots and I wasn't supposed to like it.

Whirling around, I said, "Again, we are never speaking of this or repeating these events. We have altogether too much shared past and more than enough shared present. There shall be no hookup routine between us. No future dick appointments."

He ran his knuckles down his jaw, frowned at the mattress. "That's unfortunate. I was really coming around to the idea of you making a reservation for my cock."

A stiff, slightly manic laugh shook my shoulders. "That's funny. Really funny, Jed. But let me explain the facts of this matter to you." I held up my index finger. "One, this town is microscopic. There's no room for secrets here and we both know they don't keep."

"They sure don't." He blinked at me, the kind of intentional, pointed blink that suggested we were talking about different things. "Doesn't matter how hard you try."

"Whatever you're doing, stop." Forgoing all semblance of dignity, I wiggled into my jeans. "Second, I'm not interested in a repeat performance. This was fine and it's over."

"Yeah. Your pussy was adequate at best."

My jeans halfway up my thighs, I stopped to glare at him. "You're an asshole."

"Just following your lead."

Returning to my jeans, I murmured to myself, "I knew I shouldn't do this in my backyard."

"Right, because the entire town is your property."

Not bothering to look away from my button fly, I replied, "Unnecessary."

"Yeah? I'm being unnecessary?" He sat up, leaned against the headboard. The sheets pooled at his hips. "How about you going on a rant about how I'm not allowed any more *dick appointments* with you when I don't recall asking for this one?"

"Oh, so, now I forced you to have sex with me? Really, Jed? After you spent a goddamn hour asking me whether I wanted it, you're the one who didn't?"

His jaw worked as he glared at me. "That's not what I said."

"No, it's not what you said at all. You made a rude little quip about my pussy and then had the good sense to bring up my family owning the entire town." I jammed my feet into my shoes and wished like hell I could find my sweater. "This happened once—"

"Twice," he interrupted.

"—and it's not happening again."

He kicked off the sheets and swung his legs over the side of the bed. Still glaring at me as if he intended to draw blood, he stepped into his jeans and buckled his belt. "Seems like you're having some trouble understanding me, sweetheart. I'm not interested in fucking you again."

"Perfect." I stormed into the hallway and toward the front of the house with JJ right behind me. My sweater lay in the middle of the hardwood floor, a pathetic heap of cashmere and regret. I snatched it up, pulled it over my head. "I expect you'll keep these events private. There's no reason to share this with anyone."

From behind me, he said, "Least of all Annette."

Fuck. "As I stated, there's no reason to share this with anyone."

"Agreed."

He stepped around me, fetching his boots from beside the door. At some point in the past few minutes, he'd donned a shirt. A tiny part of me wished he'd left it off. When he tugged the boots on, I asked, "What the fuck are you doing?"

"A real piece of work," he said, laughing to himself. "I'm walking you the fuck home, Brooke."

I dropped my hands to my hips. "I'd rather you not."

"That's tough shit, sweetheart. It's almost four in the fucking morning. The last thing I need is you getting mowed down by a moose. That would really screw up village traffic and I got a big beer delivery coming in from Harpoon this morning."

"All right, Jed," I said as indulgently as I could manage. "You can keep an eye out for *moose*. You do that."

I flung open the door and stepped into the chilly night air. Early fingers of dawn poked at the horizon. I hugged my arms to my chest as I headed toward home, walking as briskly as I would in Manhattan. People around here didn't understand the sidewalk laws of the city. They favored leisurely strolls in these parts. They'd survive ten minutes in the city.

Behind me, I heard a whistle, a door shutting, and footfalls on the pavement. And also—panting? I glanced over my shoulder and found a dog walking beside Jed. "Where did you get a dog?"

He shoved his hands in his front pockets, shrugged. "She found me."

"Like, right this instant?"

Jed seemed to share a laugh with the dog. I didn't know much about dogs, but she looked like a Labrador or a retriever. One of those big, sturdy dogs who understood commands and herded children when need be.

"About three years ago," he replied. "She showed up behind the tavern."

I stopped to gaze at them as they caught up with me. "You're telling me there was a dog in your house—the whole time?"

"Yeah, Brooke." He touched his hand to my lower back, urging me forward. "Is that a problem?"

"Uh, no," I replied. "I just don't know how I didn't notice a dog."

"Butterscotch conks out around ten o'clock and doesn't wake up until I tell her it's morning. A band of pirates could've stormed my house and she would've slept through every second of it."

I glanced at him as we crossed into the village. "You named your dog Butterscotch?"

"I mean, look at her." He gestured to the dog's golden coat. "Also, she'll steal an ice cream sundae out of your hand if you're not careful."

"I suppose that fits," I conceded. "But I didn't know dogs ate ice cream."

We walked up the hill to my father's house—which sat on a parcel of land that'd been in my family for hundreds of years and covered almost half of Talbott's Cove—in silence. When we reached the entrance, JJ eyed the house and dropped his hand to Butterscotch's head, scratching behind her ears.

I spread my hands out in front of me. "As you can see, no moose."

He snickered. "You're welcome."

"Yes, Jed. Thank you. Your generosity is appreciated."

"Yeah, well..." His voice trailed off as he glanced toward the water. "Good night."

He turned to leave, but I couldn't let him go. Not without killing this with fire. "Jed?"

Stopping, he studied me with a wary smirk. "What is it, Bam Bam?"

"The next time I try to pick someone up at the tavern, you won't interfere." I offered him a sharp grin and marched up the walkway, not waiting for a response.

When I closed the front door behind me, he was still standing on the sidewalk with Butterscotch.

One last shot fired.

CHAPTER SEVEN

JJ

*Reserve: an accounting entry that properly reflects
contingent liabilities.*

BARRY O'CONNOR TURNED in a wide arc, his head
tipped back and his gaze fixed on the exposed beams
overhead.

The beams, the birds' nests, the bursts of sunlight
streaming in through gaps in the roof. The old cider
house presented my business partner with plenty to see.

"You think this will work?" he asked, still staring at the
remains of the roof. "Or are you thinking we knock this
popsicle stand over and start from scratch?"

"I think this will work," I replied, working hard to
keep the impatience out of my tone.

If I'd wanted to start from scratch, I would've shown
him any one of the many parcels of vacant land available
in this town. This distillery project wasn't about building

something new. It was about building on that which already existed.

Barry ambled to the far side of the cider house. He rapped his knuckles on a post, tapped his shoe against the cracked cement floor. "It's gonna need a lot of work," he said. "It might be cheaper to knock it down."

"But that forecloses the possibility of selling on the story," I argued. "No one makes a destination out of a new-construction distillery. That's no different than any number of breweries along the seacoast."

"That's only part of the pitch," he argued back. "Even with new construction, we still have the locally sourced angle, the Prohibition Era bootlegger angle, the charming small town angle. We have enough angles to do without the most expensive one." He frowned at a dark stain on the floor. "Was someone killed here?"

I shoved my hands in my pockets, ignoring the tug of well-used abdominal muscles. I couldn't think about Brooke or the things we did to leave me sore today. Not while I dealt with my part-time pain in the ass business partner. "Ever in the history of the cider house? Probably, yes. That I know of, in recent times? No."

"That's positive," he muttered.

Barry painted himself as a hometown guy, someone who grew up a handful of miles down the coast and cared about seeing this region thrive. These days, he lived in Boston and developed commercial real estate. He talked a big game about investing in Maine-based passion projects intended to grow the local economy, but a solid year after our first meeting and his verbal commitment to this distillery, he hadn't written a single check.

Each time we met, he insisted he needed one more thing before pulling the trigger. More detailed financial projections, preliminary approval from the town council for a liquor license, a site walk-through. It made sense—I was asking for tens of millions of dollars to make this happen—but I was growing tired of the hurry up and wait routine. I couldn't determine whether Barry was a flaky guy or not fully committed. His interest seemed to shift with the lunar cycle and that didn't fill me with much confidence.

"Tasting room," he announced, drawing invisible lines along the west side of the space. "We'd put the tasting room here. Keep it intimate, a little dark. Like a speakeasy. We want a space that evokes that air of secrecy and sin, you know?" He turned toward the ocean, facing east. "Save the sunlight for the restaurant. We can add twenty percent to the price of everything on the menu when we're garnishing with ocean views like these." He pivoted, holding his arms open to the wide space. "And the rest of it, well, that's where you show off racks of distilling barrels. Make the work of a distillery part of its art."

Whether flaky or not fully committed, when Barry was on, he was all the way on. His instincts were solid, and ideas—an on-site display garden to emphasize the locally grown ingredients—strengthened my plans.

"Love it," I agreed. "Let's walk the perimeter." I gestured to the wide doors on the opposite end of the space. "Back when this was a functioning cider house, this is where the wagons came in from the orchards. As you can see, it would make for the perfect patio area. Big enough to host large events like weddings and live music. With the right setup, it could house summertime farmers markets, food truck nights, and festivals. Bring in some potted trees and bushes and it's small enough for cocktail parties or bridal showers."

Barry glanced around, nodding. "The ocean view is worth the price of construction."

I was counting on it. This whole thing was a gamble of unbelievable proportions and every time our meetings ended without an exchange of funds, the stakes increased.

"Why not cider?" he asked.

I frowned at him as we rounded the building. "I'm not sure I follow you."

"This is a cider house." He shook his hands at the structure, as if his point was obvious. I knew where he was going with this, but I wasn't copping to that. He proposed crafting something different every time we met. "We should make cider. The hard cider market is—"

"Declining," I interrupted. "It boomed three years ago and it's on the way down. Beyond that, it's more labor intensive. Gin and vodka are mainstays."

Opening a distillery hadn't crossed my mind until a few years ago, when a tourist insisted on buying all of my house-made gin. I'd never sold my honey-steeped liquor by the bottle before, but this woman wasn't exiting the tavern without it. She offered a deranged amount of money, an amount that made refusing even more deranged. Before leaving, her husband told me it was time to expand beyond fried seafood and beer if someone was willing to drop that kind of cash on a case of gin.

As I didn't enjoy unsolicited advice, I ignored his

suggestion. I went back to tooling around with small-batch liquors in my spare time and convinced myself there was no place for a high-end gin joint in Talbott's Cove. But then the deranged woman's friends showed up. They'd heard about this scenic town and its artisanal gin, and they'd traveled here from Boston to see it for themselves—and buy a case of their own.

That was when I realized it wasn't isolated to opening an upmarket gin joint. These deranged people spent the weekend at the local inn, shopped all over the village, chartered sunset boat cruises around Penobscot Bay. They poured money all over a region reckoning with warmer ocean temperatures and permanent shifts in the fishing industry, with declining employment and rising hopelessness. If they came for gin, others would too.

"Right, right," Barry murmured. "And you're sure we can't get in on the hard seltzer market?"

"As a marquee product, no, we can't get into hard seltzers." How I managed to respond without snapping at him was a mystery. "We could work on adding a specialty seltzer to the menu once we have the right equipment in place."

"Yeah, something seasonal and locally inspired," he replied, snapping his fingers. "It would coincide with the rotating menu."

"We'd need dedicated equipment for seltzer," I added. "It requires testing."

Barry laughed as if developing a carbonated liquor beverage with organic ingredients was a simple task. "You can do that now. Test it out at your tavern. Do some market research."

I didn't respond to that. Instead, I steered Barry toward the northernmost tip of the property which backed up to a thick grove of maple trees. "This land makes for the perfect pollinator garden and apiary. It's the right distance from the primary outdoor spaces so we won't end up with bees buzzing around the clientele, but still close enough to include it in the educational walking tour."

"People fuckin' love bees," he mused. "Can't we do rum with bees?"

"Do *what* with bees?"

I marched away from the intended garden plot and toward the area I'd sketched out for deliveries and parking. The purpose of this meeting was to visit the site and then work through other elements critical to the business plan. We needed to make headway on licensing and zoning, as well as the paperwork necessary for overhauling a historical building. We needed to hire contractors, agree on budgets, and formalize partnership agreements with all the area farmers I'd tapped for this work.

"Rum," he repeated, jogging to catch up with me. "Doesn't Maine have a long, sordid history with the rum trade? Weren't there stories about rum barrels washing up on the shores after pirates and privateers intercepted ships? Capitalizing on a pirate connection would be a better way to leverage local history than the cider house angle."

I stopped at the front side of the building, dropped my hands to my waist and ignored Barry's presence for a second. After walking Brooke home, I'd managed three hours of fitful, furious sleep in which I'd dreamed about marching into the massive estate sitting atop the hill bearing her family's name and throwing her on the first bed I found. Telling her that, as long as she was in my tavern, I intended to interfere as much as I fucking wanted. I woke up with the kind of erection powered by regret and masochism. The kind that couldn't be helped.

That left me standing here, hot despite a brisk snap in the air, exhausted and aching all over. And I still had to put on a good face for the man with the money.

"Not sure about rum, Barry," I answered, exasperated as hell and working my ass off to keep it contained. I ran a hand over my head as I blew out a breath. I needed to chug some water and get a sizeable lunch in my belly if I was going to survive the rest of this day. "I think that was farther south. Cape Cod or Block Island Sound, maybe. I'll check into it, but you should know rum distilling also requires specialized equipment. The more we add, the higher the bill."

He considered this. "And it muddies the message. Are we rum or gin or cider? Who knows? Too confusing. You have to home in on one core competency."

I gave him a thoughtful look as I bit the hell out of my tongue. "Yeah, you're right about that."

Barry shifted to study the side of the building that would greet visitors. He lifted his arms, holding his hands out wide. "Down East Distillery," he announced. "The home of fine artisanal spirits."

I wasn't getting my hopes up, but— "This is the place?"

"This is it," he agreed, clapping his hands together.

"Lots of history and local lore to play with. I love it." He smiled at me, the kind of grin that made me wonder whether he knew exactly how much he'd jerked me around this past year. "Let's do this thing."

RIGHT SMACK in the middle of the lunch rush—before I'd gotten around to eating or drinking much of anything myself—Sheriff Jackson Lau strolled into my tavern. Moseyed up to the bar and gestured for my attention as if I had all the time in the world for him. He kept the peace well enough, but he didn't have to do it with that holier-than-thou, merit-badging Boy Scout routine. Being the next best thing to Captain America had to get boring.

Regardless of my feelings about Lau, I had some trouble with his type. My record was clean and my closets free of skeletons, but I kept my distance from authority figures. More often than not, their power was like a penis. Always taking it out and waving it around, slapping people in the face with it, shoving it down other's throats. The worst of them would shove it right up your ass and then expect you to thank them for their service.

I met his gaze briefly before turning back to the taps. "What brings you in, sheriff?"

He rested an arm on the bar, leaned in close. "I need a moment of your time, Harniczek."

"Never would've guessed," I muttered. "As you can see, my hands are full. Sit a minute, order a sandwich. Then, we'll talk."

He offered a brisk shake of his head that annoyed the

actual fuck out of me. "No can do, Harniczek. I'm on duty and have a tight schedule to keep."

Always by the book with this one. I glared at him as I loaded a tray with freshly poured beers. "Uh huh. Yeah. So, you want avocado on that BLT or no?"

The sheriff mulled this over as he settled onto a stool. "I wouldn't mind some avocado, if it's no trouble." When I shook my head, he continued, "And an iced tea, if you have any. I'm trying to cut back on the soda."

I reached for the pitcher of herbal tea produced by a local grower. They were hooking me up with juniper berries for house-made gin. I was experimenting with some tea-scented vodka too, but I wasn't convinced I could pull that one off in small batches. Wasn't convinced I could make it sound appealing either. "Is that so?"

"Annette brings a lot of sweetness to my life," he said, laughing. "In more ways than one."

"And that's why you're cutting back on the soda." This conversation was four minutes old and already far too long. "Got it." I punched his order into the point of sale system and kicked it up to the front of the queue. "That sandwich will be up in a minute. Mind giving me the general reason for your visit while we wait?"

I set a glass of tea down in front of him and grabbed the next set of tickets waiting for me. I glanced back at the sheriff while I lined up pint glasses under the taps. Waited. Cleared my throat. Waited a bit longer.

"Here's something you don't know," I said, lifting a pint glass in his direction. True to form, he waved me off. "I wasn't offering you a beer, sheriff. I understand you're a principled man and I'm not about to test those principles by pouring you a brew while on duty. Feeding you a sandwich is a big enough challenge. Now, since you're sitting here, I'm gonna teach you something. See this here?"

He followed my finger to the foam at the rim of the pint glass. "The head?"

"The proper term is barm," I said. "'Fill the barm to the brim but make it slim.' That's some bartender wisdom for you."

"I'll put that to good use the next time Annette and Brooke drag me out to trivia night," Lau replied. "It's always nice to have an ace in the hole with those two. They'll run roughshod if I'm not careful."

The mention of Brooke's name had me bobbling the trio of pint glasses pinched between my fingers. The idea of her and running roughshod...well, that was how my boots ended up soaked with beer. "Motherfuck," I hissed. I turned away from the sheriff to wash my hands. "It's brave of you to take on both of them at once. I wouldn't do that without an athletic cup and a case of Sauvignon Blanc."

"They're a package deal," he replied, shrugging. "If I didn't enthusiastically enjoy Brooke's company, Annette wouldn't have the time of day for me."

"And you do? Enthusiastically enjoy Brooke's company?" I added.

The sheriff paused long enough for me to take pleasure in his silence. Brooke wasn't for everyone. No one operated at her speed. Few could handle her. Even fewer understood her. I was positive I didn't.

"Your silence says it all, sheriff."

"No, you have the wrong idea," he insisted. "Brooke is a dear friend to Annette and she never ceases to amaze me with the things she says. But Annette worries about her and that makes me worry." I accepted a plate from one of my servers and set it in front of Lau. "I'm happy to have Brooke join us for trivia if that means fewer worries."

Nodding, I stepped away to revisit the drink orders I'd spilled on myself. It was important to keep the beer flowing, but it was also important to stop myself from asking why Jackson and Annette were concerned about Brooke. I had a few ideas on that matter and I could've compared notes all day, but she wasn't my problem.

Not. My. Problem.

"Why don't we step into your office," Lau suggested.

I glanced at his plate, clean save for some fries and a pickle. "You're as bad as the princess," I murmured. "Next time you come in here hungry, don't dick around with me, sheriff. Order a damn sandwich, you hear me?"

Standing, he counted out enough cash to cover four BLTs and tucked it beside the plate. "An excellent meal as always. Thank you."

I dropped the cash into the servers' tip drawer. I wasn't doing him any favors and he sure as shit wasn't doing me any.

"Make it quick," I said, waving him down the hallway toward my office. The hallway in which I'd found Brooke lurking last night. I needed to open a distillery just to work in a place free from her fingerprints.

I dropped into my desk chair while the sheriff sat across from me. "I'll make this quick," he said.

"Music to my ears," I muttered.

"Nathan Fitzsimmons is scheduled to leave rehab at the end of next month."

"Already?" I barked. The Fitzsimmons kid needed help. Real help. He needed professional people who knew how to help him unwind his addiction and live his life without going back to the pills again. "He's only been there, what—"

"Four months," Lau interrupted. "When he's discharged, it will be five."

"That doesn't seem like enough." I gripped the arm rests. That kid's parents went through hell trying to get him help. I couldn't count the number of times they'd checked him into detox. Couldn't count the number of times the sheriff's deputies were out at the Fitzsimmons house, hauling him away after a fight with his parents turned physical or they'd found him stealing the rug out from underneath them to pay for drugs. But I remembered the last time, when they decided enough was enough. "How does someone learn how to live a new life in only four or five months?"

Lau jerked a shoulder up. "Most opioid dependency programs are less than a month. Twenty-eight days, usually. This one treats both dependency as well as other mental health diagnoses. He was lucky to get a bed in this facility. It probably saved his life. Certainly kept him out of prison."

"That's great but how is he allowed to leave without— I don't know—going to some kind of transitional living or halfway house to help him back into the real world?"

"There are a slew of conditions to his release. He has

court-ordered drug tests every week for a year as well as counseling, sobriety support groups, and regular meetings with his probation officer." Lau glanced down at the floor. "His PO believes he'll succeed, but he won't be able to do it alone."

Fuck me. Just...fuck me.

"The reason for your visit is revealed." I waited for Lau to deny it, but he only sat back with his hands folded in his lap. "I don't know how you'd like for me to help this kid. In case you haven't noticed, I run a tavern. It's not a good old-fashioned tavern because we don't put up travelers for the night, but we hold with the tradition of serving beer, wine, and spirits alongside food. That is no place for a young man making a run at sober living and I'm the farthest thing you'll find from a social worker."

"Think about it," the sheriff prompted. "Do you think he has any chance of succeeding if he goes back home to his parents' house? That's his only option right now and we both know that won't work." He ran his hand through his hair, huffed out a rueful laugh. "Trust me, I've already tried that angle and it's a nonstarter. I've also approached a number of other residents. I'm asking you a favor, Harniczek."

"What are you suggesting, sheriff? I'm not in the market for a roommate."

"Maybe not, but you do have that vacant apartment on the back side of this building," he answered. "If my understanding of your zoning and property tax filings is accurate, that is."

That goddamn power penis. I did not need this shit today. Not on a couple of hours sleep and not with my muscles humming with every move and a woman in need of some roughshod no more than a five-minute walk from this very spot. "You want me to put this kid up in an apartment above a tavern? You think that will support his recovery?"

"According to the probation officer, Nathan's dependency is isolated to opioids. He's never been a drinker and doesn't see alcohol as a coping mechanism."

"How convenient." I leaned back in my chair, blew out a ragged breath. I hated this. I hated the sheriff coming into my business and asking for help. More than all that, I hated knowing the kid was in a bind and no one was willing to stand up. "What about your girlfriend's old apartment? She's not living there anymore."

He ran a hand along his jaw, his brows drawing together as he nodded. "That was one of my first considerations," he said. "But five other people have been asking after that apartment and she doesn't own the building. It's not her call."

"Now, that's convenient."

"I'm also hoping you're in need of a dishwasher," Lau continued. "Nathan needs a job and one that won't get hung up on his prior convictions."

I touched a hand to my chest. "And you think I'm that employer? You also think I'm willing to hire and house a kid who has spent the past five or six years of his life hooked on drugs and hope he doesn't replace that addiction with booze? You've gotta be out of your damn mind, Lau."

"You could set him straight, Harniczek." The sheriff had the balls to give me one of those *I believe in you* nods reserved for the soccer coaches of small children. "He's pissing in a cup weekly, so we'll know if he's drinking. I'm sure you'd also notice any variations in your stock. If it turns out this situation is too complex for him, we'll find something else. But I've given this a lot of thought and I think it could work. You run a tight ship and you don't let anything slip through the cracks. You won't let him fuck up or fall off the deep end. You could give him the reset he needs."

"If I agree to this, will you stop waltzing in here and taking up my time during the busiest parts of the day?"

"I'll do my best." He shrugged. "Would it help if I brought some homemade muffins or brownies? I'm sure Annette would be happy to make something special for you."

I cocked my head to the side. "Could you fucking not?"

"What? Her muffins are amazing."

"I'm not discussing her muffins with you."

"All right." He held up his hands, let them fall. "No muffins."

"This better not blow up on me, Lau. My hands are full right now and I don't have time to big brother all over a recovering twentysomething. Like I said, I'm no social worker. If this starts going south, I'm expecting you to relocate this kid to your couch if need be."

"Let's hope it doesn't come to that," he replied.

"That's not an agreement, Lau."

He chuckled, but I wasn't sharing his amusement. "I can't guarantee my couch, but I can promise I'll step in if there's an issue."

"I suppose that's all I can ask," I said with a sigh.

The sheriff pushed to his feet. "Thanks for the talk. I'll follow up when I have more information from Nathan's probation officer. I'm on a tight schedule today, so I have to cut this short. I'm taking Annette and Brooke down to Portland for the weekend."

Despite knowing better, I asked, "What's the occasion?"

A wide grin split his face. "Didn't you know? It's Brooke's birthday today. The girls will be celebrating with spas and shopping and more club hopping than I'd prefer."

That information landed in my gut like a harsh blow. "Best of luck to you," I managed. "You'll have your hands full with those two."

"I will," he agreed, laughing. "But they'll sleep the whole drive back home on Sunday. It will be my only moment of peace all weekend." He moved toward the door, held up his hand in a crisp wave. "Thank you for taking the time to talk."

"Next time you need to sort out some community problems, could you do it around three or four in the afternoon? I'd appreciate it."

"I'll work on that as well." Lau pulled the door open. "Have a good weekend, Harniczek."

The door whispered shut, but I didn't return to the bar. I needed some time to think about Brooke-Ashley Markham and all the ways in which she'd ruined my life. On her birthday.

CHAPTER EIGHT

BROOKE

Coverage Ratio: a formula used to express the adequacy of earnings-based cash flow relative to meeting debt obligations.

Annette: Well?

Brooke: Well what?

Annette: It's been more than a few hours without an update from you. That's uncommon.

Brooke: ...and?

Annette: And I require an update!

Brooke: Since I'm responding to you now, it's clear I'm still alive.

Annette: Oh my god, you're a pain in the ass sometimes.

Brooke: Sometimes feels like an underestimation.

Annette: Did. You. Have. The. Sex.

Brooke: Yeah.

Annette: That's it? Just "yeah"?

Brooke: I'm not sure what you're looking for, my love. I didn't keep the condom or snatch some of his pubes for the scrapbook.

Annette: You found someone at the Galley?

Brooke: Oh yeah.

Annette: I told you!

Brooke: You have no idea how right you were about the Galley...

Annette: I notice you're not thanking me for that advice.

Brooke: I'll pick up the tab the next time we go out for lunch. That's your thanks.

Annette: You always pick up the tab. You slapped me the last time I tried to grab the check. If you recall, I had a welt on my arm all afternoon because you make more money than everyone in this entire town combined.

Brooke: Yeah, sorry again about that. I'd hoped Jackson would slam me up against his patrol car while cuffing me.

Annette: Is it a law enforcement fetish? Is that it? Because Jackson has a handful of deputies. I'm sure we could find one to slam you up against cars, walls, couches. Refrigerators are also great options.

Brooke: Considering I've known all those guys since they were toddlers, I'm going to pass. There's something about knowing Heath Carroll used to stuff his pockets with food from the cafeteria trash barrels that turns me off from a sexual relationship.

Annette: That was kindergarten.

Brooke: That's the problem with small town living.

Annette: Okay. Back to the sex. How was it?

Brooke: Rather good.

Annette: Did you sign a nondisclosure agreement or something? Why can't you tell me anything?

Brooke: I'm in a bad mood.

Annette: You had "rather good" sex last night. You shouldn't be in a bad mood.

Brooke: One night of good sex isn't changing my desire to burn shit down.

Annette: Why are you in a bad mood today? What's wrong?

Annette: This guy was decent, right?

Brooke: He was decent. Annoyingly so.

Annette: I can appreciate an annoyingly decent man.

Brooke: You should know. You're living with one.

Annette: Stop trying to change the conversation from you to me.

Brooke: It's nothing. I'm fine. I'm looking forward to the weekend.

Annette: You're so cute when you lie.

Brooke: I'm not lying. I'm actually looking forward to the weekend. I can't wait to get out of here for two nights.

Annette: Can I say happy birthday yet?

Brooke: Can we not make this about my birthday? Can't it be a girl's weekend away—with Jackson—and not dip the whole thing in birthday sprinkles?

Annette: Can I just send you a screenshot of the conversation we had about this last year? Because I have a ton of orders to get out the door before taking off for your birthday weekend and my argument hasn't changed.

Brooke: That seems like a lot of work. Scrolling through a year's worth of messages.

Annette: I am going to celebrate the fuck out of your birthday. You can't stop me, so you might as well join me.
Brooke: Why do you do this?
Annette: By this, I'm guessing you mean not letting you get back on your bullshit.
Brooke: No. I mean, why do you care so much?
Annette: Because there's nothing you can do that will ever push me away, so stop trying.

SAME STOLEN ROBE, same wet hair, same bare feet, same ocean view. But it was a different day and I had a new set of regrets to keep me company while the autumn sun heated my skin and dried my hair. A different kind of hollowed-out loneliness to keep me company.

It was unusually warm for late September. As the story went, I was born on a day much like this one. A bright, clear sky overflowing with sunshine while only the slightest hint of cool, crisp air lingered in the breeze. The trees were a riot of red, orange, and gold, and the barren grayness of winter seemed impossibly distant. The kind of day captured in postcards and photography books and B-roll footage.

It was the perfect miracle of a day for a perfect miracle of a baby to be born.

And I *was* perfect. Not in any of the ways that meant something, but in all the ways that'd made my parents happy. I was beautiful. My hair was platinum blonde and my eyes sapphire. My skin barely tanned, never freckled. I was tall and lean, but never so much that anyone took note of either. Add to that some high cheekbones, full lips, and luck of the draw facial symmetry and I was one beautiful baby who grew into a beautiful child and then a beautiful young adult whose awkward phase lasted all of a week. It was the easy, shallow kind of beauty that signified nothing.

I was a miracle too. As that story went, I was so much of a miracle, my parents named me twice. They'd known on that sunny day in September that I'd be their only child—the only one they'd carry out the hospital doors—and that was all the reason they needed to saddle me with two first names. They'd hoped their little miracle would fill all the voids they'd identified in their lives, mend their differences, and save their marriage. But babies never saved marriages. They didn't make up for falling out of love after two decades of bitterness and disappointment and they didn't fix the things that'd broken along the way.

I wasn't the perfect miracle they'd needed, but dammit, I'd tried to be. I tried to be everything, anything. Whatever it was, I did it until I couldn't do it anymore. Until rendering my entire existence down into the glue necessary to keeping a broken family together succeeded only in burning off every last bit of my miraculous shine. But it was a challenge I'd been born to best and even now —more than sixteen years after walking away from Talbott's Cove and dysfunction and miracles that weren't —I was still trying. Still failing. And still angry as hell that I had to hold it all together for everyone else.

The sour irony of this challenge was that no one outside my father's house expected anything from me. Most people looked at me and expected nothing more than my face. Once they tossed in the cutesy hyphenated name and the family known for settling in provincial Maine a full century before the Mayflower departed from Plymouth, the expectations ceased to exist. I didn't need to be generous or smart or capable. Pretty and privileged were impressive enough for the world, but underneath all this blonde hair and behind these blue eyes was a mind overqualified for my appearance. I wasn't supposed to say that, but it was the straight truth.

I wasn't the person anyone expected. I wasn't the version they wanted. More often than not, I wasn't the version I wanted either.

I dragged a hand through my hair, pushing it over my ear as I watched the water. I did this every day. Not the wet hair, bare feet, stolen kimono, whole life navel-gazing thing, but trying to find the farthest visible point from Talbott's Cove and imagining myself there. On cloudless days like today, I could wish myself all the way to Matinicus Island. It was nothing more than a slab of rock in the middle of Penobscot Bay, but goddamn, it wasn't here.

If I was there, I wouldn't have to be me.

CHAPTER NINE

JJ

Absolute Return: an asset's achieved earnings over a period of time.

OCTOBER

THE KID WAS PISSED and I couldn't say I blamed him.

"You want me to live in a bar? And work here too?" Nate asked the sheriff. He shifted the cardboard box he held to his hip and glanced around the tavern's empty dining room. "This was the *good* idea?"

"I recognize it's unconventional," Jackson replied, holding out a *listen to reason, son* hand. "However, I've heard time and again you don't see alcohol as a coping mechanism and Mr. Harniczek here—"

"Christ almighty, don't call me that."

Under no circumstances did I want to have a conversation with Sheriff Lau before ten in the morning. Not a single one and yet here I was, shoulder to shoulder with that shined-shoes, do-good motherfucker at nine fifteen.

I held out my hand to Nate, as he preferred to be addressed. "JJ, please."

"All right, *JJ*," Nate replied with a huff. "No disrespect, man, but I don't see how this is going to work. I'm pretty sure my father carved his name into that barstool right over there. Alcohol doesn't do shit for me, but after enough time around my father, I'd start gnawing on the wood just to get high off the varnish." He angled his body to face Jackson. "I know you're sticking your neck out there and pulling favors for me, but I can't stay in this town."

Jackson went for the *listen to reason* hand again. I rolled my eyes. "Let's not jump to any conclusions. You can—"

"Yeah, I can go to Portland or Orono or Macias, or literally anywhere but this town where no one leaves, no one changes, and no one forgets a fucking thing," Nate interrupted. He dropped the box, shrugged off his backpack. He brought his fingers to his temples, rubbing as he stared at the floor. "I appreciate you trying to set this up, but it's not gonna work. I'll find somewhere else to crash."

"Or you can decide it doesn't matter." I shoved my hands into my front pockets. "This place, these people. Your parents. You can decide whether any of it matters to you." Jackson and Nate turned toward me at the same time. "Will there be shitty moments when those things force their way into your life? Of course. My father dropped dead of a heart attack my last year of high school. If you ask anyone around here, they'll say I blew off college because of it. That wasn't the reason, but I have better things to do than chase down everyone's thoughts and waste my time trying to fix them." I bent down and picked up his box. It was much heavier than I'd expected. "Nothing good will come from running up to Orono or Macias."

He turned away from us, exhaling heavily as he went. "And staying here is that much better?"

Behind Nate's back, the sheriff and I exchanged glances. I shook my head, gestured to my watch. Jackson held up his palm and gave me a chastising stare. I tapped my watch again and hooked a thumb over my shoulder. He responded by shifting his gaze to Nate.

"We can't force you to do anything," Jackson started.

"No, you cannot," Nate added.

"And if you want to leave town, I'll do what I can to help you on your way." The sheriff tipped his head to the side as if he was about to impart some fatherly wisdom. I rolled my eyes at him. Again. "This place might not feel like home right now, but it's worth giving it a chance."

I stepped in front of Nate and clapped my hands together. "All right, kid, here's what's up. I have to run to a meeting on the other side of town. If you think the Cove never changes, you should come along and listen. After that, I'm gonna grab some lunch and run invoices for the month. Are you any good with envelopes?"

"Envelopes?" he repeated.

"Yeah, you know, folding a bill, putting it in an envelope, sealing it," I replied, miming the process. "Stamps, addresses, the whole thing. Can you manage that?"

He swung a gaze between me and Jackson. "Yeah, I can manage that."

"That's all I needed to know," I replied. "Let's put your things down and we'll head out." I shook the cardboard box as I stepped away from the dining room. "What do you have in here anyway? Bricks?"

"Books," he answered, trailing several paces behind me. "And I didn't agree to stay."

"All I want to do is put this box down and we can't leave it in the middle of my tavern where someone could trip over it. The last thing I need is a lawsuit." I elbowed the back room door open, motioned for Nate to join me. Jackson followed him, not that he was invited. "Where you rest your head tonight is your business, kid. Stay, go, transform into a seagull for all I care."

I led them past the microdistillery that'd served me well when I bottled a dozen or so batches of gin each week but now fit like a school uniform in May. We passed the lineup of empty kegs I couldn't look at without thinking about Brooke and the wicked things she'd said and the way her brow had crinkled when she wasn't getting exactly what she wanted. As I had for the past month, I kept going. Moved past it. Ignored the shit out of everything to put one foot in front of the other, through the ever-present reminders and up the steep staircase.

The apartment was freshly cleaned, but that didn't make up for the fact it was an attic with a bathroom. I went to set the box down on the round kitchen table the sheriff had lugged over from his girlfriend's old apartment, but Nate snatched the box from my hands.

"I've got it," he murmured, dropping the box beside the bed.

From the looks of the pastel rainbow blanket and small pillows with flamingos painted on them, those pieces were also courtesy of Annette's former residence. "Now that's handled, we have to hit the road." I glanced at the sheriff. "You good, man?" When he didn't immediately respond, I continued, "Okay, great. We'll see you around."

I'd almost reached the base of the staircase when I heard another set of footsteps behind me. I didn't have to glance back to know they belonged to Nate. "Where are we going?" he called.

I walked through the back room, the kegs on one side and the bottling setup on the other. I knew how to ignore a certain portion of this room, but I also enjoyed pressing that bruise. Not that one night with Brooke left me wounded, though her fingerprints were a mark I couldn't wash from my skin. Just as I savored the ache that came with remembering her touch, it also served as a reminder to stay far away from that woman.

Cutting through the alleyway exit, I pointed at my car and called, "It's not far, but we're heading out to Beddington to pick up some honey when we're finished."

"All the way to Beddington for honey?" Nate asked as he pulled the car door closed. "Do they have better bees up there?"

"Would you believe me if I told you they do?" We shared a glance as I paused before backing out of the alley. When he didn't say anything, I continued. "Do you know the old cider house?"

"Know it? I used to meet one of my dealers there. It's a great spot for that kind of action. Completely hidden from the street by the tree line."

"Good thing the sheriff nabbed him a couple of months ago."

Nate stared out the window. "Thorough, that sheriff."

I snickered. "Like you wouldn't believe." I turned down the potholed road leading to the cider house. "We're meeting a general contractor. He's going to show us all the construction issues that will require more time and money. Then, we're going to meet a plumber with his own list of issues."

Nate scanned the area around the cider house. The overgrown vegetation that'd once consumed the grounds was gone. Stakes with fluorescent tags outlined the planned walkways, patios, and gardens. Spray-painted arrows and dashes marked the underground locations of water, gas, and electric lines.

"What is this?" he asked.

I stared at the building and the hard-packed earth surrounding it. Save for text messages promising to follow up soon, I hadn't heard from Barry in a full month. Our last real conversation was right here, when he was seeing the site for himself. It was classic Barry.

"When we're done, it will put this town on the farm-to-cup tourism map with a craft distillery and dining venue. It's progress." I tipped my chin toward the building. "That's what I'm hoping it is." When I saw the contractor's truck rumble down the road, I stepped out of the car and waved for Nate. "You're welcome to come along. It might not be much entertainment, but it's gotta be better than kicking rocks."

He jogged around the back side of the car to join me. At the entrance to the cider house, he flattened his hand on the door, saying, "Hold up. It would really help my ability to process all of this if you could tell me when you're going to start hiding the knives and locking up the cough syrup."

Through his windshield, I watched the general contractor plow a glazed donut. I glanced back at Nate. "Correct me if I'm wrong, but I don't think anything would stop you if you were determined to start using again. Not me, not the sheriff, not a lock on the medicine cabinet." He dropped his gaze, banded his arms over his chest. "I'm running one business by myself while trying to get a second off the ground. I don't have the time to babysit you and even if I did, that shit sounds boring as hell. If you think I'm reporting back to Sheriff Lau or your probation officer or anyone else, you've miscalculated the time I have on my hands."

Nate hesitated before saying, "I don't know anything about bartending."

The contractor popped another donut in his mouth. Jelly, this time. "What do you know about?"

"Books. Poetry." He lifted his shoulders, dropped them with a sigh. "The treatment facility I was at this summer had a gardening program. It was nice. Everyone tended their own piece of land."

Considering this, I shifted toward the ocean. Nate did the same. "And you learned something? From the gardens?"

"I learned that flowers and fruit are the last stages in a plant's life cycle," he answered. "That tons of growth takes place underground, where no one sees it. And that it might look like nothing is happening for so long that people wonder whether it's unhealthy or the soil isn't draining well or it doesn't belong in this climate, but that plant is busy gathering the strength to bloom. That's what I learned."

The contractor slammed his truck door shut and wiped his paws on the seat of his jeans. I raised a hand, waving him toward us. To Nate, I said, "I'll teach you what you need to know about mixing drinks and pulling pints. The rest of it is listening while someone tells you how their garden grows." I clapped him on the back. "If you stick around, that is."

CHAPTER TEN

BROOKE

Covenants: The conditions agreed to in the process of financing debt, intended to protect the lender's interests.

November

Annette: Let's go to the Galley tonight.
Brooke: This isn't a good night for me.
Annette: Tomorrow?
Brooke: Maybe not.
Annette: Come on…I realize it's not the swankiest spot, but we get to drink liquor and annoy JJ. That sounds like a great outing to me and we haven't been there in ages. Like, full months.
Brooke: I need to keep a handle on things around here.
Annette: Is everything all right?
Brooke: Yeah.
Brooke: No.

Brooke: I don't know.

Annette: It's okay, sweetie. We don't have to go out. I can bring some snacks and wine over.

Brooke: That works. Thank you for dealing with all my quirks.

Annette: Don't mention it. You deal with mine.

DECEMBER

Annette: I regret to inform you that I am dead.

Annette: I've died.

Annette: Remember me fondly.

Brooke: This is fascinating for me because I'm usually the one coming out with outrageous comments and you're the one saying, Uh huh. Okay. Care to unpack that for me?

Annette: Please don't enjoy my death.

Brooke: Let's start with this. Why are you dead and how did you die?

Annette: Allow me to set the scene.

Brooke: Should I pour a glass of wine for this?

Annette: It's not even 9 a.m. yet, so maybe not.

Brooke: Seems like an arbitrary reason, but okay. Set the scene.

Annette: It's early this morning. Before Jackson's alarm goes off. We're having sex and things are good. As far as pre-dawn sex goes, it's real nice.

Brooke: I don't even remember what pre-dawn sex is like.

Annette: Oh, honey.

Brooke: Ignore me. Carry on. Seriously, I need to find out how you died.

Annette: Like I said, real nice pre-dawn sex…until a sound emerges from my body.

Annette: It was a deep squelching sound. A cross between a deflating windbag and aggressively stirring macaroni and cheese.

Annette: And it might've been fine if it happened just once. But much in the way aftershocks follow an earthquake, there were several smaller but equally noticeable squelches.

Brooke: Some might call that a queef.

Annette: No. A queef is too dainty for this noise. This was aggressive. Like a vaginal cannon blast. I don't know how he stayed inside me.

Brooke: What did you do?

Annette: I died. Right there on the bed.

Brooke: How did Jackson handle it? Did he say anything?

Annette: He paused for a second and then said, Okay, back to business.

Brooke: I love him so much. Are you certain we can't negotiate a sister-wife agreement?

Annette: We are reserving a room for you in the new house, but I don't see any polyamory in our future.

Annette: Not unless Jackson is down at the station, rethinking his life choices on account of the noise violations from my downstairs.

Brooke: What was his expression? Did he look shocked or concerned or amused? He couldn't have been that mortified since he kept going.

Annette: I couldn't see his expression.

Brooke: Ah. All right.

Brooke: Well, so what? It was a queef. A super loud one. Given that you two live together, I'm sure there are other unpleasant things he's witnessed.

Annette: It's easier to keep up the charade than you might think.

Brooke: There's one bathroom at your place. There's no room for charades when you share a bathroom.

Annette: You're forgetting that my shop is a three-minute walk from the house and there's a perfectly private bathroom there.

Brooke: Oh my god, Annette. You're leading a double life. You can't marry this man if you've led him to believe you don't poop. It's deceptive and wrong. I won't let it happen.

Annette: It's irrelevant because I'm dead.

Brooke: You're not dead. You just don't like living through a moment where Jackson thinks you're anything but a delicate little lady who doesn't poop.

Brooke: We can look at this a few different ways.

Annette: Which is why I love you.

Brooke: First, certain positions can be noisier. That has nothing to do with you or him or anything other than the acrobatics.

Annette: It's never happened in that position before.

Brooke: Which brings me to my second point. Maybe Jackson has a really big dick and it just…you know… forces a lot of air in there.

Annette: It's his fault?

Brooke: Why the fuck not?

Brooke: But why does it have to be anyone's fault? All kinds of horrible things happen during sex.

Annette: Examples, please.

Brooke: I've done all of these things during sex: cut myself on a guy's gnarly toenail and bled all over his sheets, punched a guy in the nose, forgotten about a tampon, elbowed a guy in the eye, started my period, puked in a guy's lap because his dick smelled like a sewer, and peed the bed.

Annette: You peed the bed?

Brooke: I know, I know. I was young and I didn't know how to get up and go to the bathroom in the morning without waking the guy.

Annette: So…you peed the bed?!?

Brooke: No, I stayed in bed and held it. But then he woke up and wanted to have sex. Again, I was young. Like, 21. And I figured it was fine, I'd pee later.

Annette: But that wasn't how it worked out, huh?

Brooke: Nope. In the middle of sex, peed the bed. I told him it was some special girly juice from him being super good at sex.

Annette: Did he believe that?

Brooke: Sadly, yes.

Annette: That toenail story was disgusting.

Brooke: You don't even know. I insisted on getting a tetanus shot.

Annette: The most awful thing to happen to me during sex was this morning.

Brooke: You see? It wasn't that bad.

Annette: You say that but I'm still convinced it was pretty bad. It was explosive. Vagina cannon, I tell you.

Brooke: Perhaps you have a wide-set vagina. That, coupled with the really big dick and the position, could set the stage for a vagina cannon moment.

Annette: We're just going to blame Jackson, okay?

Brooke: Remember you're having good morning sex and I'm not, okay?

JANUARY

Annette: I want to redecorate the back room at the shop. It's really dreary and boring in there.

Brooke: You're just noticing this now?

Annette: Actually, yes. I've never used it as more than a place to store boxes because I handled business stuff in my apartment.

Brooke: If you tell me that Jackson keeps you on your back too much to handle your paperwork, I'm going to die.

Brooke: Not on the spot, but soon.

Annette: Helpful clarification.

Brooke: I'll wander into the woods and wait for the elements to claim me. That would be better than hearing about the sex life you won't share with me.

Annette: Sometimes I have trouble determining whether you're being serious…

Brooke: You're doing fine.

Annette: You do realize you're hot as fuck, right?

Brooke: What does that have to do with anything?

Annette: You're going to argue with me on this, but you're a good person too. You're a little psycho, but you're kindhearted about it.

Brooke: Are you…are you hitting on me?

Brooke: Although I have yet to act on it, I've always considered myself a Kinsey 2 or 3 but I thought you were MUCH closer to a 0 than this conversation suggests.

Annette: What?

Brooke: I love you, I really, really do, but I don't think I want our relationship to change and there are times when I really need some dick in my life.

Brooke: And this is one of those times.

Annette: What are we talking about?

Brooke: You were putting the moves on me.

Annette: I was not.

Annette: I was gently reminding you that you can get a sex life of your own and stop trying to insert yourself into mine.

Brooke: I'm definitely looking for some insertion.

Annette: ANYWAY.

Annette: If I mentioned to a few people that you're look-ing, you'd have a line at your door in 10 minutes.

Brooke: omfg stop.

Brooke: Talk about ugly storage rooms. Please.

Annette: Let me forage for you.

Brooke: I love you but oh my god no.

Annette: You don't trust me to find someone you'd like?

Brooke: If I needed to cover up a crime, you'd be the first person I call.

Annette: My fiancé, the sheriff, would have some… concerns…about that.

Brooke: I'd want you to clear my browser history, reset my phone, and discreetly dispose of my vibrators if I died suddenly.

Annette: And I'd want the same.

Brooke: I'd trust you to give me an at-home Brazilian wax.

Annette: That's special.

Brooke: But I don't want you matchmaking for me, dearie.

Annette: And why is that?

Brooke: Because you believe in love and relationships and knowing the person's name before you have sex with them.

Annette: You deserve that, you know.

Brooke: I recognize what you're doing. You're giving me all the shit I gave you.

Annette: You are the smart one in this relationship.

Brooke: But the difference between me giving you shit then and what you're doing now is you had a man carrying your panties with him as a good luck charm, and I am not the subject of anyone's obsession.

Annette: That did not occur.

Brooke: Mmmm agree to disagree. Let's get back to the storage room before I have to deal with the fallout over Dad rejecting whatever his caregivers made for dinner because all of his triggers seem to be food-related. Please.

Annette: I don't like bringing work home. I'd rather do it at the shop, but the back room is depressing. It needs some warmth and motivation.

Brooke: In my old office, in New York, I had a huge reproduction of a Georgia O'Keefe painting framed behind my desk. A complicated red flower. Actually huge. At least 5 feet wide, probably 8 feet tall.

Brooke: People (and by people, I mean men) would stare at it. As per male usual, they never knew what they were seeing.

Annette: Pussy power much?

Brooke: My workplace was filled with men who used their penises to activate touch screens. Men who insulted each other with stories of fucking each other's wives and mothers. Men who loved a good rape joke.

Brooke: You bet your ass I decorated with pussy power.

Annette: Where is it now? I'm not sure I have the wall space for a giant red vagina painting, but I like the idea.

Brooke: It's in a storage facility outside Manhattan.

Brooke: Along with the remains of my hold on reality.

CHAPTER ELEVEN

JJ

Collateral: assets which can be repossessed in the event of loan default.

THERE WERE a lot of things I didn't know about starting a business. It was no skin off my back to learn, as I'd been doing that since taking over the Galley from my aunt and uncle years ago. But there was a substantial difference between figuring out the food and beverage business as I went and banging my head into walls because it was better than making sense of building codes and licensing permit paperwork.

That was how I found myself chucking a binder at Sheriff Lau's head.

"Whoa there," he called, swerving in the doorway to avoid the offending binder. It hit the wall and thumped the floor. "Should I take that personally?"

I leaned back in my chair, regarding him as he stood

before my desk. "Give it a try and don't tell me how it works out for you."

Finding no humor in my suggestion, he went on staring at me with a cool, flat expression I was certain he received with his badge and uniform. "Can I borrow a moment of your time?"

"Only if you intend on returning it." He offered more of that cool flatness in response and I wished I had another binder to throw simply for the purpose of snapping him out of it. "What do you need, sheriff?"

He settled into a chair, saying, "I've heard from several different people that you know how to stop Audee Netishen from shooting the deer and moose he lures onto his property."

"It's always something with that old fucker," I muttered. "I bet he's telling you it's legit because he's not hunting outside the state's season and bag limits, but protecting his home."

The sheriff nodded. "That's correct."

"And I bet he also has a peck or two of apples piled up on his property."

Another nod. "Also correct."

"He does that," I said, reaching for my glass of water. "He hires high school kids to harvest his apple trees every autumn, but then he leaves them in his damn barn three or four months. Because he's a crazy old fucker, he carts them all out in December and January, leaves a peck right in front of his house, and bags some deer from the comfort of his recliner. His wife sells the jerky at one of those big farmers markets up in Orono."

"Sounds like a lot of work," he said.

"Sounds like you don't know much about hunting," I replied. "I don't have an interest, but I grew up with it and I can tell you it's much easier to cart some apples out from a barn than it is to get geared up and sit in the woods all day."

"And that's how you know the magic word to getting Netishen in line?"

I barked out a laugh. "We used to be neighbors. My family lived next door to the Netishens for twenty years. My father planned his entire year around the season. He loved hunting, but he was a lot like you, sheriff. By the book." I paused, ran my tongue over my teeth. "He worked as a game warden until the day he died. Every time he saw Audee dragging those apples out of his barn, he told him he'd permanently lose his hunting license if he bagged so much as a goose. They had the same conversation two or three times each winter."

"That's all it takes?" the sheriff asked. "A warning?"

With as much patience as I could muster, I gestured at his sheriff's garb, saying, "From a game warden. Guys like Audee know the system better than the state does and they know you"—I pointed at his badge—"aren't pulling his license. Call the Augusta office and fill them in. They'll send a warden down."

He bobbed his head as he took in this information. "There are moments when I forget I'm still a newcomer here." He glanced up at me with the barest of smirks. "But then I'm sent here to get a history lesson and a shove in the right direction."

"No one in this town will give you a simple answer

when the complicated one makes more sense to them," I said, laughing. "Give it a few years, you'll be doing it too."

"I suppose I should thank you for that lesson as well," he said.

"That one is on the house," I replied.

Jackson rested his hands on his thighs and took a moment to sweep a gaze over my office. It was piled high with boxes and crates, decades' worth of accounting ledgers, and an assortment of items branded with beer logos. Hats, t-shirts, paper coasters, frisbees, you name it. I meant to clean it out every time I couldn't find something, but never remembered to get it done.

"Since I'm here," he started, "I'm interested to hear how Nate is progressing."

And since you're here, I'm interested in hearing everything you can tell me about your fiancée's best friend. "You'd have to ask him that yourself," I replied. "You could, but he's not here right now."

The muscles in his jaw twitched. "Where is he?"

"I got enough problems of my own. I don't keep track of the kid's calendar too."

I shuffled the documents on my desk, looking for nothing but an exit from this conversation. I didn't care for the routine check-ins on Nate's recovery or the constant questions about his conduct and habits, and the sheriff wasn't the only one asking. The reemergence of Nate Fitzsimmons was something of a local legend now. It wasn't uncommon for customers to ask him highly personal questions or gape at him while he bused their table. Others gave him sobriety advice after ordering their meals and a special few made it their business to watch his every move and report back to me about behavior they found suspicious.

"Got it, got it," Jackson murmured. "I'd have to assume he's doing well enough if you've kept him on this long. Knowing how you operate, he would've been on the curb if there was an issue."

I didn't like the sheriff. We were cut from different cloth. But I couldn't deny that he was suited for his job. "What do you want? A performance review? He comes in on time, he does the work, and he puts up with all the assholes this town has to offer. He's fine. Leave him alone."

He nodded thoughtfully, as if this information put everything in a new light. "I see him at the gym in the morning." He shared a laugh with himself. "The mornings I manage to drag myself out of bed early enough to hit the gym."

I gave him a blank stare. "Ha."

"He seems to like the six a.m. yoga and meditation class," Jackson continued. "The weight room too. All the times I've stopped by, he's been very focused on the weights."

"Maybe if you shared your protein shake recipe with him, he'd share his workout plan," I replied. "I'm sure you'd hit it off once he forgets he's on probation and handing in a cup of urine every week and you're the head of the local law enforcement agency receiving those piss reports."

He blinked at me. "Point taken."

"Leave the kid alone. Let him work out without the sheriff spotting him." I took another sip from my water.

"Don't you have better things to do? You're engaged, you're building a house, and you're in a power struggle with Audee Netishen. Isn't that enough?"

Jackson lifted a hand to his forehead, rubbed his brow. "Following up on Nate is much easier than building a house. The process is—I can't even explain how complicated and exhausting the damn thing is. And the ground is frozen, so there's nothing we can do until spring, but since we have that time to kill, we might as well change the plans seven or eight hundred times."

"Don't forget about the wedding," I added.

"I don't know whether I should be concerned or relieved that Annette has prioritized the house." He continued rubbing his brow. "I figure she wouldn't be driving herself nutty over closets and cabinets if she didn't intend to stick around." He glanced up at me, a look of pure dread on his face. "She wants us to visit a home design studio in Portland this weekend."

"Isn't that what you do best, sheriff? Escorting Annette and Brooke up and down the coast while they shop and brunch and whatever else it is they do?"

It was such a lame attempt at drawing information about Brooke out of him that I wanted to kick my own ass.

"We haven't seen much of Brooke lately. She has a lot on her plate." He frowned, glanced over his shoulder at the door. "Last I heard, she isn't available to compare bathroom flooring samples this weekend."

I drummed my fingers on the desk, considering my options while the sheriff and I stared at each other. They weren't good options. Everywhere I turned, I boxed myself into a new corner. I couldn't ask about Brooke and whether she needed some help without tipping my hand hard in that direction. I couldn't ask whether her father's condition was deteriorating because it was possible Jackson didn't know about it.

"Annette's baked a number of banana cream pies for Judge Markham these past few weeks," Jackson continued. "I'm told it's his favorite, but Brooke hates them. Can't stand the smell of bananas. The conversations Brooke and Annette have about those pies are, well, they're entertaining."

"It's always fun to be the target of Brooke's simultaneous love and hate."

Jackson pushed to his feet and opened the door, hooking a glance at me over his shoulder. "You would know, wouldn't you?"

And that was how I realized Jackson Lau was better at his job than I thought.

CHAPTER TWELVE

BROOKE

Prime Rate: the interest rate at which banks lend to their best customers.

FEBRUARY

Annette: Jackson just sent a million roses to the shop to celebrate six months of cohabitation.
Brooke: That sweet boy. Someone taught him right.
Annette: That's the truth.
Brooke: As you know, I love you dearly.
Annette: Yep.
Brooke: Do you think you could share with me some of the downsides of that cohabitation? Because I love you and don't want to hate you for having unlimited access to good dick and someone to take out the trash.

Annette: I wouldn't say it's unlimited access. He does work.

Brooke: And you've had sex in his office enough times to count on both hands, so let's not split hairs on that point.

Annette: Here's one. He prefers to store leftovers on plates covered in plastic wrap. He doesn't see why anyone would move food to a storage container when it's on a perfectly good plate.

Brooke: What a savage. Pyrex is life.

Brooke: Keep going.

Annette: He doesn't believe in expiration dates.

Brooke: What's that now?

Annette: Yeah, I bought a bunch of ricotta cheese in November. Two quarts. I wanted to try a new cheesecake recipe, but I never got around to it. It has since passed its expiration date, however, Jackson won't let me toss it because he believes it's still good. So, we have two quarts of aging cheese in the back corner of the fridge.

Brooke: That's an interesting belief system.

Brooke: What else?

Annette: He flat-out refuses to take any of my help when he's getting sick. I tried to give him some vitamins when he picked up that cold after the holidays and you would've thought I'd offered him heroin or a teacup of bleach.

Brooke: Men are the worst.

Annette: He won't admit when he's falling asleep. He likes to watch one of those sports news programs every night, though he's never seen an entire episode. He falls the fuck asleep. And god forbid I suggest he DVR it or turn off the television. It's right up there with illicit use of vitamin C.

Brooke: Yeah, you're a heretic.

Annette: Whenever it's snowing, he wakes up two or three times during the night to shovel. He says it won't accumulate as much that way. I understand that it's easier to shovel a few inches rather than a few feet, but first of all, we have a snow blower. Second, nothing good has ever come from going outside at three in the morning during a snowstorm.

Brooke: Literally nothing.

Annette: I don't even try to argue it with him. He's going to do what he's going to do.

Brooke: How do you manage?

Annette: He makes up for it in other ways.

Brooke: This guy has the good dick.

Annette: You're not wrong.

Brooke: Ugh this hasn't made me hate you less.

Annette: That's fine. You can hate me. It's that or put real effort into meeting men, I guess, and we both know you won't do that.

Brooke: Would you just shut up, please?

Annette: Since when have you refrained from giving anyone a pointed push?

Brooke: Yeah, because that's my thing. I'm the rude one. You're the nice one.

Annette: Only sometimes.

Brooke: Wait, are you referring to me or you?

Annette: Both seems like a fine answer.

MARCH

Annette: Can I be ridiculous and self-centered for a minute?

Brooke: You never have to ask permission to be ridiculous or self-centered as I am both with alarming frequency.

Annette: You're neither.

Brooke: Don't try to debate this with me. I'll win. I always win because I'm amazing like that.

Brooke: See? Ridiculous and self-centered.

Annette: Anyway…Jackson's sister is coming to visit next weekend.

Brooke: Rachel, right?

Annette: Yeah.

Brooke: Isn't she a teacher in some Grimms' fairy tale land?

Annette: By that, I assume you mean western Massachusetts.

Brooke: Same thing.

Annette: Right, well, Rachel who teaches middle school out in western Massachusetts is visiting next weekend and this is the first time I've spent more than a Thanksgiving meal with her.

Brooke: …and you're freaking out about what?

Annette: The list is extensive.

Brooke: Start with the most absurd shit.

Annette: She doesn't like sweets and 90% of my life is baking with tons of sugar and I don't understand how anyone could exist without pie and cookies and cake and lemon squares.

Brooke: Proportionally speaking, your life is not 90% baking. You run a small business, babe. Baking is your passion project, your stress relief, your hand work.

Annette: I don't really care about the math.

Brooke: Of course. But, real talk, she's not going to ooh and ahh all over your sticky buns and that's okay. People like you for reasons entirely separate from the treats you shove in their mouths.

Annette: I don't shove anything in anyone's mouth.

Brooke: Oh, right. I forgot it's the other way around with you.

Annette: Shut up.

Brooke: Back to the freak out of the day. What's the next most absurd thing?

Annette: I feel like the house is a weird mix of 1990s-meets-vintage-thrift. I know that's the least of her concerns and she's not coming here to evaluate the style of the place we're renting while our house is being built, but I've never had guests in our home before and I want it to be nice.

Brooke: Would you like to move into the carriage house over here? It hasn't been updated since before my mother died, but you can play house there all you want.

Annette: Jackson would never go for that.

Brooke: It's funny how Jackson is the reason it won't work and not your own lunacy.

Annette: (eye roll emoji)

Brooke: What else is bothering you?

Annette: I just want her to like me.

Brooke: She absolutely will.

Annette: Sisters never like me.

Brooke: Your sisters are the heavyweight champions of cunt. They do not count as evidence.

Brooke: Rachel will adore you. She'll get a tattoo that reads "I'm With Annie" before the weekend is over but if you think for one second that this chick is replacing me as your bloodless sister, I will wage war.

Annette: I would never go to war with you.

Brooke: Because I know all of your weak spots?

Annette: Because we know each other's weak spots, but we'd never use them.

Brooke: No. We wouldn't.

Brooke: Would you like to continue freaking out or are you feeling better?

Annette: I think I'm okay.

Brooke: I know you're okay.

CHAPTER THIRTEEN

BROOKE

Depreciation: the allocation of value over a period of time to account for the loss of value as an asset ages or is rendered obsolete.

APRIL

ANNETTE STARED at her reflection in the mirror as she pivoted on the pedestal. "I'm not sure."

"Aren't you supposed to have an involuntary reaction? Something more interesting than a sneezing fit, but less troublesome than a seizure?"

She glared at me in the mirror. "This was your idea."

"You're the one who got engaged," I argued from my perch on the tufted white sofa. "Suggesting we find you a wedding dress doesn't seem ridiculous to me."

"But this," she cried, fisting the ball gown's heavy skirts, "this *is* ridiculous."

"Oh my god, yes." I drained my champagne. Everything in this bridal boutique was blindingly white and the dresses were questionably fashionable, but at least the champagne was free. "Take it off immediately and return it to the America's Cup team. I'm sure they're pissed about someone stealing their sails."

"Perhaps a slimmer silhouette," the saleswoman offered as she flew to the racks. "Something form-fitting, like a column or mermaid."

Annette met my gaze in the mirror, shook her head. She blinked quickly as tears filled her eyes. That was my cue. "Sandra, you've been such a treasure today. We're going to pause here, but we'll be back when the bride has narrowed her ideas. Let's get her out of this giant cupcake, okay?"

Sandra stepped away from the sea of tulle and lace. "You're so lucky to have such a caring maid of honor," she said to Annette. "But *your* interests are my priority. What do *you* want?"

"I want to get out of this dress and never see it again," Annette replied.

"You are breathtaking in this dress," the saleswoman argued. "Look what it does for your figure. It's just magical." She smiled despite Annette's deep frown. "Let's try it with a veil!"

"I want to get out of this dress," she repeated.

The saleswoman shook her head. "Try to see it with your own eyes. Don't let the opinions of others"—a pointed glare in my direction as she went in search of a veil—"change your mind."

"My eyes are annoyed that I'm still wearing this," Annette replied.

I pushed up from the sofa and moved to my friend's side. Lacing my arm around her waist, I said, "I can have you out of this corset in thirty seconds flat."

"You should add that to your résumé. At least your LinkedIn profile." She patted my head. "It's strange being taller than you."

"Maybe, but now you're at the perfect height for me to nuzzle your boobs." I dropped my cheek to her chest. "I can see why Jackson wants to marry you. These are amazing."

"I know, they really are," she agreed with a laugh. "You can't hear it through the ten miles of satin fabric I'm wearing, but my tummy is rumbling like a thunderstorm."

I pointed to the front of the gown. "You pick up that end. I'll get the other end. We'll waddle back to the dressing room." The saleswoman appeared again, veils draped over her forearms and her hands outstretched as if she meant to help. "We've got this, thanks."

"Oh, well—"

"I wouldn't argue with her, Sandra," Annette interrupted. "She was president of Kappa Alpha Theta at Yale for three years and would've served a fourth year, but the bylaws didn't allow new pledges to take office."

The saleswoman trailed after us as we shuffled toward the dressing room. "Okay, but—"

"And she's the only female hedge fund manager in her firm's one hundred and nineteen year history," Annette continued. "She has a black belt in tae kwon do, speaks fluent French, German, and Mandarin, and consistently reels in the biggest catch during the bonito run. But, go ahead. Tell her she doesn't know how to properly exit me from this whipped cream avalanche."

I folded my lips together to stop myself from laughing. Once we'd wedged Annette through the dressing room door, I kept my gaze on the dress. I didn't dare look at my friend or the stunned saleswoman while I loosened the corset's lacing.

"I'll be right outside," Sandra said. "Shout if you need anything."

When the door closed, I said, "I don't speak German and I went fishing once when I was fifteen. I made Chad Bodger bait the hooks and then get the fish off the hooks because it looked horrible."

"So, you—what? Held the pole?"

"That could be the summary of my life right there," I said, giving the laces a yank. It was a wonder my girl could breathe. "I held the pole."

"But you do know tae kwon do?" she asked.

"No black belt, but I took a few martial arts classes when the guys in my office started raving about Krav Maga. They spent entire days chopping each other in the balls. I wanted to be able to poke them in the neck and have them fall to the ground and piss themselves."

"That's a noble desire." The dress fell away from her body and a breath rattled out of her. "I'm going to need some lunch now."

"Maybe we can talk about this wedding while we eat." I gathered the dress as she picked her way out of it. "You know, spitball some of the basics like colors, theme, venue. If you want to go crazy, maybe we'll even come up with ideas for the date."

Her back turned to me, Annette shrugged into her clothes. "I get it. Going dress shopping wasn't the best idea."

I slipped the dress onto its hanger. "That's not what I'm saying."

She bent at the waist to fluff her hair. "You're saying I can't choose a dress until I know when and where I'm getting married," she said, standing. "And you're not wrong, but dresses felt—I don't know—manageable. I figured we could drive down here and I could try on a dress and it would be perfect and then I'd have all the answers."

"You don't need all the answers," I said. "Let's get out of here before our friend Sandra busts in here and tries to sell you on some more meringue."

She frowned at the dress, brushed her fingers along the delicate fabric. "It is lovely," she said softly. "For someone else."

We left the boutique and headed straight for one of our favorite Portland breweries for lunch. Once we were settled with a flight of beers and three appetizers between us, I revisited the wedding topic. "You've been engaged for a couple of months now—"

"A couple of months is two or three," she interjected. "It's been more than two or three months. It's spring. Seasons have come and gone while I've been engaged."

"And I see we're sensitive about that," I said, laughing.

"A little bit," she conceded. "I just feel like I should

have this sorted out by now." She laughed into her raspberry wheat. "If you asked my mother, she'd say I'm inexcusably far behind. She leaves me voicemails reminding me to make appointments with florists and bakeries and priests. But whenever Jackson and I try to decide on anything, we get derailed."

"Let's not call sex on the living room floor *getting derailed*." I shook my head. "It's punny, but we're better than that."

"There is that, but we're also trying to build a house and figure out how to live together without fighting over every little thing," she said. "The wedding is low on our list right now."

"And between all that living room floor sex and your mother, you're opting for the sex." I shrugged. "That's fair."

"My mother can't decide how she wants to handle this," Annette continued. "She's somewhere between wanting to make this bigger and better than my sisters' weddings, and being annoyed because I'm nothing like my sisters and won't go along with her daft ideas."

She went on venting about her mother's assortment of misguided wedding initiatives. I listened, nodding and sympathizing as best I could. Her mother wasn't my favorite person. She wasn't kind to my friend and I was waiting for an opportunity to call her on that shit. But beyond my frustrations with Mrs. Cortassi, I found myself wondering about my mother and how she would've reacted to me getting engaged.

I tended to believe my mother would've transformed into a steamroller, knocking me and my fiancé out of the way while she planned a showstopper of a wedding. It would be at home, of course, as she and my father were married there and she loved tradition when it fit her interests. She would've ordered the most opulent tent and bought all the flowers in New England. Every last one of them. The cake would be banana. Fucking banana. I'd wear whatever she told me to and style my hair as she instructed, and I'd do it without complaint or argument because I had to be perfect. Had to be perfect for her, for everyone.

It was macabre to think it, but I'd always known she'd die suddenly. My mother lived for putting on a show. It was always going to be the blink of an eye or a long, epic, slow process where she died but came back to life at least three or four times because everyone loved a good sob story.

"Shit," Annette murmured.

I glanced around the nearly empty restaurant, but couldn't locate a cause for concern. "What?"

"I'm going on about my mother and how I'd rather she go back to ignoring me." She gestured toward me. "And that's really insensitive of me."

"Oh, no, don't worry," I said, waving her off. "I'm fine. It never gets better, but it's okay. I don't think I want to get married anyway."

Annette gaped at me. "What? Since when? We've had no fewer than four thousand conversations about our fantasy weddings. You've already planned your groom's cake and you haven't even met him yet." She leaned forward, peering at me. "Why are you feeling all the feels today?"

"I'm not feeling all the feels." I busied myself with the beer flights, lifting and sniffing each glass before sipping. "This is your day to try on heinous dresses and have tiny panic attacks in them. This isn't about me and I'm *not* feeling the feels."

"I'll admit I had a tiny panic attack if you admit you're having deep, boggy feels."

I drained two different beers and shoved a slab of nachos in my mouth. "Fine," I said around the chips. "Feels."

"This is good. It's progress," Annette said, pointing at the empty glasses. "Drown them in beer and cheese." She nibbled a chip. "Was it the dresses or the wedding talk that did it?"

I shook my head. "Neither, I don't think. I don't know why I've had these—what did you call them?—boggy feels."

That was the truth. I didn't know where all these emotions came from or why they seemed to flood my waking moments, but I was lonely. Not alone, but lonely. Living with my father was like living with a ghost. In many ways, he was gone. He didn't recognize me, didn't call me by name, didn't remember his own name, couldn't care for himself. He hadn't experienced a good day in many, many days.

But he was very much alive. He was obsessed with banana cream pie and *Laverne and Shirley* reruns. He played Monopoly with one of his home health aides for six hours straight last week and required help to bathe and use the toilet. He was a living, breathing person but my father was gone.

Annette snagged another chip from the nacho plate. "Getting derailed might help."

JUST ONE MORE TIME, I promised myself as I headed toward the village that night. *There's nothing wrong with it as long as it's just one more time.*

When I reached the Galley, I stopped outside and stared up at the sign over the door. Scowled at it. I couldn't remember the last time I'd paid attention to the round logo with words arched over the top and a busty mermaid with a handful of wheat and berries—which made no sense whatsoever.

Aside from the logistical issues of a mermaid holding field crops, when did mermaids become things of admiration rather than animosity? The whole of history painted them as temptresses with fickle moods and violent methods. If they weren't seducing seamen into unchartered depths, they were gathering storms to toss those seamen and their ships into riptides and rocks.

It was never the sailors who encroached upon their sacred waters. Their warning songs and brutal storms were never acts of self-defense. The fishermen who reeled in mermaids and tortured them on ship decks weren't getting their due. Rather, it was the mermaid's fault for swimming too close to their nets.

She was asking for it.

And now, somehow, that mermaid represented beauty and whimsy and mystery, and that was splendid. But it didn't erase three thousand years of men blaming mermaids for their existence. And it didn't explain why this one was holding wheat and berries.

I found the tavern mostly empty when I pushed through the heavy door. Not surprising. This town marked its days by sunrises rather than sunsets, and anyone who worked on the water was tucked into bed by now.

Several familiar faces dotted the tavern, but the game playing on the television consumed their attention. Nate Fitzsimmons stood behind the bar, busy marking notes on a clipboard. No one noticed as I slipped into my usual seat on the far end.

I wasn't concerned about finding JJ. I'd put eyes on him when the time was right.

I checked my phone and then tucked it into my back pocket when I found no new messages. Jackson and Annette were watching a movie—rather, having sex while a movie played in the background—and my father was asleep. Barring any disasters, I'd have a couple hours before anyone noticed me missing.

Nate tapped his clipboard on the edge of the bar. He looked older than I'd remembered, with lines creasing his forehead, the edges of his eyes, his mouth. Tired too, but he'd bulked up since the last time I saw him. His shirt strained over his chest and his legs looked like tree trunks. "What can I get you?"

I hesitated. "What do you have for white wines tonight? Anything you'd find outside of this one-stoplight village where dreams go to die and conventional wisdom predates the Civil Rights movement?"

It took him a moment, but he chuckled. "Let me see

what I can find. Are you looking for something dry or something sweet?"

The door to the storeroom burst open as JJ backed in with a keg in tow. "Nothing sweet about that one." To Nate, he said, "Put the empty out back with the others going to Allagash."

My chin propped on my palm, I watched while Nate removed one keg and JJ tapped another. He did it with an eye on the ball game and that was when I knew I really needed to have sex because there was nothing hot about him distractedly tapping a keg.

Still watching the game, he asked, "What brings you in here tonight, Bam Bam? Where's Annette?"

"It's just me," I said.

"Haven't seen you without your sidekick in months."

He had to call me on that. Had to make note of the fact I hadn't crossed the tavern's threshold without using my best friend as a human shield. Yes, I'd hidden behind Annette since leaving JJ on the sidewalk outside my father's house *months* ago. And it'd worked. She was a glowing bounty of goodness and light, and it wasn't unusual for her to shine like the center of the Cove's solar system.

As the moon to her sun, it was easier for me to fade into the background, especially now that she was engaged to the sheriff. The townspeople couldn't stop dousing her in well wishes and I was happy for her—and happy for the reprieve. While the endless familiarity often bothered the hell out of me, the folks around here were mostly kind and decent and they always asked after my father.

There was only one problem with those questions: no one knew about Dad's dementia. As far as this nosy, in-your-back-pocket town was concerned, Dad was involved in a single vehicle car accident a little more than two years ago which resulted in a badly broken leg and long-term mobility issues. They didn't know he'd emptied the contents of his refrigerator into the trunk before driving away, barefoot, and losing control of his car in the middle of nowhere, about eighty miles inland. They didn't know he'd been restrained and then sedated after punching a medical assistant in the mouth. And they didn't know I'd chartered a plane from New York City to get here as soon as possible, only for him to demand I keep his secret.

That was one of the last lucid conversations we'd shared, and it'd left me carrying a burden of unimaginable weight while those good, decent Talbott's Covians kept peppering me with their questions and concerns and prayers. So many prayers. Sooner or later, those prayers were bound to kick in. Right?

JJ shot a glimpse in my direction before testing the keg. "I was beginning to think you and Annette were joined at the hip."

"We would be if Jackson didn't mind me sleeping with them." I shrugged. "Strange as it is, he draws the line there."

JJ stepped away from the keg and turned to face me, his hands fisted on his hips. "What do you want, Brooke?"

"As I mentioned, some wine would be nice."

He shook his head. "I don't think so."

"Excuse you?"

"You heard me," he replied. We stared at each other

until Nate returned from the back room and crossed between us. To the other man, he said, "I'm going to check on the small batches. Work on hustling Lincoln out of here before his wife comes looking for him. I'm not interested in staging any more domestic disputes."

"Amen to that," Nate muttered.

JJ spared me a glance that came across as one part irritation, one part impatience, and one last part interest. I could work with the aggregate. "Drink your wine and go home, Brooke."

He set a glass in front of me before turning on his heel and marching into the storeroom. Nate and I stared at the door swinging shut behind JJ. "Put this on my tab," I said.

Nate tucked a dishrag into his back pocket. "You don't have a tab, Miss Markham. Boss's orders."

"Your boss is needlessly rude." I slipped off the stool, yanked a twenty out of my bra and dropped it on the bar. He eyed the cash as if it was contaminated with boob sweat, which it was. "I need to have a talk with that boss of yours." I paused at the door to the back room, my palm flat on the slab. "Do me a favor, Fitzsimmons. Stay out here, even if you hear yelling and glass breaking and all kinds of mayhem."

He glanced at the cash again. "Is that supposed to cover mayhem?"

"It is if you interrupt." I didn't wait for him to respond, instead pushing into the dim room. The last time I'd visited, I'd missed the entire chemistry lab setup back here. There were tanks and beakers and devices I couldn't name. A floor-to-ceiling rack stood off to the side with a dozen rows of glass bottles, each bearing a scribbled label. "What the hell is all this?"

I heard an exasperated sigh before setting eyes on JJ. He crossed his arms over his chest and scowled as if he could warn me off with an angry pose and some bared teeth. He had the audacity to do all that while also wearing million-year-old jeans, a button-up with sleeves rolled to his elbows, and a goddamn tweed vest. He was so fucking grouchy and it made me want to push at him, poke and scratch that mood. I wanted to antagonize him until he pushed and poked and scratched right back. Until he snapped.

"Jesus Christ, Brooke, what do you want?"

I circled his work table, dragging my fingertips over the surface as I went. "Did you order that vest from the Bartenders of Brooklyn catalog?" I moved behind him, my fingers ghosting over his shoulders and earning me some major side-eye as I went. "It looks very official. I mean, Brooklyn as fuck, but also official."

He hooked his hand around the waist of my jeans as I passed him, jerked my body flush against his. "Admit it," he ordered, his teeth pressed to my neck and his palm low on my backside. *More of that, please. More more more.* "Admit you lied."

"I'm sure I don't know what you mean," I replied. "I'm also sure you have no business questioning my integrity."

His fingers followed the seam of my jeans down, between my legs. *More.* "You said never again, sweetheart, but look at you." His other hand slipped under my sweater, his knuckles brushing the underside of my breasts. "Admit it. You came out to play, didn't you?"

A fractional piece of me wanted to say yes, to surrender. To get what I needed. But the rest of me knew better than to surrender to any man. "Just as soon as you explain why your mermaid is carrying wheat and berries."

"My fucking what?" he growled into my hair.

"Your sign, Jed. You have a mermaid on your sign and she's holding wheat and berries, and I shouldn't have to explain to you that neither grow close enough to the coast for mermaids to be in possession of either."

"Mmhmm." He palmed my ass and boosted me up onto the table. "You came here to argue about the plausibility of mermaids getting their hands on some fruit? That's what you want, Bam?"

I raked my hands down his tweed vest, laced my legs around his waist. "I'd like your signage to make sense, even if it is promulgating misogynistic mythology."

He planted his hands on the table, caging me in his arms. "I'll give you a fight if that's what you want. Just tell me, sweetheart."

I met his gaze, tipped my chin up. "Admit your sign— the one with the outrageously voluptuous mermaid—is inaccurate and illogical."

He bowed his head and bit the side of my breast through my sweater. "Meet me at my place in half an hour and we'll talk about the right kind of voluptuous."

"Are you mocking me?" I shoved him away from the sweater covering my barely B-cup breasts. "No amount of dick is worth dealing with a dickhead."

He rasped out a growl as he returned to my cleavage. "I haven't forgotten how much you liked the dick *and* the dickhead, Bam. You haven't forgotten either."

"You know what? I don't need this." I scooted forward to get off the table, but JJ fisted the hem of my sweater, held me in place. "I don't know what you think you're doing, but I don't need you for this."

"You wouldn't be here if that was true." He twisted my sweater around his hands until it tightened against my body. "I'm not mocking you and I'm not taking your shit either. I want your tits in my mouth and I'll debate some fuckin' mermaids with you while I do it if that's what you need to make it work in your head." He turned his hands once more, banding the cashmere under my bra like a tourniquet. He leaned close, his short beard tickling my neck, and pressed his lips to my jaw. "But if your ass isn't waiting for me at my house within thirty minutes, don't think you'll ever play this game with me again, Bam."

A gasp shuddered out of me as he tightened the sweater once more and kissed my cheek, right at the corner of my lips. Then he was gone, the door swinging behind him.

My fingers pressed to my not-quite-kissed lips, glanced down at the wrinkled, stretched-out mess he'd made of my sweater. "Look what you've done now."

CHAPTER FOURTEEN

JJ

Compound Interest: interest paid on previously earned interest as well as principal.

"YOU'RE CLOSING UP, KID," I called to Nate as I blew into the bar.

I'd spent twenty minutes pacing the short length of the walk-in refrigerator. I'd solved all of jack shit in there. I stepped up to the point of sale system as I adjusted the unflagging bulge behind my zipper, but that didn't escape the notice of my bar hand.

"Did you hear me? You're closing."

He eyed me up and down before saying, "This seems like the type of situation where I should advise you to run far and fast in the opposite direction."

"From Brooke?" I asked, hooking a thumb over my shoulder toward the storeroom of ill-repute. "Nah, I've tried that. Doesn't help. She's the kind of storm you ride out."

"You're sure about me closing? I'm allowed to do that?"

I tapped the screen to run a day-end report. He'd been on the job more than six months now and I'd learned enough about him in that time to know he could handle more than his history of guilty pleas and rehab stays suggested. His humor was dark and his work ethic was mile-long, and he hadn't slipped up once since leaving his treatment program. "Why the hell not?"

Nate continued unpacking a crate of freshly washed glassware. "Would you like that in brief form or bullet points? Chronological order or degree of severity? My parents prefer chronological, if you were wondering."

I squeezed my eyes shut, rubbed my thumb across my brow. I knew everyone had their limits, but I couldn't understand why Nate's parents insisted on persecuting him for his mistakes while he worked his ass off turning his life around. It was a fine thing that they'd stopped coming in here, because that shit wasn't helping anyone. "This isn't the time to be self-deprecating. Just tell me whether you can handle the close-up checklist."

"Yeah. I have this under control." He glanced between me and the door. "I'd thank you for trusting me with the responsibility, but I don't think this decision has anything to do with me."

I closed my hands around the edge of the countertop, dropped my head between my shoulders. My entire body throbbed. Every last inch of me. This fucking *hurt* and I was the only one to blame. I could've stripped off Brooke's clothes and given us what we needed right there in the back room. All I needed was five minutes to finish her off and send her on her way.

But the same part of me throbbing from nothing more than her skin under my lips couldn't accept five minutes in a storage room. It'd taken me months to admit it to myself, but I wanted her naked between my sheets, mouthing off about everything, taking her sweet time as she struggled on my cock.

And I fucking hated that.

My life was too busy and my head too full to add the complication of Brooke-Ashley Markham. I had a tavern to manage, a distillery to open, a business partner obsessed with pirates and hard seltzers, a foster child bar hand trying to find his sea legs, and now that months had passed without her looking me in the eye once, Brooke was back and starved for attention. That was all she wanted from me—attention. Sex was part of it, sure, but not the entirety.

"If I didn't trust you, I wouldn't ask," I said to Nate. "This is your last chance, kid. Tell me if you're prepared to close."

He swung his gaze from side to side, a frown deepening as he scanned the tavern. "Can I call you if there's a problem?"

I didn't need the complications that came with Brooke. I didn't need the distraction or the drama, or the months-long sexual hangover that followed a night with her. But needs and wants were two separate, distinct creatures.

I folded my arms over my chest, gave a quick shake of my head. "There's not a chance in hell I'm answering my phone after I leave here."

Nate stared at the door to the back room, narrowed his eyes. "Is she still in there?"

"Probably not," I replied. "There's a delivery bay, an exit to the alley, and four windows. I'm sure she went through one of them. She's crafty."

"That's—well, okay." His brows arched up his forehead. "Yeah, all right. I can do this."

"You're a good man, Nathan." I clapped him on the back. "If everything goes wrong, just lock the doors behind you. Try not to start any fires or floods."

"I can do that," he replied. "I can lock the doors."

"Yes, you can," I called as I backed across the tavern. I was ready to sprint my ass home. "No fires, no floods."

I didn't wait for Nate's response, instead breaking into an easy jog through the village. It was late enough that most people were at home, zoned out in front of the television or tucked into bed, not minding the likes of me hauling ass for a woman who'd always demand but never appreciate that hustle.

And there she was, kicked back on my porch with her legs stretched out in front of her, ankles crossed. "That was thirty-nine minutes, Jed."

I stepped over her on my way to the door. "You can take your complaints up with my cock, Brooke."

"I'm merely pointing out you asked me to be here within thirty minutes," she continued. "Either you don't respect my time or this is some kind of dickhead power play, and I have to tell you, I'm not interested in either."

I opened the door, flipped on the lights, greeted Butterscotch with a head scratch. It was odd to find her awake at this hour. "It's always something with you, Brooke," I said, mostly to myself. The dog wasted no time on me, instead rushing to the woman's side as if she'd been waiting for her. *You and me both, Scotchie.* "At least the dog likes you. I'd have to say good night if she didn't."

Brooke glanced up from dousing the golden retriever in affection, smirked at me. "It's a wonder she likes you."

I kicked off my shoes, shrugging. "I feed her. Speaking of which, have you eaten?"

Brooke knelt down, raked her fingers through the dog's shiny coat. "Don't ask me questions like that."

"And why is that?"

Still focused on my dog, she replied, "You're not my keeper. It's none of your business."

"I was asking because *I* haven't eaten but this is a fine reminder you're an awful lot of work." I ran a hand over my head. "What are you doing here again?"

"Take your pants off and I'll show you." She stood up, sanded her palms together, and tipped her chin in the direction of my jeans. "You can eat after I leave."

"Or right now." I pointed at her jeans, her top. "Off."

She flicked a glance at my belt. "Same."

Neither of us moved. Butterscotch paced between us, alternately licking our hands and nudging our legs as she whined.

Brooke held out her palm and Butterscotch went to her. "Your dog wants you to stop screwing around."

I whistled, snapped my fingers in the direction of the kitchen. "Scotchie, go lie down." The dog gave Brooke one more lick before taking off for the kitchen. "Are you going to get what you came for or are you going to stand there and prove a point only you care about?"

"Why is your mermaid holding wheat?"

"Why did you move home from New York?"

That one landed like a slap across the face. It wasn't the reaction I'd wanted, not the one I'd intended, but she recovered quickly. "My question requires considerably less explanation, so you're welcome to answer first."

"You might think it's simple, but I reckon it's just as complicated as the one I want from you. There's some history, some family shit, and some laziness, and that's the answer."

She glared at me, the air between us heating and rippling with hostility with each breath. Then she charged toward me, her head shaking as she seethed, "You are the *worst*."

My back hit the wall as she reached for my vest, weaving her fingers between the buttons, dragging me toward her. I didn't doubt she'd tear it to shreds if she wanted. "And I keep good company."

I grabbed her waist, thumbed her fly open. I stared at her lips, and for a moment, I thought about kissing her. Nothing sweet or precious, but the kind of biting, brutal kiss she deserved—and wanted. I didn't doubt that for a second. She wanted me rough and rude, not giving a good damn whether I ruined her sweater or marked her skin. But I didn't kiss her. Not yet, not this time. Kisses were promises, even the vicious ones. Especially those.

"There's no confusion as to why you're here, sweetheart. Either get undressed or get the fuck out. I want your bare ass in my hands right now or we're not doing this tonight"—I shoved my hand down her panties and flicked her clit hard—"or any other night."

"What the fuck was that?" Brooke wailed.

"Exactly what you want," I replied, forcing her jeans down to her knees.

She yanked the vest open, sending at least one button flying across the room as it snapped free of the thread. I had her sweater over her head and off while she worked my shirt open. "Why the fuck did you stop wearing long-sleeved thermals?" she yelled. "You know, the ones without buttons? You used to wear those thermals every damn day unless it was summer, but no, you had to go and complicate your life with buttons."

The next time my cock wasn't throbbing a hole through my jeans, I planned to make sense of Brooke's accounting of my attire. But right now, I had her bra unhooked, but I couldn't discard today's fine lingerie until she gave up the button fight. "Would you fucking stop with the shirt?"

"You stop with the bra," she yelled. "Let me do this."

"Let go of the goddamn shirt. I'll take it off myself." I closed my fists around the delicate bra cups, tugged them apart. "If you think I won't rip this thing in half, you're not paying attention."

She dragged her gaze up my chest, to my face. "Don't you dare."

"Have it your way." I grabbed her hands away from the shirt and freed the bra from her arms. My shirt was quick to follow. "Just so you know, your way does not involve you fiddling with buttons for an hour."

I pinned her wrists behind her back and held them there with one hand. I shoved the other into her panties and strummed her clit as I walked her toward my bedroom.

"Rude," she muttered.

"Yeah, just the way you like me, Bam." I kicked the door shut and wasted no time yanking her jeans all the way off, bending her over the bed, pressing her cheek flat on the quilt. I traced the line of her panties from waist to hip to crotch. "What am I allowed to do? Or do you still not know what you need?"

"Bag up your meat and fuck me," she answered. "Don't act as if you know anything about me."

I fisted her panties, twisting the fabric until it wedged between her folds. She sent me furious glares over her shoulder, but she also squirmed like crazy to get the friction she wanted.

"You're cute like this," I said as I kicked off my remaining clothes and fished a condom out of my bedside table. "Never cuter than when you're bent over and snarling mad."

She wiggled out of the panties. "Is that supposed to be a compliment?"

I kicked her ankles apart and took my cock in hand, pressed it to her opening. Of all the things I hadn't been able to get out of my head in the past few months, the way her body opened to me was the most vivid. I remembered it like a punishment.

"It's true." Pushing that thought from my mind, I

slammed inside her. I stayed there, my head bowed and every inch of me throbbing as she shifted beneath me. I listened to her uncomfortable gasps and frustrated sighs, holding myself steady as she adjusted to me. I thought I wanted this. I thought I'd enjoy watching her struggle like she did the last time, thought I'd get some satisfaction out of it. I didn't. I wanted to make it better, make it good for her. *So fucking good.* "It's true, Brooke."

"If you think calling me cute will soften me up, you're extremely confused."

"Not confused." I eased out of her, hooked my arms around her shoulders and behind her knees, and chucked her on the bed. "I know how to soften you up."

She went with a yelp and a curse—"Motherfucker!"—but her legs fell open when I crawled over her, a clear and welcome invitation.

I rested my weight on one arm as I fisted my cock, moving inside her with slow, easy rolls of my hips. She barely had half of me, but that half was heaven. There was a reason men were content with just the tip.

"This is better for you," I said. She licked her lips, hummed in agreement. "Then it's better for me."

"Don't bullshit me," she said, canting her hips up to take more. "The last thing in the world I want is your patronizing, nice guy bullshit."

"I don't know how I went from being the asshole to the nice guy, but I'm not patronizing you with any amount of bullshit, sweetheart." I dropped my forehead to her chest, ran my lips around her nipple. "Is this all right?"

Instead of speaking, she arched up, feeding me her

small breast. I licked and sucked her nipple to a stiff peak while I snared the other between two knuckles. Now this, *this* was all right. She was wet like a river and all her tightly wound tension was melting away.

I couldn't claim to know everything about Brooke's mind or body, but I knew it took time for her to relax enough to enjoy this. She came to me with a head of steam and enough stress to form a diamond, and none of that disappeared when I dropped my pants. I couldn't argue it away and I couldn't fuck it away; I had to learn how to unravel it. I had to learn Brooke, and I was beginning to believe I wanted to make room for that challenge in my life. It was foolish and definitely in service to my dick, but I liked this. No matter what happened when it was all said and done tonight, it wasn't ending here.

"Your cock is not as great as you think," she said, her nails cutting into my biceps. "You need to do something with it. You need to move. You can't just stick it inside me and think you're done."

This fucking woman. Goddamn, I did not want to like her.

"And you can't just lie there and expect me to know what you want," I replied, giving her a slow roll of my hips. "Speak up, sweetheart."

"Keep doing that," she said, her head thrown back and her eyes closed. "Keep doing that and—*mmmm*."

"That is the right fuckin' answer, Bam."

BROOKE SIGHED at the ceiling approximately thirteen seconds after I rolled off her.

"Time for me to go. This was, well"—she glanced at me—"you know what it was. No need to explain."

My dick was half hard and still wet, and there was no reason for anyone to leave this bed. "Nah, you're staying right there."

"In fact, I am not. I'm leaving." She said this, but she remained where I'd left her.

"Give me two or three minutes." I moved my hand to her thigh, dragged my fingers over her silky skin. God, she felt good. "Don't move. The blood flow will return in my extremities and then I'm licking your pussy."

She shifted to her side, which put my hand between her legs. No complaints from either of us. "That's a real nice offer, but I'm leaving."

"Do I have to teach you how to enjoy that too?" I slipped a finger inside her, grinned at the way her eyes popped wide in response. "I don't mind, Bam. I'll put in the hours. I'll do the work."

"Your opinion of yourself is not proportional to the quality of your dick," she replied. "It would be nice if the two had a stronger correlation."

I brought my hand between her breasts, pushed her back down as I shifted to my knees. "Let's see how my tongue rates."

I was still shattered from the orgasm she snapped out of me like a sea witch's curse, but I wasn't passing up an opportunity to win an argument. Not a fucking chance.

I settled between her legs, careful to scratch my beard

up her inner thighs as I found a comfortable position. She made some quiet noises, little gasps and whines that suggested she liked these moves, but the best indicator was the way her belly jiggled. There wasn't much to her, not an inch to pinch, but the area around her belly button was barely soft enough to telegraph every clench and release.

"I know it's lovely down there and I do put some effort into keeping things tight and tidy," she said, "but I was under the impression you were doing more than rubbing your beard all over my leg and making eye contact with my clit."

I blinked up at her for a second. I thought about arguing with her, but quickly determined the best course of action required no words. I shoved both hands under her ass, dragged her center to my mouth, and got my first real taste of her. Her clit was the most perfect little pearl. I couldn't stop circling it and sucking it while her body shook in my hands. That clit tasted like I was meant to obey it and fuck me if I wasn't ready to kneel.

In no time at all, I had her belly quivering and her most delicate flesh throbbing under my tongue. And since I was here, I was getting that ass too.

"Jed," she cried, her hands fisting around my hair. "Jed, I'm—almost—what—oh my, *fuck*."

The spasms crested and I backed off when she pulled my hair harder. I knew she could take more, but I wasn't going to tell her how to own and operate her body tonight. I'd save that for tomorrow night.

My head resting on her thigh, I looped an arm around

her waist and pressed tiny kisses on her mound. "How'd I do?"

"This isn't the Olympic ice dancing qualifier. Stop waiting for a score every time you put on a show." She said this, but she also brushed her hand through my hair with more plain, transparent affection than she'd ever offered.

I flopped down beside her on the pillow. "When should I expect you again?"

"Expect me?" She sat up, an arm banded over her breasts as if I couldn't identify them in a blind taste test. "Why the hell would you *expect* me?"

"Because you'll be back." I dragged my gaze down the heart-shaped curve of her ass. "We both know you will be, so there's no sense in pretending otherwise. You're not a silly woman, Brooke. Don't play silly games with me."

"Is that because you believe I'm fond of your dick? Because I'd skip the victory lap if I was you. I can count the single guys in this dismal, hole-in-the-wall town on one hand and that includes old widower Lambertson, the Mulcaheys' grandson, who can't be more than twenty, and your little friend Nate, who is also too damn young for me." She climbed off the bed and stood in the middle of my bedroom, completely nude, and said without a hint of humor, "You're the least offensive option in the bunch."

I shouldn't have fallen for the obvious trap she laid, but I couldn't stop myself. Her words annoyed the shit out of me, so I laid a trap of my own. "Here's what I can't understand, Brooke. If you hate living here so much, why don't you leave? Go back to New York?"

She scooped a stray shirt off the floor, held it to her chest. She refused to meet my eyes. "I have my reasons."

"Such as? While you're at it, why don't you fill me in on why you came back here in the first place." I watched as she slipped my shirt over her head and took great pains to keep her gaze away from me. "I have some ideas, but I'd love to hear it from you, sweetheart."

"You don't get to call me that," she said, her voice barely audible. "And you don't know anything about me."

"You're not that difficult to understand, sweetheart."

"Uh, yeah, okay. Whatever. Believe what you want, but I don't have to sit here while you make all these accusations."

"I've accused you of nothing."

She snatched the only remaining pillow from the bed and winged it at my head while I pulled on my clothes. "It sounds like you're accusing me of something."

Tell me the truth. Tell me what's happening with your father and I'll help you. "Nothing you're not guilty of."

"Oh my god. I'm so finished with this." She pushed past me, into the hall. "What the hell is wrong with you? We had sex, that's it. You're not entitled to explanations. You don't have to go and explore issues and make sense of things." She stepped into her jeans, wrapped her sweater around her shoulders as if she'd planned on wearing it that way all along. "All you have to do is get your dick out and shut up, and apparently, that's too much to ask of you."

"It's a reasonable question, Brooke. You don't hide the fact you hate it here. What's the problem with asking why you stay?"

She shook her head and then flung the front door open. "Do not follow me."

The door banged shut behind her while I shoved my feet into shoes and whistled for Butterscotch. We stayed a fair distance behind Brooke, but that didn't stop her from tossing furious glances over her shoulder every few minutes.

"Why are you in such a rush?" I called. "It's the middle of the night."

"Oh, well, since you asked," she shouted back, "I'm going to get some work done. I'd planned on enjoying the post-orgasmic haze, but someone ruined that for me with a bullshit conversation that's none of his fucking business. I'm awake and I'm aggravated, so I might as well make some money."

"You could turn around and come home with me. You won't be aggravated when I'm done."

"One cannot be the source and the solution," she said. "I'm finished with you."

"For tonight," I added.

"Forever. I'm done with you *forever*. There are no circumstances in which you will ever see me naked again."

"You say that, sweetheart, and I know you think you mean it. But I also know you'll be back."

She stopped near the village, pivoted, and stared at me for a solid minute. Then, "Jed, I'd rather trip and fall into hot garbage in Midtown during a heat wave than get on your dick again."

Butterscotch galloped to Brooke's side and nuzzled her thigh. She murmured something to the dog and scratched her head, and they continued into the village side by side. They stayed together all the way up the hill to the Markham estate, Butterscotch's head brushing Brooke's hand every few steps.

I shoved my hands into my pockets and trailed behind them, content to follow—and wait.

CHAPTER FIFTEEN

BROOKE

Marketable Securities: financial instruments that can be readily converted into cash.

Annette: Were you walking a dog last night?

Brooke: Good morning to you too.

Annette: Were you walking a dog in the middle of the night? Because one of Jackson's deputies swears he witnessed that exact thing and I...have so many questions.

Brooke: Can you describe the dog?

Annette: I didn't ask for details. All I heard was dog.

Brooke: Sounds unlikely.

Annette: And yet it wouldn't shock me if it was true.

Brooke: That says more about you than it does me.

Annette: Are you sure about that?

Annette: Did you walk any dogs last night?

Brooke: I did not, no.

Annette: Will you be walking any tonight?

Brooke: Can't see why I would…

Annette: I wasn't sure whether it's something new you're doing, like goat yoga.

Brooke: I'm not doing goat yoga. That sounds horrible. I don't want a goat in my face while I'm in downward dog, thank you.

Annette: But middle of the night dog walking? That's an option?

Brooke: Probably not.

Brooke: You know what's hard?

Annette: It feels like you're walking me into a dick joke.

Brooke: Ha. I wouldn't have this issue if I had some good dick available.

Annette: Go back to the Galley. That worked out well the last time.

Brooke: You don't fish in the same pond twice. It's a well-known proverb.

Annette: You just made that up.

Brooke: Maybe but I'm having real problems.

Annette: All right. Tell me what's hard.

Brooke: Trying to have some alone time with my new vibrator when Dad is taking a bath across the hall and having a loud conversation with his health aide about the town council being a pack of fools.

Annette: Yeah, that's rough.

Brooke: I'm almost certain he's referencing a council from the 1970s, but he's talking like it's today and it's messing with my orgasm.

Annette: Wait. Is the problem that you can hear him while you're visiting your amusement park or is it that he's talking like it's the 1970s?

Brooke: Honestly, a bit of both.

Annette: I'm sure you could leave the house, go to the Galley, meet someone, and fix that situation.

Brooke: Nah. I don't feel like putting pants on.

Annette: Also valid, but try some noise-canceling headphones.

Brooke: I've tried those and discovered dead silence is not an improvement over rants about lousy small town politicians.

Annette: Then put your damn pants on!

Brooke: You know what's funny? The idea of putting pants on in order to find someone to take them off.

Annette: You're stalling. Do not make me come to your house and dress you myself. I will. I'll also drag you down the street and force you to flirt with people at the Galley.

Brooke: omfg Annette, when did you get so militant?

Annette: Everything I know, I've learned from you.

CHAPTER SIXTEEN

JJ

Fixed Costs: a cost that will remain constant regardless of the amount of goods or services produced.

BROOKE WAS in one hell of a rotten mood.

I knew it the minute she blew into the tavern, all thunder and lightning. I saw it in the scowl permanently twisted across her lips, the stiff line of her shoulders, the joyless chill in her eyes. It was the same way she'd blown out of my house four nights ago.

I cataloged her every movement as she swept across the tavern toward her usual seat at the bar. She worked hard at dodging my gaze, but that wouldn't last long. Once could be forgiven, twice was a mistake, three times was a pattern—and she was here for her third.

Turning away from the territory she'd claimed as her own, I sidled up to Nate. He was running the bar tonight and having a tough go of it. It was barely ten o'clock and we'd wasted more beer on foamy pours than I wanted to price out in my head. My pet project had also forgotten the ingredients to the most basic drinks—gin and tonic, anyone?—and looked damn close to melting down on several occasions, including this one. "How goes it, kid?"

Nate shook his hands at the taps. "Not great," he whispered, mostly to himself. "It's not great."

I glanced between him and the handles. "What's the problem?"

"That's a question I'd really like to answer, but I have no clue why I can't pour more than one beer at a time."

"Then don't pour more than one at a time." I clapped him on the back. "You run the ship, kid. It sails as fast or slow as you want, and these people"—I tipped my head toward the regular crew—"are just happy you're pouring them."

He closed his eyes, pressed the palms of his hands there. "I'm sorry."

"For what?" I asked. "For making some suds? That's nothing."

"For—it's just everything. You gave me a chance and I'm just fucking it up," he replied, still hidden behind his hands.

I turned in a half circle, scanning the bar and tavern. "That isn't reality, Nate. Look around. You have this under control." I elbowed him toward Brooke. "I'll handle these pours. Go get Miss Markham's order."

He dropped his hands to his hips. "Is it still on the house?"

I responded with a quick nod and pushed him in her direction. I didn't want to elaborate on that piece of legislation. It made sense to me in a convoluted way: any woman who shared my bed and consumed my waking thoughts drank for free. But more than that, I didn't want Brooke's money. She had a whole fucking lot of it, more than most people would see in ten lifetimes, and I wasn't prepared to mix that with sex. I didn't even like thinking about it. She didn't like anyone thinking about it either, but she came from old money and found a fuckton of new money for herself in Manhattan. No doubt about that.

Forcing myself to keep my focus away from Brooke, I went to work filling pint glasses. It gave me a moment to sweep a gaze over the corner of the bar closest to the television and gauge Bobbie Lincoln's degree of inebriation. As far as I could tell from beer-wet splotches on his shirt and his inability to simultaneously focus both eyes, he was far beyond his usual state. He seemed to be the only one getting more than foam from Nate's pours.

Lincoln was drunk every night of every week, but it tended toward pleasant, mild drunkenness rather than this evening's version of morose and increasingly hostile. He'd started bitching about sports to anyone who would listen, but the urge to instigate got the best of him and he'd transitioned to divisive political topics. No one was engaging—hell, I wasn't sure they were listening—but that didn't stop him from ramping up the rhetoric.

If I was smart, I'd ring the sheriff or one of his deputies to escort Lincoln home. But my bar hand spooked easily, and calling in the sheriff's deputies was certain to jangle his nerves even more. I didn't want to wash another keg down the drain. Add to those issues the fact I was short-staffed in the kitchen and playing phone tag with both Barry and the marketing coordinator he wanted to hire for the distillery's branding, and every aspect of the project was taking five times longer than planned.

And Brooke was in a ranty, pouty, jerky shoulders, rolling eyes mood. God, I wanted to fuck it right out of her. I would. But not yet. Not until I contained a few issues.

Once I'd cleared the pending beverage orders, I headed into the back room without glancing in Brooke's direction. Ignoring her served two purposes. First, it annoyed the hell out of her and I enjoyed nothing more than turning her screws. And second, I didn't trust myself to get a mouthful of her salty mood and not drag her out of that seat.

Free from the oppressive heat of Brooke's gaze, I fired off text messages to the Cove's innkeeper Rhys Neville, gently begging him to take Lincoln off my hands. When he agreed, I ducked into the kitchen to assess the situation there. The dinner rush was behind us, thank god, but running a kitchen without enough hands on deck was a nightmare. I checked the walk-in fridge for prepped goods, sent messages to suppliers to adjust tomorrow's deliveries, and returned to the back room. I took my time inspecting the kegs, bottled beer, and liquor stored in there.

When I emerged, I made a point of looking out across the dining room—and avoiding the devastatingly irresistible woman seated in her usual spot. I scanned the occupied tables, the patrons seated at the bar, the orders waiting to be fulfilled. I checked on Nate and found him managing a bit better now that he was out of the weeds.

Grabbing the day's inventory list from beside the point of sale system, I headed toward Brooke. I stopped two seats away from her, braced my forearms on the bar while I thumbed through the pages. It was enough distance to make it clear this mood didn't earn her my undivided attention. From the corner of my eye, I saw her fingertips tapping the walls of her glass in a quick, erratic rhythm.

"Here's what you're going to do," I said, flipping to another page. "Go to my house. There's a key under the mat at the back door. Get undressed and wait for me in bed."

"And how long will I be waiting, good sir?"

I lifted a shoulder, let it fall. Continued staring at the pages without seeing. "Until I get there."

"That's not going to happen," she replied. "I'm not going to wait around in your bed—naked—until you're content I've learned some kind of lesson."

"And why would I be teaching you a lesson, Brooke?"

The electricity behind her stare dragged my focus up, away from the inventory. I wished I hadn't surrendered to that pull because even with her forehead creased and a snarl on her lips, she was unreasonably beautiful. It was unfair for one woman to be granted so many gifts and advantages.

"I'm certain you have a reason or twenty-nine." She tossed her platinum hair over her shoulder and I had to draw a breath because the memory of those strands on my skin twisted my gut. "You've never lacked for reasons to resent me, Jed."

"We're not having this conversation," I replied.

She clasped her hands under her chin. "It seems that we are."

I leaned forward, lowered my voice. "And yet conversation is the reason you stomped out of my house in the middle of the night, swearing up and down you'd never be back."

"Hmm." She arched an eyebrow up as if granting me a point in this match. "Perhaps I should go to your house, lube up my preferred vibrator, and take matters into my own hands. I'm sure I'd learn a lesson from that." Another arched eyebrow. "Or perhaps the lesson would be yours."

I gathered the inventory, pushed away from the bar. "You're welcome to do that, Brooke, but you should think of it as tonight's appetizer. You'll get the main course when it's good and ready for you."

I HELD out for ninety-three minutes.

It would've been longer if Nate hadn't spilled a full tray of whiskey shots on my jeans and boots, but I could live with ninety-three minutes. It was enough time for Brooke to simmer down or boil over, and I was prepared for either version of her.

I wasn't prepared to find her curled up on my bed with Butterscotch tucked in beside her, fully dressed and fast asleep. Her hair was everywhere, mouth open, arms tucked inside the body of her sweater, one shoe on, one off. For an unreasonably beautiful woman, she slept like a blacked-out teenager.

Leaning against the doorframe, I watched her longer than I should have. My clothes were wet and reeked of whiskey—and everything else at the tavern. My body was exhausted from sixteen solid hours of work and my head ached from the hours I needed to catch up on distillery business. But I went on watching while she slept with my dog until watching wasn't enough. Until I had to touch her.

I pushed away from the door and stood by the bed. "Are you tired from being angry all the time? Or angry because you're so damn tired? Which one is it, Bam?" I tucked her hair over her ear, dragged the strands between my fingers. "And how can I make it better?"

Even as the words passed my lips, I knew I didn't mean them. I didn't want to help. Truly, I didn't want that trouble in my life. Helping people wasn't my thing. This town was packed to the gills with nosy neighbors who lived to help each other, one pot roast and diaper drive at a time. That wasn't me. It wasn't my place.

But Brooke was asleep in my bed. She came to me in that storm of a mood and she let it drop long enough to curl up with my dog, put her head down, and close her eyes. She came to me. She asked for me, albeit in her supremely fucked-up way. She needed me.

I stayed there longer than I should have, rubbing her hair between my fingers and studying this open, unpracticed version of her. Eventually, I stepped away to discard my liquor- and grease-scented clothes. I thought about showering the day away, but more than anything, I wanted to know how it felt to sleep beside Brooke. I pulled on a pair of flannel pajama pants and a t-shirt and slipped into the bed behind her. It took a bit of finagling with the blankets to get her underneath them without waking her and Butterscotch, but I managed. She must've been absolutely exhausted.

"Sleep well, Bam." I kissed her shoulder over her shirt and retreated to my side of the bed. A soft canine snore huffed out. "You too, Scotchie."

CHAPTER SEVENTEEN

BROOKE

Drawdown: the percentage loss from a fund's highest value to its lowest over a given timeframe.

I WOKE up to a tongue on my face.

I wasn't opposed to oral wake-up calls, but face licking wasn't my preferred form of oral. Call me particular, but I also preferred that tongue to belong to a human being rather than a dog.

"Good morning to you too," I said to Butterscotch. "What the hell am I doing here?"

"Scotchie," JJ whisper-yelled from the other room. "Leave her alone."

"It's fine, she's awake," I called back. I sat up and crossed my legs, and rubbed the sleep from my eyes. Blinking, I ran my hands through my hair and spotted the hazy outline of JJ in the doorway. "What happened? Why is it"—I glanced at the clock—"oh my god, why am I here at six in the morning?"

"You fell asleep." He wagged a spatula at me. "I let you stay asleep."

"Why the hell would you do that?" I cried. "I came here for a dick appointment, not a sleepover."

He crossed his arms over his chest. "You were out cold. Sorry, but I'm not fucking you while you're unconscious."

"It sounds like you want me to congratulate you for that. I'm not going to." I drove my fingers through my hair again, groaning. "Did it not occur to you that I needed to get home? That people might be looking for me?"

He pushed his tongue against the inside of his cheek. Stared at me. Waiting a long damn time to say, "Your phone is plugged in on the other side of the bed. If anyone was looking for you, they would've called. No?"

"Maybe I had to work," I continued.

"In the middle of the night, Brooke?"

I held out my hands. "The beauty of international markets is that one is always open."

JJ rolled his eyes and glanced over his shoulder. "Come get some scrambled eggs."

I followed him into the kitchen, calling, "I didn't come here for the breakfast buffet."

He held his hand over a cast iron skillet on the stove, nodded, and poured the contents of a glass measuring cup into the pan. Over the sizzle of the eggs, JJ said, "We've established that, sweetheart, but it seemed like you needed some rest." He jerked a shoulder up. "A good breakfast wouldn't kill you either."

Hipshot and arms crossed, I said, "It's not your place to tell me when I need to sleep or eat. Having sex with me a handful of times doesn't entitle you to make my decisions."

"How do you feel about marble rye?"

I blinked at him. "What are you asking me?"

He stepped away from the stove to retrieve two wax paper-wrapped loaves of bread. He lifted one of them. "I have a fresh loaf of marble rye from a husband and wife bakery over in Charlotte, Vermont." Lifting the other, he said, "They also sent a whole grain raisin walnut with my order, but I don't get the impression you're a fan of raisin bread."

I took the raisin bread from him and unwrapped the paper. "What? Just because I want you to wake me up and fuck me into a mild concussion, I can't like raisins?" I sniffed the bread. "That seems ruder and more judgmental than your usual."

He snatched the loaf out of my hands and set it on the countertop beside the stove. "I'm sorry that, rather than leaving you to stumble home with a sex-induced brain injury, I allowed you to sleep. It's terrible, I know. Can I make it worse by feeding you breakfast, Brooke?"

"Yes," I replied, surprising us both. "But I want the raisin bread, lightly toasted." I helped myself to his French press coffee and watched while he scooped the eggs onto a plate. "I'd also like a rain check for that dick appointment you missed."

"That *I* missed," he grumbled.

While he sliced the bread, I drifted into the adjoining dining room with my coffee. Binders, boxes, and file folders sat on several chairs. Architectural blueprints covered half the table, but I couldn't make sense of the plans. It seemed too big for a house and I couldn't imagine him tearing down the Galley and starting from scratch. It was a Talbott's Cove institution.

I was surprised I didn't notice any of this last night.

JJ came up behind me and set two plates on the table. "Your raisin toast," he said. "Sit, please."

I gestured to the blueprints. "What is this all about?"

He stared at the documents as he settled into his chair. After a moment, he replied, "I'll explain if you sit down."

Nodding, I dropped into the chair. He shot a pointed glance at the toast and I took a bite to appease him. "This is some quality raisin bread," I said. "Now, tell me what you're building."

He forked up a heap of scrambled eggs, still staring at the plans across the table. Eventually, he replied, "I'm building a distillery with a tasting room, restaurant, and event space."

Shocked, I gazed at him with the toast suspended an inch from my open mouth. "A distillery...and some other things? And where are you doing this? And how, exactly?"

His brows furrowed as he poked at the eggs. "Here in Talbott's Cove, on the site of the old cider mill, the one on the far end of the village. It's set back from the street, but close enough that people who come here for craft gin and vodka will stay for the bookstore, the gift shops, the inn, everything else." He took a bite, but still hadn't managed a glance in my direction. "It's contingent upon a million things. Inspections and feasibility studies and licenses and financing and my incredibly flaky business partner's daily whims."

I tore the toast into small pieces, bobbing my head as I considered this information. "You have a business partner? An accredited investor?"

And now he chooses to look at me.

"Yeah. Is that particularly surprising to you, Bam?"

I popped a piece of toast into my mouth. "It's not surprising, no. But I want to know who it is so I can look up his SEC filings."

He leaned back in his chair, layered his hands over his belly. "Why do you care? You're just here for the sex."

We gazed at each other for a moment that felt as heavy as midnight, and for once I yielded first. "Because this is my world. This is what I do. If you're working with someone who is promising to bring sizable capital investments to the table, I want to confirm whether this person is one of the good ones and he has a record of doing it right."

He tipped his chin up, studied me through narrowed eyes. "Again, why do you care? Why does he need to be one of the good ones, Brooke? As you've said, I'm the worst and this is a hopeless, dead-end town. Why does it matter whether we're doing it right?"

I hunched forward, flattened my hands on the table-top. "You want me to confess something deep and meaningful, I can tell. Instead of doing that, why don't you run your business plan by me?"

He laughed into his coffee. "Isn't it a little early for a

ritual beating?" For a minute, we ate in silence. Then he dropped his fork to the plate and said, "All right. Fine. Here's the quick version. Small-batch gin and vodka crafted entirely from locally sourced ingredients. Grains from nearby family farms, honey from an apiary in Beddington, juniper berries and herbs from growers all over New England. Clean, organic, sustainably produced."

"That's what you're brewing in the back room of the tavern?" I asked.

He bobbed his head as he sipped his coffee. "Yeah. It started out as an experiment, turned into a hobby, and now a solid percentage of the monthly profits come from distribution agreements with bars and restaurants all over the region."

"Nice. Word-of-mouth demand is the kind of proof point that opens more doors than any data set," I said.

He peered at me, frowning. "I thought you worked on Wall Street. Stocks and bonds and funds and...the rest of that stuff no one understands."

"Yeah, I do," I replied. Then, thinking better of it, I added, "I mean, I did. Obviously, I'm not there right now because I work out of my childhood bedroom as everyone truly aspires to do. My firm is at Broadway and Wall Street and they let me do this remote thing because being in New York City is not essential when one has a decent Wi-Fi connection, and I make a lot more money than their cadre of #MeToo miscreants. But yes, stocks, bonds, funds, and the rest of that stuff. Hedge funds, in particular. Before hedge funds, I managed a handful of different international market derivative desks. Derivatives trading bores the shit out of me, so I got the hell out of there. I spent a little time in venture cap, but I found all the idealistic people asking for money to be exhausting."

He polished off the rest of his eggs, wiped his mouth on a cloth napkin, and retreated into the kitchen without a word. Since this was JJ, I didn't question it. The boy liked to walk away and come back when it suited him. True to form, he returned with the French press and topped off my coffee.

"Thank you," I said. He waved me off as if he couldn't be bothered with my manners. "I want to hear the rest of your pitch. How does the cider house figure in?"

"The idea is to make a destination out of the production facility. Tasting room, restaurant, gardens, tours, the whole thing. The location has to be worth the trip and it has to photograph well because, like you said, word of mouth converts to social proof." He rounded the table and tapped his fingertips on the blueprint. "This is one of the proposed floor plans. This one allocates space to a fine dining restaurant as well as a fast-casual venue, both focused on showcasing the products and goods from local farming partners. I don't think we can sustain two dining facilities but my partner wanted to get an idea how it would look."

I couldn't make sense of the blueprint, but I nodded anyway. "If you get this right, it's going to be huge for the local economy."

"That's a big *if*," he said, laughing. "There's a lot of movement that needs to happen before the local economy feels a damn thing."

"And your investors? I know you mentioned a partner

with a sense of whimsy and that troubles me. You shouldn't rely on someone like that. The kind of money I imagine you need is no problem for me. I'm willing to invest and—"

He brought his hand to my shoulder, drew it up my neck and into my hair. "I don't want to get into that with you. I need it to be separate."

"You need that separate from me?"—I tapped my chest—"Or *me*?"—I circled my hand between us.

"Yes and yes." He gathered my hair in his fist, held me steady as he barely brushed his lips over mine. It wasn't lost on me that we'd shared a bed and our bodies, but not a real kiss. This was the closest thing to it since high school and I didn't know what it meant that he was almost kissing me while asking me to stay the hell out of his business. "Please understand."

"I do, I mean, yeah, I get that. It's fine," I stammered. I did not get it and it was not fine. "You don't want to tell me who is bringing the capital to the table and I'm certain that makes sense to you, although I am going to offer you some suggestions because I invite myself into other people's problems. I know a number of investors who are big into food and beverage tourism ventures. I'm talking about people who open bars and restaurants every week, people who scout emerging foodie tourism markets, people who know the heartbeat of this business. Just off the top of my head, I can think of four or five investors who are actively looking for homegrown, niche market startups, especially ones with a sustainability angle. It's as easy as making email introductions if you're interested."

JJ was quiet while he rubbed his fingers over my scalp.

I couldn't determine whether he was insulted or excited or his usual brand of grouchy. Then, "Thank you for... everything. I appreciate it. It's good to talk this out with someone who knows the town. But I have to say no. I'm all set."

I pressed my lips together and went right on staring at the blueprint I couldn't decipher. "Even if you won't take my money, I could help you. I could offer technical assistance on the financial side or connect you to talented branding and marketing people and"—I paused, glanced up at him as I found the words I never found for anyone else—"and I could fund this entire venture right now if you wanted to bail on that partner of yours. I could just *give* it to you."

He leaned forward, pressed his forehead to mine. Of all the touches we'd shared, this one made me feel the most exposed. "Bam, sweetheart, I'll give you all the rain checks for angry insult concussion sex you want. I'll let you bitch and moan about this town and I'll stop asking you why you came back, even though I think you want to get it off your chest. I'll set aside all the raisin bread I get from Vermont for you. But there is no way in hell I'd let you invest a penny in this project."

I twisted out of his arms as tears filled my eyes. I didn't know why I was crying, but I knew I had to leave immediately. "If you change your mind, you know how to find me," I called as I stepped into my shoes.

"Brooke, come back here and—"

I slammed the front door shut behind me.

CHAPTER EIGHTEEN

BROOKE

Duration: the measure of a bond price's sensitivity to shifts in interest rates.

Annette: Hello, madam. You're awake early. Or was it a very late night?

Brooke: I'm always awake early. I make a lot of money in China. Their morning is our night.

Annette: Yes, this is true. However, I don't usually see you walking through the village first thing in the morning. Because you're usually so busy with China.

Brooke: Oh, yeah. I just went out for a walk.

Annette: You went for a walk? Since when do you walk?

Brooke: I walk. I walk all the time.

Annette: Yeah, from one room to another. You don't walk for, you know, the practice of walking.

Brooke: Well, I went for a walk today. Fresh air, birds, sunshine. It was glorious.

Annette: I have several questions about this but I'd like to start with this—how dare you?

Brooke: How dare I what?

Annette: Do whatever you're doing without telling me!

Brooke: We cannot be those women who walk together in the mornings. Honey, no. I love you but we can't get a set of matching visors. That's not our look.

Annette: Let's presume it was a very late night. Let's also presume that it was a satisfying outing for you, even if it's not one you're willing to discuss with me.

Brooke: Why is it so hard to believe that I went for a walk?

Annette: If it was an early morning outing of the amorous variety, I applaud you. Morning sex for me is an experience made possible by virtue of already being in bed. Getting up and going out for sex at that hour is commendable. If we gave out awards for outstanding performances in getting some, you'd win in the Early Morning, Out of the House category.

Brooke: How much coffee did you drink today? You're wired, sweet pea.

Annette: You only deflect when I'm close to the truth.

Brooke: I'm worried about you. Go over to the pharmacy and get your blood pressure checked.

Annette: I'm keeping an eye on you, Markham.

Brooke: Don't stop with one eye. Use both of them. That's why you have two.

Brooke: This is going to sound ridiculous, but I'm asking anyway.

Annette: I'm here for it. Give me all the ridiculous.

Brooke: Where can I get really good fried chicken?

Annette: Quantify "really good."

Brooke: I have to tell you a story in order to do that.

Annette: I love your stories. I'm going to refill my coffee and sit down with a cupcake for this.

Brooke: Dad has been talking about his time in the National Guard recently. When I say recently, I mean it's the only thing he's talked about for the past week and I'm ready to start plucking my eyelashes out if it will make him stop.

Annette: Your father was in the National Guard? I didn't know that!

Brooke: Allegedly. I haven't done any digging to confirm or deny the story, but this is the first I've heard of his service.

Annette: Weird. Go on.

Brooke: It seems he enlisted after high school, trained with the state National Guard during college in Orono, and then spent a few months in Texas after graduation.

Annette: He was deployed to…Texas?

Brooke: It's hazy. Can't be certain. Dementia is a liar. This could be a story he read once upon a time or something he watched on television. It could be a mashup of things he believes to be true.

Annette: I know he's older than my parents, but not so old that he would've been down at the Alamo.

Brooke: Who fucking knows. But he claims he had the

best fried chicken of his entire life while in Texas. In one retelling, it was near Galveston. In another, it was Plano.

Annette: And now he's craving some Texas-style fried chicken.

Brooke: It's not about the chicken, but it also is about the chicken. Right now, he wants that memory and the safety and familiarity that comes with it, but he can't access it without the chicken. For the past few days, he's been somewhere between aggressively angry and ugly cry sad at all times.

Annette: Oh, honey. I'm so sorry. You should've reached out earlier. I can help with things like chicken and whatever else. You have enough on your hands. Ask for some damn help, woman.

Brooke: I never know when these things will spin out of control. Sometimes they're quick blips.

Annette: I love you and I know you're trying your ass off, but it sounds like it spun out of control several days ago. Give me the context so I can help you fix this.

Brooke: As the story goes—and I can't believe I'm saying this—he and a bunch of other National Guardsmen brought a chicken to a shop where they fried it for them.

Annette: You mean a package of chicken from a butcher.

Brooke: That isn't the way the story was told to me, no.

Annette: They brought a live chicken to a fry shop?

Brooke: Maybe that's how it goes in Texas. Maine has general stores where you can buy ammo and wedding dresses.

Annette: Forgive me for being obvious, but have you tried any of the fast food chicken options?

Brooke: There are grease stains on the wall in the dining room and bits of chicken stuck in the chandelier. One of the home health aides is on personal leave because Dad stabbed her with a drumstick. My hair smells like fried chicken and I'm afraid I'll never wash that scent out.

Brooke: We've tried everything.

Annette: Then…we need to find a live chicken fry shop?

Brooke: I have looked, but as you know, certain parts of this region don't maintain much internet presence.

Annette: You need someone who knows how to fry chicken in volume and saves the oil.

Brooke: What does that mean, saves the oil?

Annette: It's a flavor thing. Trust me. I'll ask around.

Annette: I'll also see if anyone has a hen they want to sell.

Brooke: What does a hen cost? I'm sure I have the cash on hand, but I'm wondering what the going rate is for live chickens.

Annette: Let's work on finding a chicken and a fryer first, okay? Then we'll get into the economics.

Brooke: Good plan. Thank you.

Annette: You're welcome and stop letting it get this bad before asking for help.

Brooke: I'm trying.

Annette: Try harder.

Annette: Jackson and I are going to that pub in North-port tonight, the one with the Trivia Tuesday. Are you in?

Brooke: Ugh, no. I can't.

Annette: What's going on?

Brooke: I'm just swamped. I'm sorry. I know how Jackson loves it when I tell him he's wrong about everything.

Annette: Are you all right?

Brooke: Yeah, totally. Just a lot on my plate right now.

Annette: How's your father doing?

Brooke: No major changes. He's watching the original Hawaii Five-Oh and Quincy, M.E. and that's giving him something to talk about. I'm just torn between being really fucking happy I can stream these old shows and really fucking appalled at the shit that was acceptable back then.

Brooke: Also, the hairstyles. Did flat irons not exist until 2004?

Annette: I wouldn't know. They don't work on my kind.

Brooke: You curly-haired girls are all alike.

Annette: What's happening with work? Do you have any big pitches or, I don't know, whatever happens in your world?

Brooke: I have a number of SEC filings coming up.

Annette: We're not talking about college football, right?

Brooke: Securities and Exchange Commission.

Annette: Right. That SEC.

Annette: Are you sure we can't convince you to come along?

Brooke: Not this time. Have fun at trivia.

Annette: Have fun on your morning walk.

CHAPTER NINETEEN

JJ

Margin: the difference between the revenue produced by a good or service and the cost of production.

BROOKE-ASHLEY MARKHAM RUINED my life on an unseasonably warm night last September. She dismantled all the good sense I had with the simple command of "Take off your pants" and tore down the years of distance I'd put between us since high school. Since kissing her once and wanting more.

Now, she ruined my life with her hair on my pillow and my dog's affections and text messages that simply proclaimed, *I want you to fuck me tonight.*

As if I was just a cock waiting around for some pussy to invite me in from the cold for the evening. As if the only things we exchanged were soft and hard, yes and no. As if we weren't building a new world from the old, broken one behind us. As if we meant to stop.

And I let her do this. I asked for it. I went willingly, knowingly.

Same as I did every time she asked, I responded with, *I'll be home in forty-five minutes. Let yourself in.*

Brooke-Ashley Markham was ruining my life, and I didn't want her to stop.

CHAPTER TWENTY

BROOKE

Secured Debt: a debt which is covered by specific assets in the event of a default.

JJ GRABBED the backs of my thighs, pushed them to my chest. My ankles bounced on his shoulders as he slammed into me again. My body was stuffed and folded like tortellini, and all I could manage was, "What the hell kind of position is this?"

He turned his head, pressed his lips to my calf. He got what he deserved there, as I hadn't shaved my legs in *days*. "The kind that shuts you up long enough for me to use you the way you like."

I reached for sheets, blankets, anything to keep me anchored. "I'm not sure I requested *this*."

"The fact you have"—he rocked into me like he was trying to demolish walls—"something to say"—and dislocate my hips—"proves you want me to use you even rougher."

"No, Jed, not rougher," I begged. "No, I can't—"

"No?" He pulled out but kept his hands on my thighs, brushed his thumbs over my backside and the spot where my legs met my center. It was uncomfortable like this, contorted and empty. I wanted to be filled, moved. And yes, used. "You want me to stop? You've changed your mind?"

It hurt, this emptiness. It was an ache, deep and true, and I couldn't go on this way. I couldn't live another minute without him inside me. I clawed at his chest, reaching for as much of him as I could get. Anything I could get. "You owe me," I snapped. "You still haven't made up for the time when you didn't wake me up."

His thumb tapped my clit once, twice—and then he went back to kissing my damn leg. "Do better," he said. "I know you can do better than that."

"No, not when I'm still mad about it," I replied. "If I wasn't enjoying it, I would've woken up and told you as much. I wanted that one, Jed."

Scraping his beard up my leg, he laughed into my skin. "You know this isn't a punch card situation, right? You're not working up to a free fuck, Bam."

Still chuckling, he shifted my leg to kiss my ankle. My damn ankle. "Oh my fucking god, Jed. If you don't put that rolling-pin dick inside me and keep going right now, I'll leave here and set fire to the tavern."

I wasn't finished issuing that threat when he was seated all the way inside me and we were crying out, a chorus of groans, growls, wails. The way he bent me made it feel like his cock was everywhere. It was almost too much, but only almost. It reduced my world down to him, me, us. It emptied my mind and took away the itchy need to control anything.

"There you go, Bam." He grinned down at me as if I'd learned to tie my shoes and rewarded me with a slow, slow slide of him inside me. "That's how I want you."

"You like that?" I asked. "You enjoy the idea of me burning down the tavern?"

"I do," he admitted. "I want you so desperate that arson makes sense and then I want to fuck you so good all you can do is take it." He pressed two fingers to my lips. "No more talking. You're not the boss here. This isn't one of your conference calls."

I raked my nails over the octopus inked into his shoulder. He answered with a rumbly groan and I clenched around him without thought. "I hate you."

"Go ahead and let yourself believe that, sweetheart."

IT'D HAPPENED ONCE or twice and I'd written it off each time, never paying it any mind. It wasn't a big deal and there was no reason to create drama where none existed, so I didn't. It didn't mean anything. *This* didn't mean anything.

But as I lingered in JJ's bed more than thirty minutes after orgasms had been achieved and the condom was discarded, his arms tight around my body and my head tucked under his chin, the word *significant* pulsed behind my eyes. This was becoming significant, and I didn't know how to find space for more significance in my life. I didn't know whether I wanted to find that space.

He ran his palm down my flank, over my hip. "Are you good, Bam? Are you going to be able to walk all right?"

"Why? Are you tossing me out?" My words came out like the crack of a whip, much harder than I'd intended. "It's fine, I mean, I should go—"

"You really know how to wind yourself up," he murmured. "It's the middle of the night and it's snowing. You're not going anywhere but I want to know if you need a hot bath or something. This time was a little—"

"Savage?"

He shrugged, pressed a kiss to the crown of my head, my temple, the corner of my mouth. "Nothing wrong with savage if it gets you where you need to go."

"Tell me more about that, Jed," I joked, expecting him to say something about turning women into pretzels in order to give them black-out quality orgasms. "Where do I need to go?"

"You need to get out of your head," he replied softly. "So far outta your head, Bam."

Significant.

For the second time in far too recent history, tears filled my eyes. "I have to go," I said, fighting his embrace. "Seriously, this isn't one of those situations where I want you to hold me down and ignore my protests. I have to go."

"It's the middle of the night." He locked his arms around me, pinned my legs with his strong thigh. "It's snowing. It's been twenty minutes since you were semiconscious and ten since you stopped shaking. You're not going anywhere."

I was prepared to argue, to kick and fight. To do all the things I usually did to keep people away.

But then he said, "And I don't want you to go, Brooke."

Resentful, overwhelmed, significant tears streaked down my cheeks and I turned my face toward his arm. "You don't get to say things like that."

"Why not?" he asked, his lips skating over my neck, my shoulder. "You're allowed to hate me just as much as I'm allowed to want you. It's always been that way."

"That is not how"—my phone's sharp, distinctive peal cut me off—"I have to get that."

Without argument, JJ untangled his limbs from my body. He watched as I scrambled off the bed to locate my device in the heap of clothes discarded on the floor. "Don't you have people who can answer your calls? I know you're important, but aren't you allowed a couple of hours when the world doesn't need your opinion on where to put money to make it grow faster?"

"This isn't work, it's my father," I shouted, snatching the phone from my coat pocket. I pressed it to my ear, still kneeling on the floor with the coat clutched to my chest. "What happened? What's wrong?"

The first thing I heard was crying in the background. High pitched sobs and wails that I would've recognized anywhere. Then, I heard the words. *Accident, inconsolable, bleeding.* I was certain the home health aide was speaking in full, thoughtful sentences, but I couldn't comprehend any of it.

"I'll be there in five minutes. Please try to keep him from injuring himself any further," I said, pushing to my feet. I ended the call and flattened the phone against my breastbone, my eyes shut as I searched for a calming breath.

"I'll drive you." Even with my eyes closed, I knew the sound of JJ stepping into his jeans and fastening his belt. The rustling that followed was the black thermal I'd ripped off him hours ago, the one he'd added back into the rotation after I'd complained about its absence. "You're not hoofing it through a spring snowstorm."

Unable to find that calm breath, I opened my eyes. I slipped into my clothes, stuffed my underwear and socks in a pocket. "That won't be necessary."

JJ held out my boots to me. "It wasn't a question."

"Neither was my refusal." Wobbling, I gripped his forearm as I jammed my bare feet into the rubber wellies. Gross, but necessary. "Stay out of it."

"Please put your outrageous arrogance aside for a minute and acknowledge when it makes sense to accept help," he said, following me to the front door. "The roads haven't been plowed and the sidewalks are buried under six inches of snow and ice. You can be right about every-thing else, Brooke, but you can't—"

I didn't wait for him to finish that thought. I walked straight into the storm.

CHAPTER TWENTY-ONE

JJ

Net Operating Loss: excess of business expenses over revenues.

ONCE AGAIN, Brooke was going to do what she wanted, how she wanted. It was up to me to decide whether I'd chase after her this time.

By the time I rolled up beside her, she'd waded all the way to the end of my street. Lowering the window, I called, "You're being ridiculous. Get in."

"Go home, Jed."

I wanted to let myself believe I wouldn't have followed her if it wasn't an emergency, but I didn't know about that. At this point, there wasn't much I wouldn't do for her, even when she insisted she didn't want it. And this was the tricky truth about Brooke: she *did* want it.

I pulled ahead of her, stopped the car, and stepped out into the snow. I pressed a hand to my heart and watched as she slipped and bobbled on the slick road, a fine layer of snowflakes crowning her head. Fickle, headstrong, and too fucking breathtaking for me to stand. And then I darted toward her, grabbing her around the waist and tossing her over my shoulder while she screeched and flailed. I dropped her into the back seat like a beautiful bag of potting soil.

When I settled behind the steering wheel, Brooke shouted, "That was unnecessary."

"I asked you nicely," I replied. "Several times."

"I know how to handle myself in a snowstorm," she argued.

I glanced at her in the rearview mirror as I drove through the village. "It's a good skill to have."

"I don't need anyone coming to my rescue."

I could hear her pouting. "Never crossed my mind that you would." I pulled into her driveway, turned off the car. Shifting to face her, I said, "I told you I wasn't letting you walk home alone in this storm and I didn't. I'm not letting you deal with this"—I hooked a thumb over my shoulder, toward the sprawling estate—"by yourself. Understood?"

Instead of agreeing outright, she climbed out of the car and said, "This is Vegas. What happens here, stays here."

I pocketed my keys and followed her to the door. "Everyone knows that mandate to be false."

She glanced at me, shrugged. "It's not false when I'm in charge."

I matched that shrug. "Whatever you want, Bam. I'm not going to fight you on the validity of tourism slogans."

Gripping the door handle, her expression tightened. Her lips parted as if she was ready to drop a counterstrike on me, but then she narrowed her eyes and said, "Promise me I can trust you."

"There's never been a time when you couldn't trust me," I replied. That wasn't good enough. The unyielding shine of her eyes told me so. She wanted me kneeling before her, pledging sword and skin. "Yes, I promise you can trust me, Brooke."

She pushed open the front door and we stepped into chaos. Every light in the house seemed to be lit. Competing televisions blared. The scent of fryer grease was thick in the air. People dressed in a rainbow of scrubs were everywhere, streaming in and out of rooms, moving up and down the front staircase, and they were all talking at once. A snowstorm raged outside, and it was the dead of night, but the Markham estate was hopping like Times Square.

Brooke jogged up the stairs, ignoring everything around her. I followed her into a room at the end of the hall where we found Judge Markham sitting up in bed, sobbing, with a gash on his forehead and blood running down his face and chest, smeared on his arms and hands. His shirt was soaked red, the bed linens much the same. Three health aides were positioned around the bed, their hands gloved and ready to block and tackle.

"Oh my god," Brooke whispered before quickly recovering. I ran my hand down her back, but she shook me off. To the aide closest to her father, the one with *Sherry* embroidered on her orange sherbet scrubs, she asked, "What the hell happened?"

"We think he fell out of bed and nailed his head right here," Sherry said, gesturing to the corner of the bedside table. "That, or he was sleepwalking. If that's the case, we're not sure where the injury came from. He won't let us get a good look at it. He was aggressive with Windy and Kayla when they tried to apply pressure and clean him up, which is why we called you."

"You should've called me regardless," Brooke said, not looking at the woman.

Before Brooke moved home, Judge Markham would come into the tavern almost every night. He'd sit at the same small table near the bar and order the catch of the day with a side of seasonal veggies. He drank one scotch on the rocks and requested the dessert menu on Fridays. He'd kept to himself, but the people of Talbott's Cove believed he belonged to them the way the sea and the sky belonged to them. The Markham family was a Talbott's Cove institution stretching all the way back to Talbott himself, and the Judge embraced that legacy. He weighed in on every local matter brought to his attention, recited town history, and lobbied for the region's development.

I'd watched him do this nearly every night, and I'd watched it slip away from him. It'd started with him forgetting his wallet four days in a row. Then, he yelled at one of my servers to turn off baseball reruns and switch to the football game—in July. Not long after that, he came into the tavern wearing slippers with his trousers, dress shirt, and tie.

Two months later, he crashed his car into a tree. Two months after that, Brooke moved back home. I knew it was bad, but I had no idea it was this bad.

Brooke grabbed a wad of gauze from the table and

approached her father. "But *how* did this happen? Why weren't his bedrails up? There's no reason this should—"

She yelped when he slapped her hand away and kept slapping until I looped my arm around her waist and moved her back. The gauze fluttered down as he cried, settling on the sheets. She wrapped her hand around my arm and she kept it there.

"As you can see," Sherry started, "he's not receptive to touch right now."

"Maybe not, but we can't let him bleed until he cycles out of this," Brooke replied. "What are we supposed to do? I don't want to subject him to an ambulance and medics because it will end with sedation and we know how miserable he is when he's coming down from that."

"Can't be sure," I started, "but it looks like he needs a few stitches. At the minimum, a butterfly closure. I bet Yara Gwynn is"—I paused, not wanting to explain my knowledge of Yara's insomnia to Brooke at this moment —"able to come over if you need her."

Brooke glanced back at me, her brow wrinkled. "Who?"

"Yara Gwynn," I repeated. "She's the doctor who visits all the islands in the Bay. She lives down the street from the sheriff. Doesn't Annette know her? I assumed you all knew each other. She's strange. You'd like her."

"Annette and I don't socialize with other people." She shifted out of my arms, turning to face me. It was a wonder she'd let me hold her that long. "What kind of vampire is she that she wouldn't mind you calling at this hour?"

"The kind who makes house calls on remote islands

for a living." I reached into my pocket and retrieved my phone. "I'll text her, if you want."

"Yeah. All right. That would be good." Glancing back to Sherry and the other aides, she said, "Let's see if we can't move him to a chair and get this bed stripped. Someone get an episode of *Matlock* going. He'll move for *Matlock*. Or *Murder, She Wrote*. He likes that Jessica Fletcher. He thinks she's a tough broad."

I stepped back from the action to message Yara. True to form, she replied instantly. The woman did not sleep unless she was on a boat. I glanced up from my phone as Brooke shepherded her father from the bed to a chair by the television.

"It might seem like a small matter, but it's dividing the town," he said, wagging a fist as he shuffled across the carpet. "There's nothing small about running a pipeline through someone's backyard."

"Not at all," Brooke murmured. "Did the people sue the town to bar the pipeline?"

It took me a minute to make sense of that question, but then I realized they were talking about an issue from years—maybe decades—ago. She was asking questions to which she knew the answer, leading him into the well-worn territory of Talbott's Cove political and legal history. It made sense there was a nostalgic comfort associated with those old stories, but nostalgia had to be bittersweet when losing your mind.

"Fifteen minutes," I mouthed, pointing to my phone.

"You better believe they did," he replied. "And I'll tell you something else, young lady, they won." He brushed the back of his hand over his forehead and wiped the blood on his pajama pants. "What's your name?"

I saw the split second where she wilted under that question. Her eyes were cool and distant and lines formed between her brows. "Brooke," she replied evenly.

"That's a lovely name," he said. "Do I know your family?"

She stared at me as she shook her head. "No, you don't know them. They're not from around here."

I arched my brows up, silently telling her, *We both know this isn't okay. We know you can't handle this on your own.*

She shook her head again. Instead of arguing with her, I waited by the front door for Yara. It was easier than watching small pieces of Brooke wither and die.

I saw headlights flashing through the first floor windows, and I held the door open for Yara. She bounded out of a souped-up Jeep, doctor's bag in hand, and climbed through the accumulated snow.

"Hey, JJ, hi!" she called, waving as she stomped her boots on the doormat to dislodge the snow. "Wild night, huh? You just can't predict the last snow of the season, can you? I always think it's over, I put the snow pants away, take the chains off my tires, and then poof! More snow. Can't even believe it."

I crossed my arms over my chest as I watched her shake off her coat. "How much coffee have you had tonight?"

"Oh, I don't know! Maybe a quart or two? Not much." She plucked her hat from her head, freeing her long black ponytail. "Why haven't I seen you around recently?

Where are you hiding, sir?" She gave my chest a playful whack. "I don't even know what's happening in your life anymore. I've missed you."

"Hello."

One word. That was all it took. One word to snap me out of Yara's cloud of bouncy ball energy and drop the temperature in the house by twenty degrees. My girl was multitalented like that. "Brooke, this is Yara Gwynn. Yara, Brooke. Her father is the one with the injury."

"Thank you for coming." Brooke gestured toward the grandfather clock on the landing between the first and second floors. "Especially at this hour."

If she could've accompanied that gesture with a spray of ice from her hand, she would've. And I loved it. This frigid ray of jealousy was the highlight of my month.

Oblivious to the frost radiating from Brooke, Yara said, "That's what I do! That's what I'm here for!" She grinned at Brooke. "Okay, let's get going. Where's my patient?"

As I'd expected, Yara handled the shit out of the situation. She got on Judge Markham's good side by starting a *Murder, She Wrote* debate and managed to clean and patch the wound with some medical-grade Krazy Glue. She recommended feeding him some ice cream laced with two crushed sleeping pills and waited around to make sure he nodded off without incident.

For Brooke's part, she pretended I didn't exist for the entirety of Yara's visit. As much as I marveled at her transformation into a frozen block of resentment, I remembered how much I hated being invisible to her.

Once Yara was headed home and the Judge was

secure in his bed, I dragged Brooke into the first room I could find. It was a bathroom, but I didn't give a damn. "Come on." I backed her up against the door, pressed my lips to her neck. "Ease up, Bam. It's just you and me."

"I have one question for you," she said. "How is it possible to have sex with someone who doesn't stay still for more than five seconds at a time?"

"You're so cute when you're jealous," I replied. "I've never seen this look on you before. I fucking love it."

She laughed, her whole body quaking against me. "I'm not jealous of anything. I'm merely pointing out that you know Dr. Gwynn more intimately than you might've suggested at the outset." She tilted her head back, batted her lashes as she hit me with an evil pout. Absolutely evil. "And she *misses* you, Jed."

I didn't stop to think before driving my fingers through her hair and kissing her as if I wanted to steal those words from her lips. She stayed rigid for a half second, but then all that ice melted away. She fisted my shirt, my belt, pulling me closer and forcing out the last of the distance between us. I held her, I kissed her, I drowned in her.

"Brooke," I rasped against her skin. "Talk to me, sweetheart. Tell me you're all right."

"I'm not talking about anything until you tell me something first."

I went back to her lips, kissing, biting, tasting her tongue. "Anything."

"When was the last time you got in Yara's snow pants?"

I ducked my head to her neck and kissed her there. I

stopped short of sucking a mark into her skin. "About two years ago." *I could give you the exact date if you wanted it.* "Maybe a little more than that."

"Why weren't you surprised when you walked in here tonight?"

"Why did you think I wouldn't know?" I asked. "I've known since the day the Judge came into the tavern for dinner and asked whether I thought it was time for Nixon to resign. I've known since before you came home and since before his accident. I know you can't handle this on your own, but more importantly, you don't have to, Bam. You don't have to be the one picking up the pieces and holding them all together."

"Does everyone know? Is it the worst-kept secret in town?"

"I can't speak for the whole of the town, but I've never heard anyone suggesting anything other than the Judge is getting on in his years. People around here love him and they've granted him a wide berth. Even when he made odd comments or went out in town wearing mismatched clothing, they've assumed the best." When she bit her lower lip, I continued, "I'm telling you the truth, Brooke."

She nodded, but it was hesitant. "He made me promise I wouldn't let people watch him deteriorate and I wouldn't send him away. That's why—that's why I'm here. Why I do this."

"You can keep that promise without shouldering the world on your own. You could've shared this with me." When she started to protest, I swallowed her words with a kiss. "Don't you see? You've let me inside you, but not to any of the places that matter."

Her gaze dropped to my chest, and for a moment, I thought she was going to throw me out of her house. The possibility always existed. But instead of kicking me out, she pressed her face to my chest and let the dam break all over me.

"Bam," I said, pressing a kiss to her temple. There were more tears stored up in her little body than I would've thought possible. "I've got you, sweetheart."

"Will you stay?" she asked through her sniffles and hiccups.

"I'm not going anywhere." I gathered her in my arms and carried her out of the bathroom.

In the hallway, I heard the Judge snoring away like a chainsaw. It was a relief to know he was sorted for the remainder of the night. At the other end of the hall, I found Brooke's room and set her down on the bed. I curled up beside her, my arms tight around her body as she shook with sobs.

We fell asleep on top of the blankets, fully clothed. Somewhere between night and day, we reached for each other, discarding clothes and sliding beneath the sheets. Our bodies twined together, came together, stayed together.

CHAPTER TWENTY-TWO

Present Value: the current value of cash to be received in the future.

MAY

"WHAT ARE WE ORDERING?" Annette asked as she flipped over the menu. "Is it too early for sangria?"

"It's brunch," I replied. "By definition, it's not too early for anything."

"No, I mean, is it too early in the season for sangria," she said. "It's not appropriate to drink sangria until summer, but white peach sangria is on this menu even though it's too early to harvest peaches."

I set my menu aside and laced my hands on the table. I couldn't do this anymore. Not one more minute. "Can I talk to you about something?"

She peeked up at me, smiling. "We can totally skip the sangria. I was getting carried away with the idea of peaches. Would you rather have mimosas?"

"The sangria is fine—or mimosas. Or both. Order everything. I don't care," I said.

"Oooh, look! They have a blackberry mojito," she said. "You'd like—"

"I can't talk about mojitos with you right now because I have a standing dick appointment with JJ Harniczek," I yelled.

The server stopped at our table, glanced between me and Annette, and said, "I'll come back in a few minutes."

Annette blinked at me, her lips parted and the menu clutched to her chest. "Do...you have to leave?"

I pressed my fingers to my temples. "What are you talking about?"

"You said you have a dick appointment," she replied, jerking a shoulder up. "I'm wondering whether you need to leave or if this is taking place here." She glanced around, frowning. "The restrooms, perhaps? The back seat of a car? I don't know. I don't know how it is with you two."

I sat back, dropped my hands to my lap. And then I laughed, deeper and harder than I had in months. Tears clouded my vision as Annette joined in, rocking back and forth in her chair as her shoulders shook.

"I fucking love you," I said to her, mopping my cheeks with a napkin. "I mean it. I fucking love you, Annette."

"You should," she replied. "Now, start from the beginning and tell me everything. Just as you should have when it started. When was that, exactly?"

I glanced down at the menu. "It started last September."

The server returned to the table when Annette said, "It started in *September*? And you didn't tell me until *now*? I was prepared for you to say two weeks ago or maybe last month. *September*? You've hidden this from me since *September*?"

"Aaaaand I'll be back in a few more minutes," the server sang.

"No, don't go," I cried, clawing at the air in the server's wake. "She needs sangria. A really big pitcher of sangria. And a straw. Please. *Please*."

The server turned around, nodding. "Sangria," he said. "With a straw."

Annette glared at me, her eyes narrowed and her lips flat. "And one of those blackberry mojitos for the keeper of secrets."

"Sangria with a straw and a blackberry mojito." He gestured to each of us and then brought his palms together. "Can I interest you in a local creamery cheese plate or the rainbow chard dip with crudité and house-made breads?"

"Yes to both." I directed a pleading, hopeful smile toward Annette, but she held on to that glare. "And an order of fries for my very tolerant, very loving friend."

"Perfect." He glanced between us, nodding. "I'll get those orders in for you."

Once we were alone, I leaned forward to layer my hand over hers. "I'm so sorry."

"Just tell me why you've been hiding this from me since *September*."

"It was late September and it only happened once," I said. "It was actually your idea."

Laughing, she asked, "How was it my idea?"

"You told me to go to the Galley." I held out my hands toward her. "I went to the Galley."

"I specifically told you to aim for tourists," she said, still laughing. "I told you to steer clear of townies. How did you mix that one up?"

"Believe me, I tried. I brought my best game and JJ went ahead and cockblocked me," I replied.

"So, you slept with him?" she asked, shaking her head of dark curls at me.

"Yeah, that's basically what happened. I yelled at him and he yelled back, then I went to his house and told him to get naked and we yelled at each other some more," I admitted. "But it only happened the one time and I swore it wouldn't happen again. That's why I didn't tell you. I didn't want it to become part of the Talbott's Cove narrative."

Annette stared at her water glass for a moment. Then, "First of all, fuck you for suggesting I'd introduce any of your private affairs into the local lore. You know me better than that."

"You're right," I agreed. "You're right and I'm sorry."

"I'm not done with you," she said, wagging a finger in my direction. "Second, it's not cockblocking when a guy gets in the way of you having sex. You can cockblock a guy, but he can't cockblock you."

"That's true," the server said as he set a glass in front of Annette, filled it with sangria, and nestled the pitcher between us. "It's called clamjamming."

I stared up at him as he set the blackberry mojito in front of me. "Thank you for that insight," I said flatly. I turned back toward Annette. "Apparently, JJ clamjammed me. That is why I spent that evening expressing my frustration to him."

"That's reasonable." She reached for her drink. "It must've been good, right? Otherwise, it wouldn't have turned into a regular thing."

"It's not a regular thing. Except it is a regular thing. It is now." When she motioned for me to continue, I said, "Nothing happened for months and months, but then you suggested I go back to the Galley. You said something about getting derailed."

Annette pressed her hands to her cheeks. "I love how you're pinning the blame on me. That's adorable."

"I'm not blaming you so much as highlighting your influence on my life," I replied. "It happened a second time, and even though I promised myself it wouldn't turn into a regular thing, it did."

"Stop doing that! Stop telling yourself you can't have nice things. It's unhealthy." She rolled her eyes at me as she sipped her sangria. "You still haven't told me whether it's any good. I'm assuming it is, since you keep going back for more, but feel free to fill in the blanks."

"It's good," I conceded. "We argue all the time and he drives me crazy, but he's also—he's JJ. He insisted on going back home with me the night Dad fell out of bed and split his head open. He saw it all and…he was great. He helped out, he did everything I needed, and he stayed the night." I took a sip of my drink, shrugged. "But it's not a thing. It's not a relationship, it's not going anywhere.

We're just two people who are super bored with Talbott's Cove and we happen to be in the same age band with complementary sexual interests. Of course, we're having sex. It's JJ or...who else, really? Either I hit up the widowers or start robbing cradles. However, the high school cross-country team jogs past the house every afternoon around four. A few of them are *men* and they've grown up *right*. There. I've said it. I'm not apologizing."

Annette propped her chin on her fist and stared at me, totally silent, for a full minute. Finally, she said, "It's unreal to be sitting in this seat."

"What is that supposed to mean?"

"It means I've been there, done that, and bought the t-shirt and I'm not letting you take the same trip. Now, listen. I know some people have casual sex and that's how they operate. I know you were that person at some point, but you're not that person right now. You are in a serious, heavy place in your life and while it might sound like a good idea to find someone light and casual to balance it out, that isn't what you need. You would've hopped on a hookup app and found a grad student from one of the college towns nearby if you really wanted casual and light."

I glanced around the restaurant in search of our server. This would've been an awesome time for him to appear with some cheese or unwelcome contributions to our conversation. "It's not?"

"Also," Annette continued, barely stopping for a breath, "JJ isn't a casual-sex guy. You might think he is—"

"Have you met Yara?" I interrupted. "Because I have."

Annette dismissed me with a wave. "Yara is a doll. We

should invite her out with us sometime. Once you get to know her vibe, you'll agree."

"Her *vibe* wants to climb my man like a mainsail."

She steepled her fingers together. "Did you hear that? How you just went all possessive mama bear on a woman he hasn't touched since before you moved home? Because I did and I think it's time for me to rest my casual-sex case."

"I hear what you're saying and I know it sounds like I'm in this real deep, but he wants to keep it low-key," I argued. "He's working on expanding his business and he's doing all these things to help Nate and he's got too much going on for a serious relationship. He was there for me in a pinch, but that doesn't mean he wants to sign up for anything else."

Annette leaned in, whispered, "You, my darling, are full of shit. You are assigning opinions and attitudes to JJ that he probably doesn't possess and you are deciding how things are going to go down without asking what he wants." She stabbed a finger in my direction. "Have you even asked him?"

"I know you're trying to kick me in the ass the way I kicked you, but I'm not planning on staying here that long. I'm not having a heartfelt conversation with JJ about his wants and desires when I know damn well I won't be the one fulfilling them."

"That's news to me," Annette chirped. "What's your endgame? Are you moving your father to an assisted living facility? Are you leaving him in Maine or taking him with you to New York? What's the plan, Brooke?"

"I don't know," I replied. "I don't know, but I can't stay

here forever. This isn't home for me anymore and I can't go inventing relationships where none exist because it's where I am right now."

"You'll have to forgive me," she said, tapping her index finger against her lips. "I didn't realize the relationship I thought I had with my maid of honor was a figment of my imagination."

"That's not what I meant," I said. "You know that, Annette."

"What do I know?" she asked. "In the past few minutes, you've announced you have no intention of staying in town and you have no real relationships."

"You are my other half. You're my soul sister. We don't have a *relationship*, no. We're way past that and you know it."

"Maybe I do know it." She lifted her shoulders. "Maybe I want you to be as honest with JJ as you are with me."

"I don't know about that," I said. "Sisters and misters exist on different planes. But I swear to you, Annette, I am going to rock the shit out of my maid of honor duties. Whatever it takes, I'm here for it. Bridal showers, bachelorette parties, dress fittings, cake tastings, seating charts —you name it, I'm there. I'm holding your dress while you pee."

"It's really convenient how you can commit to events that won't take place for twelve to eighteen months, but you won't commit to anything with JJ. Super convenient."

"Oh my god, Annette. Can we talk about sex now? Please. There are so many things I want to tell you. Is

Jackson licking your ass? If not, go home and ask for that, pronto. You can thank me later."

"And here are the local creamery cheeses," the server announced.

"Right on time," Annette murmured.

Once we were alone with the cheese, I gestured toward her with a chunk of bread, saying, "His dick is unfortunately large."

She stared at the table, shaking her head. "I know I'm going to regret asking but...what's the threshold between fortunately and unfortunately large?"

"I haven't studied that in exact terms," I admitted. "I just know I've crossed it because there are times when I'm certain he's rearranging my intestines."

"That's really great for you. Not so much for your digestion, but it sounds like a good problem to have."

"Yeah," I said around a bite of cheese. "I mean, I've left his place feeling like I need to hold my vagina together because I'm sure he's hammered some dents into it and I don't want to risk it falling out."

Annette brought her fingers to her temples. "Oh my god, Brooke. *Oh my god.*"

"See," I replied. "You know what I mean."

She tipped back her glass, gulping the sangria. "I might, but I'm not going there with you."

"If I had sex with him every day," I continued, "I'd need a strict program of warm baths, physical therapy to keep that shit tight, and voodoo. And lube."

"It sounds like you have your priorities in order. That should be helpful going forward."

"Well, we're not going forward." I speared my knife into the goat cheese. "I'm riding out a phase."

"I see what you did there and it is hilarious," Annette replied lightly. "Riding out a phase. Nice."

"In all seriousness, how do you have sex every night and keep your vag from falling out? Wait, is Jackson's penis unfortunately small?"

Annette held up a finger. "First of all, it's more than enough."

"I figured as much. Those uniform trousers don't leave much to the imagination."

"It's great that you're inspecting my fiancé's trousers with such thoroughness," she said. "Thanks for that."

I shrugged. "I'm just looking out for you, love."

"Again, thank you," she said. "And second, we don't have sex every night."

"I'm sorry to hear that," the waiter cooed as he stepped up to the table. He shifted our plates and beverages to make room for the veggie dip and fries. To Annette, he said, "I hope things improve soon."

I reached into my wallet and pulled out two bills. "Here's one hundred dollars. Take this and exit yourself from this conversation." I glanced back at the table. "After you bring us another round."

He plucked the cash from my fingers. "Gladly."

I pushed the fries toward Annette. "Explain this to me. You're engaged, you live together, you can't get enough of each other—and you're not having sex every night? Why the hell not?"

"We don't need to," she replied. "Being with someone doesn't mean you have three-hundred-and-sixty-five days of sex. It means falling asleep beside them is just as meaningful as sex. Sometimes, more meaningful."

I stared at her, baffled. "You're steering me toward a long-term, committed relationship and *now* you're telling me it doesn't involve dick on the daily?"

As she hefted a handful of fries onto her plate, she replied, "That seems to be what I'm saying, yes."

"Are you out of your mind? Why would I entertain that sort of thing?"

"I love you," she said, laughing, "but you're crazy."

"I think you mean eccentric or free-spirited. Crazy has such negative connotations."

She grinned as she bit into the fries. "Mmhmm."

Holding out my hands, I leaned toward her. "Since we're here and we're having this conversation, I need your insight. Your married lady insight."

"I'm not married. We haven't even set a date yet. You know this, darling."

An exasperated grunt sounded in my throat. "You know what I mean."

"Yes, fine. I know what you mean." She fluttered her hands at me. "What do you need?"

I rubbed my thumb over my fingernails. "He does this thing where he waits for me."

"Waits where?" she asked around a mouthful of fries.

Still focused on my fingernails, I said, "You know. During sex."

There was a long pause and then, "Ah. Okay."

I glanced up at her, my lip snagged between my teeth. "Is that weird?"

She shook her head, waved her hands. "No, it's generous. It's *respectful*. Men who participate in sex like it's a team sport are the best kinds. Oh my god, the *best*."

I dropped my chin onto my fist. "I've never thought of it that way. The team sport way. I've always thought of it like an individual competition that happened to involve another person."

She grinned, her eyes sparkling. "Oh, so you're the selfish partner in the bed?"

I glanced away. "I guess so?"

"But JJ isn't selfish," she remarked. I shook my head. "I promise you, it's a good thing. It's awesome. Let it happen." When I didn't respond, she continued, "Do you know that expression, Big Dick Energy?"

I revisited the cheeses. "Ugh. Yes. Why?"

"Men who wait transcend that. They have a different kind of energy altogether. It's like Mighty Good Dick Energy."

I wagged a piece of cheddar at her. "Are you invoking Salt-n-Pepa right now?"

She shimmied her shoulders, arched her brows. "I am."

"Well done, madam." I smiled at her. I fucking loved this girl. "Well done."

Annette mimed a curtsey, saying, "To summarize, you have some Mighty Good Dick Energy on your hands. If you're careful, it's going to develop into some Mighty Good Husband Energy."

Skipping right over the husband comment, I replied, "It's not in my hands, Annette. A woman over thirty shouldn't be giving handies. Understood?"

She gave me a stiff, fake grin, the kind that made her

eyes squint and her lips stretch into a thin, sarcastic line. "Sure. Let's make that the point of this discussion."

"Listen," I started, "I don't show up to meetings that can be held without me, you know?"

"I do. I really do," the server murmured. "And here's the blackberry mojito."

CHAPTER TWENTY-THREE

BROOKE

Capitalization: the sum of an organization's stock value, long-term debt, and retained earnings.

Brooke: I just found an unnaturally long hair on the back of my leg.

Brooke: I thought it was head hair I'd shed and it was stuck on my leg. When I tried to remove it, I discovered it was growing out of my leg. What the fuck is this about?

Annette: Welcome to your mid-thirties, love.

Brooke: I reject that explanation.

Annette: I'd like to reject it too, but I have a pimple on the inside of my nose and it feels like I'm driving a stake through my skull every time I touch it.

Brooke: This is some bullshit.

Annette: You have it easy. You're blonde.

Brooke: How? My unnaturally long thigh hairs are nearly invisible?

Annette: That's one benefit, but your grays will blend in. Mine look like tinsel.

Brooke: What are you talking about? You have no tinsel.

Annette: Oh, I have tinsel. Curly hair is forgiving, but when they come through, they shine like a disco ball.

Brooke: I'm not ready to start growing old. We'll do that in thirty or forty years, when we've bought a pair of cottages and wear matching track suits.

Annette: There's a difference between growing up and growing old. We're not growing old yet, my friend.

Brooke: Remember being twenty-one and thinking you were a grown-ass lady?

Annette: I remember being thirty-three and thinking that. I've learned a few things this past year.

Brooke: Right there with you.

Annette: I'm looking forward to those twin cottages and wearing stretchy pants every day. We're going to need rocking chairs too.

Brooke: Have you mentioned any of our plan to Jackson?

Annette: Not yet. I have to find the right moment. Have you mentioned it to JJ?

Brooke: Why would I do that?

Annette: I have to explain this to you as well?

Brooke: You don't have to explain anything. We have different perspectives on how long I'll keep this dick appointment.

Annette: No, my dear, you don't have a perspective. You have a good man who adores you and you reduce that to "dick appointment." I, on the other hand, have a clear vision of us living in our cottages and wearing our track suits while Jackson and JJ bicker about sports and politics and the color of the sky, but grudgingly enjoy each other's company.

Brooke: I don't want to fight with you about this.

Annette: Then stop pretending you don't care about him.

Brooke: Okay, so...should I pluck it? Cut it? Douse it in apple cider vinegar?

Annette: We're talking about the hair again? Not JJ?

Brooke: Yes, the hair. I wouldn't douse him in vinegar.

Annette: I didn't think so, but since you refuse to acknowledge your feelings for him, I wasn't sure. I'd pluck it because those things drive me nuts, but it will grow back.

Brooke: Then...vinegar?

Annette: I'm not sure how that would fix anything.

Brooke: Me neither! But the internet really likes that shit.

***

Brooke: I won't be able to get out of here for a few hours. Another one of Dad's caregivers quit.

JJ: What happened?

Brooke: Nothing. She just couldn't handle it anymore.

JJ: Are you all right?

Brooke: Of course.

JJ: You're sure?

Brooke: Yes. Don't make it seem like I can't manage some staffing changes. I can.

JJ: It's not the staffing changes I'm referring to when I ask if you're all right.

Brooke: Then what the fuck is it? Get to the damn point

because I need to talk with the placement director at the nursing service to find a replacement.

JJ: Why do you expect more of yourself than professionals trained to handle these conditions?

Brooke: Why do you think you're entitled to ask those kinds of questions?

JJ: Consider it an objective observation.

Brooke: If you don't approve of the way I'm handling my father's care, you are welcome to fuck right off.

JJ: Got it. Get your ass over here when you're free.

Brooke: No. Not tonight.

JJ: Fair enough. I'll go there after I close up.

Brooke: That option isn't on the table.

JJ: I'm not fucking you on the sidewalk, sweetheart. Too damn cold, even in the springtime.

JJ: I'll be there by midnight and don't try to pull this bullshit.

Brooke: It's not bullshit.

JJ: It's not logical and you damn well know it.

I WALKED out of Dad's house in the middle of the afternoon. Just grabbed my shoes and walked the fuck out of there. I had no idea where I meant to go, but I knew I had to go somewhere. I couldn't stay another minute. Not in the house where things went from bad to worse, from severe to end stage. And not in the town where I didn't belong, not really. This wasn't for me, not a single inch of it.

Except for Annette. I couldn't live without her.

Also, Jed was growing on me in fascinating ways.

And I couldn't forget about Jackson.

The three of them were my de facto family, but I couldn't shake the sense that this wasn't where I belonged. Not this small town, not Dad's house, not this compressed, bitter version of myself. I didn't want to resent my father's dementia for stealing him away and leaving me with a living ghost. I didn't want to resent my father for making me promise to keep him at home, keep his condition quiet. I didn't want any of this.

I blew through the Galley's front door, not wasting a second on the fact I'd walked myself here without conscious thought, and marched up to the empty bar. When Jed spotted me, he stopped what he was doing, his hand paused over the knot at the nape of his neck. I loved it when those strands slipped loose. It checked a box I didn't know I had.

"You're going to light something on fire with that look, sweetheart," he said.

"What are you doing tonight?"

He dropped his hand, blew out a breath. "Don't ask me questions when you already know the answer. I don't have time for that."

"And I don't have time to repeat my mistakes but here I am."

He braced his hands wide on the bar. "Do you need to be hauled over my shoulder right now? Is that the kind of attention you need from me? Because that's what it sounds like, Bam."

"I need your dick paying extra-close attention to my vagina tonight. Do you think you can do that or is this another one of those instances where I'm supposed to intuitively know the answer?"

Nate sidled up beside Jed, swung an amused gaze between us. "I'll be here until closing, but I'm free after that."

Jed turned a glare in his direction. "Go somewhere else. Right now. Go and stay gone for ten minutes."

Nate glanced back at me. "It makes my day when you come in here and yell at him."

"Go away," Jed barked. When Nate pushed into the back room, Jed said to me, "I expect to find you in my bed tonight. Awake, please."

"Give me something worth staying awake for," I replied.

He pressed his fist to his mouth, but he couldn't hide his wicked smirk. My entire body clenched at that smirk.

"Bam, you don't know what you're asking for," he said.

"Explain it to me." I took a step back and then two more. I needed the distance. Without it, I'd vault my ass over that bar and drag him home right now. "Then make me regret it." I was almost certain those jeans of his were getting tighter by the second. "Don't make me wait." I hit him with a dick-eating grin and dodged Jackson at the door. To Jackson, I said, "It's a pleasure to see you, sheriff. Are you here in an *official capacity*?"

He responded with the same bewildered smile he'd been giving my innuendos for the past year. "Good afternoon to you as well, Brooke."

"You really don't know what you're getting yourself into," Jed called.

He was right about that. I didn't know what I was getting into with him, but I knew I could drop a few words on him and flash a feral stare and he'd be mine. Even if it only lasted a few hours, he could belong to me and I could pretend I belonged to someone too.

CHAPTER TWENTY-FOUR

JJ

Due Diligence: the investigation of an organization or financial opportunity prior to the consummation of an agreement.

FOR NEITHER THE first nor the last time, I seriously contemplated running through a damn wall to stop Brooke from strutting out of my tavern with my balls in her back pocket. It wasn't about the balls. Goddamn, she could keep them if it meant I could keep her long enough to unravel the issues tying her in knots today.

"Harniczek. A moment, please."

"For fuck's sake, sheriff, why are you here?" I shouted, dragging my gaze away from the door and settling it on Jackson Lau. "In case you didn't notice, I just had a moment. I don't have one for you too."

Laughing, he dropped into a seat at the bar. "I have to admit I'm somewhat afraid of Miss Markham. I can't help but believe she'd reach into my belly and tear out my liver if I crossed her."

"You best believe she will."

"She might scare me, but you should know I won't stand for anyone screwing her over," he said.

Well, that was unnecessary. "It's funny you say that," I started, "because no one screws Brooke over. She can spot that shit from a mile away and she screws back a hundred times as hard. But it's not Brooke you're worried about here. It's me." When he responded with nothing more than his usual cool stare, I continued. "I don't dick women over, sheriff. Not my style."

"Then we won't have a problem," he answered.

That was really unnecessary.

Out of the fucking blue, Jackson said, "I've kept an extra set of patrols on the Markham estate since last summer. Every four to six hours, just to keep an eye on things." He gave me a meaningful nod. "If there's a need for Dr. Gwynn to make another house call during a blizzard, I expect you'll let one of my deputies escort her."

Without fail, the most annoying portion of the sheriff's lectures was when I realized we were on the same team. "Will do."

"The white-out conditions aside, I'm pleased the good doctor was on hand to assist when Brooke needed it. Not that Brooke would ever admit to needing help."

Instead of taking that bait, I grabbed a set of glasses, filled one with iced tea and the other with club soda. "To women."

Jackson tapped his glass against mine. "And their red flags."

"And the bulls who love them," I added.

"Too right," he murmured into his tea.

I drained the club soda in two gulps and went back to the taps for a refill. "Now, what the hell are you doing here? Did you miss lunch again?"

He waved me off, saying, "I'm curious about Nate's progress and whether you've noticed any signs of relapse. His probation officer sent a glowing report last week, raving about him meeting all the terms of his probation. I share that enthusiasm, but I know the realities of addiction. I want to hear your take."

I didn't care whether we were on the same team. I didn't have any patience for this shit. "You want my take, sheriff? Here it is. I believe in the kid and I believe in second chances. Third, fourth, fifth chances too. People can fuck up. People can do terrible things. And they can learn from them. No one should be thrown away or erased simply because they did the wrong thing. I don't care if they did the wrong thing for *years*. The minute they decide to turn it around, I'm gonna let them." I tossed a lime wedge into my glass with enough force to send half the liquid sloshing over the sides. "He didn't kill anyone, he didn't maim anyone. He harmed himself. Sure, he stole from his family. He hurt his relationship with his parents in ways that won't easily mend. But he's still alive and so are they. He gets another chance, and if he relapses, he gets another one after that."

Jackson regarded me for a moment and then said, "All right. I also have concerns about Bobbie Lincoln. He keeps drinking himself into trouble. Wandering down dark roads at night where he's bound to get hit by a car.

Arguing with everyone who crosses his path. We're called out to that house at least once a month."

"It's not as simple as him drinking himself into trouble," I replied. "There's more to the story than you think."

He knocked his knuckles against the bar top. "That's why I'm here, Harniczek. Tell me the story. Let me help from my side while you help from yours."

"If you're looking for a buddy cop setup, you should know I'm not one for team sports."

"You make it sound like that should surprise me," he quipped.

I poured more iced tea into his glass. "When did you get a sense of humor?"

"It was probably around the same time you took up team sports with Miss Markham," he replied.

"Since that's a fully unacceptable line of discussion, let's get back to Bobbie Lincoln. All I can tell you is he's sorting through some issues. There's the unhappy marriage, the job that sucks the life out of him every day, the elderly mother-in-law who invited herself to move in a couple years back." I lifted my glass, motioned toward him with it before taking a sip. "I don't think the guy should be drinking it away to the point of walking in traffic but you can't fault him for bellying up to the bar if for no other reason than getting out of the house."

"I don't want to fault him either, but he picked a fight with a trash can outside the O'Keefe place shortly after one a.m. last night. The O'Keefes called the station thinking it was a bear. Lincoln pummeled the damn can until the boys rolled up. He broke both hands in the process." He laced his fingers around his iced tea, glanced up at me. "Did you see him at any point?"

"I did, but he left before nine o'clock," I replied. "He had a couple of beers, bitched about the Red Sox, and took off before the fourth inning. If he was tanked enough to beat up some cans after midnight, he didn't get there on my watch."

Jackson lifted his shoulders. "I didn't expect so, but I think it's time someone had a conversation with Lincoln about getting help. I'm going to gather some resources and see about sitting down with him and his wife, but I wanted to give you the heads-up."

"What would it be like for you to leave an *I* undotted? Have you ever tried?"

"Is it safe to come out now?" Nate asked as he swept in from the back room. Seeing the sheriff seated at the bar, he stopped, glanced around the tavern. "First the blonde, now the cop. This is a lot of excitement for one afternoon." He fluttered his hand over his chest, but I knew his sarcasm was too dry for the sheriff to translate. "It's a lot for me to process."

Much too dry. "You're right about that, kid."

"My apologies." Jackson pushed to his feet, nodded at Nate and me. "I'll keep you updated on these matters. I expect you'll do the same." He stopped several paces from the bar, turned back toward us with a grin. "Give my best to Brooke when you see her tonight."

WHEN I MADE my way home that night, Brooke was

awake and waiting in my bed as I'd requested. She was stripped down to her skin, her knees bent and her hand lazily moving between her legs. That picture was enough to incinerate me on the spot, but it was the screaming sadness in her eyes that slowed me to a stop.

Her legs fell open. "Make me regret this." My jeans hit the floor. "Make me regret it *all*."

There was no thought, no plan. Only Brooke and the absolute certainty I wouldn't allow her to regret anything, ever.

I wrapped her legs around my waist and watched while she taught me how her clit preferred to be treated, glancing away only long enough to snag a condom from the drawer.

"Keep doing that, Bam." With one hand on her waist and the other supporting her backside, I positioned myself at her entrance. "I want those fingers moving while I fuck you."

I thrust into her and that immediate wave of heat rolled up my spine and stole everything from my mind but Brooke. Everything but this woman and the way she was destroying my world.

"Maybe you should fuck me better," she said. "Then I wouldn't have to take matters into my own hands."

My hips moved in slow rolls, giving her the kind of deep, dragging slides of my cock I knew she loved. "You want that? Earn it."

Her eyes darkened at the challenge but it didn't stop her from trembling when I angled her hips to hit the soft spot that made her wild. "You're the *worst*," she said, her words dissolving into a beautiful moan. "The fucking worst, Jed."

"That's right, baby. The worst," I agreed. I shifted my hold on her, pressing my index finger to her back entrance. "You hate it when I tell you what to do, when I throw you on the bed, when I make those French panties of yours all wet, when I tease your ass. You hate it so much, Bam. *So much.* But you come on my cock like you think you can break me."

With her free hand, she parted her folds, exposing that perfect pink pearl and the place where her most intimate flesh stretched around me. Still rubbing her clit, she said, "Save the sermons. I'm the one doing all the work here."

"You want me to take over?" I asked, my index finger sliding between her cheeks. She clenched and, yeah, this was the kind of pain I wanted in my life. "You want to stop arguing and let me do this?"

She turned her face to the pillow, her eyes closed. "I want you to shut up and fuck me like I am the biggest mistake you've ever made."

"That's what it is for you, Bam? That's what you need? You've been getting it since the start. Never once has this been anything but a mistake." Brooke ground into me, her hips snapping to meet my thrusts while the headboard pounded the wall. "And never once did I think I'd be able to stop. You bring me this cocktease body and I'm gonna want it every damn time. Doesn't matter whether it's any good for me—"

"It's not," she whispered. "It's not, Jed."

"Doesn't matter," I said, bowing my head to drag her nipple into my mouth. "Doesn't matter. I'm not stopping.

You hear me, Bam? You can't make me stop. Don't you try."

She blinked up at me, her sapphire eyes as clear as the dawn. "Don't stop. Please, don't."

"Never." She nodded, her hands still working between her legs. My balls were full and aching, and I was long overdue to empty myself into her. I gradually pulled out and then drove into her, lingering on that sweet spot, the one that felt deep and tender and *all fucking mine*. I stayed there as the cords holding her together frayed and she broke apart, as gorgeous and strong and fucking furious as I'd ever seen her.

CHAPTER TWENTY-FIVE

BROOKE

Initial Public Offering: a company's first sale of stock to the public.

Annette: Jackson just told me the most fascinating story!
Brooke: Let me guess. Someone was walking along Old County Road last week and they were struck in the leg with a golf ball. They contacted the sheriff directly because what else would you do about a non-event in the Cove? And the sheriff determined a few teenage boys were practicing their chip shots in their backyard. No charges were pressed.
Annette: Nope, not that one.
Brooke: Okay, let me think.
Brooke: Was it the car stopped between Jeffries Point Road and Main Street a little before midnight last night? The one where the guy had a craving for meatballs but

wasn't sure where to go at that hour so he stopped in the damn intersection?

Annette: I hope you find this amusing, my dear.

Brooke: It's not amusing. It's the official Talbott's Cove sheriff's log. It's printed in the Talbott's Cove Times.

Annette: Wait, so…you read that? For funsies?

Brooke: No, I sure don't but my father does. Since he only knows how to read on the best of his days, I get to read those entries to him every bloody morning.

Annette: Wow. Okay. I hadn't heard about the guy with the meatballs.

Brooke: I want to know if he got any. The sheriff's log really needs to provide more follow-up details. Can you ask Jackson about that?

Annette: I'll see what I can do.

Annette: The story he did tell me involved you and JJ. Believe me when I tell you he was completely scandalized by the conversation he observed.

Brooke: Whatever he heard was out of context, I assure you.

Annette: There was no ultimatum issued? Nothing about giving you something worth staying awake? And he didn't offer up a semi-threatening response about making you regret that ultimatum?

Brooke: Pillow talk.

Annette: …in the middle of a tavern?

Brooke: Um, okay, Miss Judgypants.

Annette: Stop it.

Brooke: I didn't realize you'd apply your contempt and condemnation like strawberry jam all over my toasty sex life.

Annette: No contempt, no condemnation. Just really amused to find your under-the-radar, no-strings, no-big-deal dick appointment is now an in-public, sexy-ultima-tums-and-threats kind of relationship. If I had to guess, I'd say you'll be sharing a Netflix account within two months.

Brooke: Is that what couples do now? They share streaming accounts? What is this world we live in?

Annette: It's crazy, I know.

Annette: In other news, I have some fabulous ideas for double dates!

Brooke: I didn't understand a single word in that sentence.

Annette: Just you wait. I'll extract my vengeance for your months of secret-keeping.

Brooke: Fuck, you are evil. Diabolical. Why does anyone think you're the nice one?

Annette: Because I let them believe it.

Brooke: Wow. Just...wow.

Brooke: The Good Witch wasn't good, was she? It was an act and she had the right look for it.

Annette: And the Wicked Witch wasn't wicked, honey. She'd just taken too much of everyone's shit to play nice anymore.

Brooke: My sister-wife heard about the conversation we had at the tavern yesterday afternoon, from Jackson.

JJ: Please don't call her that. I'm sure it's some kind of appropriation and it also weirds me out.

Brooke: You don't like bloodless sister either.

JJ: What is wrong with her name? Why can't you simply say you talked to Annette?

Brooke: Because I'm cheeky like that.

JJ: All right. Fine. What are you trying to tell me?

Brooke: Jackson was a little concerned about the things he heard and passed that info along to (let me see if I do this right) Annette.

JJ: Yeah, I had a great chat with him after you left.

Brooke: You didn't mention that last night.

JJ: No, I was more interested in fucking you than recounting my conversation with the sheriff.

Brooke: I won't disagree with that logic.

JJ: Good girl.

Brooke: Don't tell me I can't use sister-wife when you toss around good girl. That one is just as bad.

JJ: Funny how you didn't object last night.

Brooke: All I wanted to tell you is Jackson told Annette everything he heard and now Annette is cooking up some devious double dates for us.

JJ: I'm not sure I want to ask but—what the actual fuck are you talking about?

Brooke: Don't worry. It'll be fine. She won't act on those threats.

JJ: Great. Have your ass in my bed before midnight.

Brooke: Excuse you.

JJ: Be a good girl and do as you're told.

Brooke: Oh, so you want to play?

JJ: Any day, Bam. Any day for you.

Annette: Hey, you two!

Brooke: omfg. Annette. What is this? A group text? Are you serious?

Annette: I'm inviting you both to a dinner party!

Jackson: We'd be thrilled to have you over.

Annette: Right! Yes! WE are inviting you two to a dinner party!

Brooke: What do you mean by "dinner party"?

Annette: Jackson and I want to have you over for dinner on Thursday and it's a party!

Brooke: That's enough exclamation points, lady. You're killing me.

JJ: What distinguishes dinner from a dinner party?

Annette: We're expecting you two at 7 on Thursday!

JJ: Will there be party hats at this dinner party? Is that what carries it over the line into party territory?

Jackson: We'll skip the hats.

Annette: Can't wait to spend time with both of you, together!

JJ: Are gifts exchanged at a dinner party?

Annette: And don't think you can get out of this!

Brooke: Any chance you have a food and beverage emergency you'll need to handle tomorrow evening?

JJ: Are you trying to get rid of me?

Brooke: I just don't want to do this.

JJ: I'm the last one to willingly break bread with law enforcement considering Lau is a pain in my ass more often than not, but I don't mind your sidekick Annette.

Brooke: I think I'm her sidekick, actually.

JJ: Either way, I'm guaranteed a good meal from her. That's more than I can say for you.

Brooke: Yeah, feeding people isn't one of my gifts or talents.

JJ: Aside from me joining in, how is this different from any other evening you'd spend with them?

Brooke: I'd rather not view it through that lens.

JJ: The logic lens?

Brooke: Call it what you want.

JJ: Should we bring something?

Brooke: How the hell should I know? See, this is how it's different. I've third-wheeled it with them plenty of times and never once worried about sacrificial offerings to the dinner party gods.

JJ: I was thinking more along the lines of a bottle of wine or something, or some flowers. Not so much in the sacrifice lane.

Brooke: Again, call it what you want.

JJ: I can grab a bottle of wine, gin, vodka. Two, even. A combo pack if you want to go wild. I have plenty in the storeroom.

Brooke: No, that's boring. Unimaginative.

JJ: Your confidence in me is inspiring.

Brooke: You don't need any additional confidence. You're doing fine.

JJ: Okay. We won't bring wine.

Brooke: I'll figure something out. Don't worry about it.

JJ: I wasn't worried.

Brooke: You're never worried.

JJ: That is untrue.

Brooke: You never worry about things that matter.

JJ: Yeah. Imaginative dinner party gifts for your best friend are the things that really matter.

Brooke: Exactly what kind of Meet the Parents shit are you trying to pull?

Annette: I haven't a clue what you mean.

Brooke: You have many clues.

Annette: Listen. There was a small bedroom accident this morning and I nailed my head on the footboard. I have a terrible headache and an obnoxious goose egg that customers won't stop asking about. I'm going to skip our slow-walk-to-the-conclusion routine and give you some real talk.

Brooke: How...did you hit your head on the footboard?

Annette: It was a reverse cowgirl accident.

Brooke: Paint the picture, honey. Talk me through this.

Annette: Okay, so I'm on his dick and things are fine until I reach down and start playing with his balls and...other points of interest in that vicinity. Things got a little rowdy and I lost my balance and flew head first at the footboard post.

Brooke: The bronco bucked you off?

Annette: Pretty much.

Brooke: You know, I am not having that kind of sex. I think I'm okay with that.

Annette: Since we've cleared that up, I'd like to remind you that you fight back against things, all the time. It's your way of insisting the people in your world prove how much we really love you. We have to get past many levels of you pushing us away in order to prove we actually want to be with you. Because you'd rather reject people than be rejected. So, yes, we're having this dinner party, and yes, you are attending. Because Jackson and I love you so much, we'll go find you and drag you to the event if you don't come willingly.

Brooke: This makes me sound incredibly high-maintenance.

Annette: Humans are high maintenance. Some are better at putting those requirements out there than others.

Brooke: This is scary for me.

Annette: I know. It will be all right. I would never put you in a situation where it wouldn't be all right.

Brooke: I don't deserve you.

Annette: You do. You deserve many good things.

Brooke: At this dinner party…can I ask Jackson whether he's going to outfit you in pro football gear before taking you to bed again?

Annette: He feels awful about this.

Brooke: Great, I'll capitalize on that.

AFTER SPENDING the entire afternoon in small, cluttered boutiques all along the seacoast that offered everything from scented candles to quilted tote bags to wind chimes, I'd found a gift and completed the inevitable transition into my mother. There was no other way to explain the cellophane-wrapped basket that required both arms to carry.

"Would you let me take that?" Jed asked for the fortieth time as we stepped up to Jackson and Annette's door.

I nudged his hand away when he tried to free the basket from my grasp. The cellophane protested these movements with a crackle. "There's no need."

"You can't see over it. You're going to wind up falling on your ass." He reached for the basket again and I batted him away, nearly losing my hold on it in the process. "What do you have in there? It's the size of a commercial food processor, Bam."

"It's not a food processor. She already has one of those."

"Great. So, what the hell is it?" he asked.

Before I could respond, the door swept open and Annette cried, "Come in, come in, come in."

Jed glanced between me and Annette several times. "No one mentioned anything about a costume party."

Annette touched her fingertips to the wide swath of Pucci-inspired fabric covering her forehead and woven through her dark, curly hair. "It was optional," she replied. "I'm not surprised Brooke kept that tidbit to herself. You know how she hates these sorts of silliness."

"I do not hate silliness one bit. In fact, I love when sex accidents necessitate silliness," I argued, stepping inside the house. "Here." I pushed the gift toward her and nearly succeeded in knocking her down. "This is for you. And Jackson too, of course."

"Of course," Annette said over the crinkle of cellophane. "But what the hell is this and why are you giving it to me?"

At a volume not far from screeching, I replied, "It's a hostess gift. For hosting us."

"Bam," Jed murmured as he skimmed his knuckles down my back. "Take a breath."

Annette plopped down on the sofa, setting the basket beside her. "Let's see how to open this," she said, examining the basket for entry points. The cellophane squealed under her touch. It was taped and tied and ribboned to death. There was no entry. "Hmm. I wasn't prepared for a puzzle tonight."

I pressed a hand to my mouth because *oh my freaking god*, why didn't I opt for a bottle of relatively silent wine with an obvious opening?

"For fuck's sake," Jed breathed, reaching into his pocket as he crouched in front of the sofa. He took hold of the ribbon-tied top, flipped open a Swiss Army knife, and cut the wrappings off at the head. He drew the blade down the sides and front, peeling back the layers as he went. "There you go."

Annette ran her hands over the carefully displayed items, prying each from the mess of paper grass filling the bottom of the basket. Still staring at the gifts, she said, "You must be deep in the feels." She hefted the serving platter up, studied it, turned it over. "Oh, my friend. You're *deep* in your feels, aren't you?"

Folding up his knife, Jed asked, "Do I want to know what that means?"

I blinked at her, my hand permanently fixed over my lips. Nodded once. Yeah, I was in my feelings. All of my feelings.

"This is silver," Annette announced, as if I didn't know.

As if I hadn't selected the most lovely, excessive gifts I could find because that was how I managed my deep feels. I bought ridiculous things and hoped I could store my conflicted emotions inside those objects as there was no room for them within me. That was the reason for most of the shoes in my closet and the Brooklyn townhouse I'd purchased a week after my mother's funeral.

"This is a silver platter that's big enough for a giant Thanksgiving turkey. I mean, a big ass turkey. I could feed the entire town off this platter. And it's *silver*." She set the tray aside and chose another item from the basket. "What do I do with this?"

"It's a wine canister," I said through my fingers. "You put, you know, a bottle of wine or champagne in there. Mineral water, maybe. To keep it chilled while it's on the table."

Jed chuckled as he ran a hand down his face. "You're somethin' special, Bam."

"Okay." Annette bobbed her head as she set the canister down.

It was the type of "okay" that also said "I'm going to let you think I agree with that" and "In case you didn't notice, this is ridiculous." My soul sister could get away with a packed "okay" and make it sound as pleasant as pie, but I knew what she was thinking. *I knew*. And I was relieved I'd talked myself out of adding an ice bucket to this purchase.

"These must be coasters. Silver coasters." She grinned

up at me, saying, "I take it they were out of gold and platinum options."

Her snark snapped me back into this moment. "Nothing encrusted with jewels either. It was annoying. I wouldn't have this problem in New York."

She glanced back to the basket of silver, shaking her head. "No, probably not, though I appreciate the absence of monogramming. There's some next-level crazy at work here, but I admire your ability to draw the line at engraving 'Jackson and Annette' or some combination of initials. That's how I know this is from the heart."

"It is," I replied softly. Jed squeezed my shoulder. "From the heart, I mean."

"Get over here and hug me." Annette pushed to her feet and held her arms out as she crossed the room toward me. She gathered me up, folding me tight to her body. "Come into the kitchen. I made a cheese plate. We'll handle your feels tomorrow." Leaning away from me, she asked Jed, "Do you like cheese?"

He rubbed his hands over my shoulders as he kissed the crown of my head. "What's not to like?"

"I always knew I liked you," she said, laughing.

Behind me, I heard the door open and then close. Footfalls on the floor. "It's good you learn the truth now, Harniczek. There's no tearing these two apart. The best you can do is hold on and hope for some scraps, even if that scrap means being the ass-end of a group hug."

"I don't think you should be telling anyone how to hold on," I said to Jackson. "Not when you're throwing Annette off beds and nearly cracking her skull open."

"Cheese!" Annette shouted, taking me and Jed by the

hands. "It's time for cheese. We're going into the kitchen, we're eating cheese, and we're not talking about bedroom injuries."

"Jesus, Annie. Tell me it's better," Jackson insisted.

"Is that not how dinner parties work?" Jed asked.

"It's fine. Stop asking," Annette replied.

"Well, I'm gonna ask," Jackson grumbled as he made a beeline for the refrigerator. As he swung it open, he jerked his chin toward Jed. "What'll it be? Beer or wine?"

Jed tapped my wrist. "What would you like?"

There they were again, emotions like storm waves against a sea wall.

"I've got Brooke covered, don't you worry," Jackson called. "Beer or wine, Harniczek?"

"Beer," he replied, staring at me with a half-smile that pried something loose inside me. At the rate I was going, it was probably a bone spur or a blood clot. "Thanks."

Jackson popped the tops on a pair of beers, setting one in front of Jed before he busied himself collecting white wine and two glasses. When he'd delivered the wine, he pointed his beer bottle at me and Jed. "All ribbing aside, what's the story here? When did this start?"

At the same time as I said, "Last month," Jed responded with "Last year."

I turned to face him. "That's a bit of a stretch, don't you think?"

He leaned close to me, bent his head, dropped his gaze to my neck. "Yeah, I think it was a stretch," he whispered. "Took some getting used to, didn't it, Bam?"

Heat washed over my face and down my chest. I wasn't sure, but it seemed as though I was blushing all the way to my toes. I'd never reacted that way before and I wasn't keen on doing it again. "You're right and it's good of you to open up about your complete inability to engage in foreplay."

He edged farther into my space, pressed his lips to the base of my throat. Without thinking, my hand went to the back of his head, my fingers sliding through his wavy strands. "You weren't complaining last night."

"That's because I started without you," I replied.

"As if I could stop you," he rumbled.

"That's enough cuddling in my kitchen for now," Annette called as she shoved her hands into oven mitts. "You're melting the buttercream off my cake."

When Jed swung an arm around the back of my chair, Jackson wagged his beer bottle in our direction again. "I suppose we can live without a firm date, though the lack of clarity is concerning."

"Would you stop it?" Annette said to him as she bent to retrieve a dish from the oven. "You're not working a case here, Jackson." She set the dish down, shucked her mitts. "Let's move this into the dining room. JJ, you grab the salad. Jackson, you're responsible for the pasta. Watch out for the sauce, there's a lot on there. I'm taking the bread basket and leaving the extra meatballs in the kitchen because those are for lunch tomorrow."

I held out my hands as the men followed her orders. "What should I bring?"

"The wine, sweetie. You bring the wine. I think you're gonna need it," she replied.

I didn't want Annette to be right about that.

For the first few minutes, we filled our plates and

spoke only of passing one thing or another. It was perfect. Jed and I didn't contradict each other. He didn't lick my neck in front of our friends and I didn't touch his hair. No one was yelling and the buttercream was safe.

Then, Annette asked, "What's new at the tavern these days, JJ?"

"The beauty of the tavern is that nothing has been new for decades," he replied. "It saves me the trouble of telling people to go to hell when they complain about hating change."

"I can't fathom why you'd take the humble road now, but it's not true to say you have nothing new in store." I hit him with a stern frown before glancing to Annette and Jackson. "Since he's playing shy, I'll tell you about the distillery he's opening on the grounds of the cider house."

"Brooke," Jed murmured.

"You know the one, it's just north of the village," I continued, ignoring him. "And it's not just a distillery. There's a restaurant and a bar area to sample everything. Gin, vodka. All homemade."

"Brooke," he repeated.

"Oh, and it's all local. Farm to, you know, highball glass. There will be tours and something with bees and a space for parties and wedding receptions. Oh! That's where you can get married. Wouldn't that be perfect?" I asked them. "You can finally set a date."

"*Brooke*."

I shifted to face Jed and found him with his arms propped on the table, his fingers steepled in front of his lips. "What? What was wrong with that?"

"You're opening a distillery in Talbott's Cove," Jackson

said, each word spoken as if he couldn't believe them. "I knew there was work underway on that site and I'd heard about zoning permits being approved, but I didn't realize people would be coming to town for the singular purpose of consuming alcohol."

Jed stared at me for a beat before saying, "Nothing was wrong. I hadn't intended to discuss all of this tonight. Some of it is public, but not all." He tipped his joined fingers toward Jackson. "True to form, the sheriff has seven thousand questions and he's already setting up his DUI checkpoints—"

"You're damn right I am," Jackson said.

"—but I hadn't expected that to be part of the dinner party festivities," he said. "Then again, I never know what the hell I'm getting into with you."

I heard my heartbeat in my ears, and once again a blush colored my skin. I searched for words to wield like the sharp side of a blade, but only dredged up more confusing emotions. Instead of figuring out these feelings and finding room for them, I wanted to pluck them from the air around me and stow them somewhere far away.

"It's strange that none of this was covered in the dinner party book I read." Annette sent a quiet laugh to her plate. Motioning to Jackson, she said, "You have to practice balancing work and life."

"Annie, you know I can't do that," he replied.

"Shush. It wasn't a question. These are our friends and this is my party and it's not time to get your sheriff on." She lifted her glass in Jed's direction. "Congratulations on this amazing project! I can't wait to hear more about the gin and the bees and the cider house. If we ever finish building this new home of ours, we'll be your first wedding."

"Don't start with *if*," Jackson remarked. "It's *when* we finish building the house. *When*."

"It's going that well, huh?" Jed asked him.

Jackson's answering eye roll and groan said it all. "We thought it would be fun to build a house. We thought it would be better to have everything the way we wanted it rather than fitting ourselves into an existing home. We thought it would cost less than renovating. We knew nothing. *Nothing*."

"And you," Annette said, shooting Jackson a tolerant grin as she turned toward me. "You are just the most precious mess, aren't you? You can't even help it."

I flipped my hair over my shoulder. "If I have to be a mess, I'd rather be a precious one." While Jackson and Annette laughed, I glanced to Jed, mouthing, *Sorry*.

Jed reached under the table, curled his hand around my knee. "Don't sweat it, Bam."

I laughed. I sipped my wine. I moved pasta around my plate while the conversation turned to the usual suspects of sports, weather, small town politics, moose sightings. I worked hard at restricting my comments to neutral, widely available information. I wasn't worried about inciting another incident as much as I worried about another wave of emotions dragging me down, driving me to delirium.

That strategy worked well enough until Annette served thick wedges of chocolate cake slathered in chocolate buttercream and Jackson asked, "The three of you grew up together, right? There must be a lot of history."

There was no specific reason for that question to hit me like a tsunami, but it did. It took me to the ground and slapped me with reminders that my relationship with Jed was complicated and tangled up with Annette and my family and this town, and it wasn't as new as I wanted to believe.

Jackson was correct. We had a lot of history.

"Technically, yes, we grew up together," Annette replied, passing a gigantic piece of cake to Jackson. His brows arched up to his hairline as he accepted it. "We lived in the same town and went to the same schools, but we weren't in the same friend groups and we didn't really know each other until later."

Jackson waved a hand around the table, saying, "It's difficult to imagine a scenario where you're not as close as you are now."

"Imagine a scenario where we're the most immature, concentrated versions of our adult selves and that's high school for you," Jed replied. "Surprising absolutely no one, Annette was the model student and the teacher's pet, and she was friendly and outgoing enough that no one held any of it against her."

"She was the favorite. Sweet cheeks through and through," I added.

"JJ was a bit of a loner, but in an interesting, enigmatic way," Annette said. "I remember you going through a Kafka phase. I remember your jacket—"

"The leather jacket." He bobbed his head, a self-effacing smile on his lips. "God, that thing got some use that year."

"You wore it every damn day," Annette said. "Until the

Hemingway phase, where you wanted nothing more than to be an ex-pat."

"That's a difficult goal to realize while living in Maine," he said, laughing.

"And then there was Langston Hughes and I think it wrapped up with a Dostoyevsky phase, right? Am I recalling that correctly?" Annette asked.

Before I knew what I was saying, I replied, "Yes, it was Dostoyevsky."

As slowly as someone could move while still moving, Jed turned his head toward me. "You remember that?"

"Yeah." I jerked a shoulder to make sure he knew it was a stray memory from long ago rather than proof of anything meaningful. "You wore a t-shirt with the book cover on the front and a quote on the back and—"

"'Love in action is a harsh and dreadful thing compared to love in dreams,'" he said.

"You wore it all the time." I stabbed my fork into the cake. I refused to take responsibility for knowing the book he glommed all over in high school.

"Yes, I can picture it now," Annette added. "You loved your tortured, broody writer types, didn't you?"

His gaze still locked on me, he said, "That's what happens when you have after-school jobs at the public library and the graphic design shop out near the highway. They had a full screen-printing setup there, which allowed me to experiment with quippy t-shirts before quippy t-shirts were popular."

"Harniczek was a loner with a library card. Annie was a sweet little cinnamon roll." Jackson's brows bent together. "Where does that leave Brooke?"

Annette beamed at Jackson, saying, "She was the princess."

"Oh my god," I muttered to myself.

"It's true," Annette chirped. "She traveled in an opalescent bubble whenever she decided to grace the small people with her presence."

"That doesn't even make sense." I shoved a bite of cake in my mouth. "For the record, I was friends with everyone. I hung out with all the different crowds. The last thing I wanted was to be that spoiled, snotty kid everyone expected me to be. No princess, no bubble."

"There was a party. Junior year, I think," Jed said, his gaze unfocused. "A bunch of chill, low-key kids put it together. Nothing big or special, just one of those times when we got some beers and built a bonfire on the beach. I remember when you arrived. You didn't pop out of a bubble, but damn, that's not far from the truth."

"What does that mean?" I snapped.

"It was a performance," he replied. "Wasn't that what you did in high school? Every day, you were on stage. You didn't want to be the spoiled, snotty kid, but you did want to be the center of attention. A princess of the people is still a princess. That was the role you played."

"Don't you think that sounds a little harsh?" Jackson asked.

Before Jed could respond, I jumped in with, "No, it sounds accurate. I'm sure I'm guilty of all—"

"We're not doing that, drama llama," Annette said.

"I don't think it's drama and I don't think you need to admit any guilt," Jed remarked. "We were kids who struggled and fought and bounced our ways into who we are today. You probably struggled and fought more than either of us."

"That seems overly generous." I went on hacking the cake to crumbs. "Like you said, still a princess."

I felt Jed's hand on my knee again, but I didn't look away from the plate in front of me. The table was silent, save for the metallic slide of Annette's knife against the cake tray. She dropped another slice on Jackson's plate and then one on Jed's.

"Why are you giving me more cake?" Jackson asked.

"It's for you to eat," she replied.

"Do I look like I need to be fattened up, Annie?" he asked.

"Sorry, can't hear you over the pounding in my head. I have a terrible headache because some brute threw me off a bed," she quipped.

While Jackson and Annette volleyed back and forth about sex and cake, Jed edged closer, ducking his head to catch my eye. "I've hurt you and I'm sorry. That wasn't my intention."

"It's fine. Not a problem. We were kids, and kids are assholes. No sweat, right?" I glanced up at him and found his hazel eyes gentle and earnest. It was nearly enough for me to admit it *was* a role, it *was* a performance. I was a princess and I was marital glue and I was perfect. But admitting that—saying it out loud to another person and watching while the truth seeped in—was terrifying. It meant acknowledging I'd spent years rotating through personalities as I attempted to be the person everyone else expected me to be. It meant confirming I'd never kept close, true friendships before Annette. And it meant recognizing Jed saw through everything I put between me and the world.

"Don't do that," he whispered. "You've never pretended with me. Don't start now."

Annette yanked my plate out from under my fork and replaced it with a fresh slice of cake. "Try *eating* this one." Rounding the table, she said, "Remind me where you went after high school, JJ. You saw all the big places. Rome, London, Hong Kong, Paris, Cairo, all of that good stuff. Where else did you go?"

I snapped my head up, blinking at Annette and Jed. "When was this?"

"After high school. After graduation." He forked a chunk of cake from my plate, popped it in his mouth. "I headed out of town, picked up a job with a travel company, and gave tours around Boston for a few months. Don't make me tell you about the Freedom Trail. It's great and important, but I still hear that lecture in my sleep." He claimed another chunk, ate it. "After the company sprung me from Boston, I rotated throughout the United States and Canada for a year. I hear the Grand Canyon lecture in my sleep too, but it gave me a chance to see every corner of the country."

"That sounds amazing," Annette said. "I always think I want to travel for extended periods of time, but I can't manage a weekend trip to Portland without packing my entire closet and then suffering because I forgot the one thing I actually needed."

"Yeah, you can't do that when you live on the road." Jed laughed as he stole another bite of cake. "After leaving North America, I spent a few more years touring overseas. Europe, Asia, Africa, Oceania. I had a chance to hit Central and South America, but I decided to live in New Zealand for a year instead."

I scowled at Annette across the table, but she didn't catch my meaning and scowled right back. She didn't realize I knew nothing of Jed's life outside Talbott's Cove. He saw me and he knew me, and I was busy floating around in my opalescent bubble, never bothering to ask him about his years away from this town.

"Why New Zealand?" Jackson asked. "I've always heard the best things about that country, but it wouldn't occur to me to move there for a year."

"And yet it occurred to you to move to Talbott's Cove from Albany," Jed mused. "I...I had time on my hands. I'd worked nonstop for six years at that point and I'd always loved touring through that part of the world. Always wished I had more time. Then, I had the time." He scraped up the last bite, careful to gather as much frosting as the fork would carry. "And New Zealand is as far away from this town as I could get."

"Did you stay in one city or wander like a proper nomad?" Annette asked.

"I spent some time in Wellington and then Christchurch. Everywhere in between. Later, I ended up on Stewart Island, on the far, far south end of New Zealand across the Foveaux Strait. A couple times each week, I took the ferry to Ulva Island to hike or read or whatever sounded good. They used rangiora shrub leaves as tickets. It was the most unbelievable experience of my life."

Jackson leaned back, crossing his ankle over his knee. "What did you do there? For *a year*?"

Jed lifted his shoulders, let them fall. "Lots of things. I wandered the Rakiura Track on Stewart Island. It's about twenty-two miles and it's—it's beautiful. It's nothing like Maine, nothing at all. So, I walked. I took millions of photos. Probably more. I went to pubs and drank many times my weight in Speight's. I stared at the stars and birds and trees I'd never seen before." He gestured toward Jackson with his fork. "A little bit of everything, you could say."

"Why did you leave a place you loved so much?" My voice sounded rusty, as if I hadn't spoken in days. "What brought you here?"

"It was time." He draped his arm over the back of my chair. His fingertips barely brushed my shoulder. I edged toward his hand. "I loved everything about being there, but I also loved being half a world away—until I didn't love that distance anymore. As I explored the country and made my way through one town after another, I realized I missed this place. I missed Talbott's Cove. Part of it was nostalgia. At that point, I hadn't spent more than ten days here since graduation."

I jerked in my seat, bracing both hands on the edge of the table to hold steady. I stared at Jed but he offered nothing, no assurance he remembered the day we graduated from high school and the night that followed.

Those waves, they didn't stop.

"The other part of it was wanting a place in the ecosystem. While I tended bar all over New Zealand, I watched the way people in those towns interacted. How their universes functioned, how relationships grew roots, how people changed the places around them. At the same time, my uncle was dying of liver disease after drinking his way through fifty-plus years of owning the Galley. My aunt wanted it out of her hands and I wanted a spot in this ecosystem." He shifted his arm off the chair and onto my shoulders, tucking me into his chest. He pressed his lips to my ears, whispering, "This place called me home. I'm not sure of much, but I think it might've called you too."

I shivered as if I was standing naked in the cold. In a way, I was.

CHAPTER TWENTY-SIX

JJ

Long-Term Debt: a liability with a maturity greater than one year.

LATER THAT EVENING, after surviving a delicious but turbulent dinner party, I asked, "What happened that night? After graduation?"

Brooke glanced back at me over her shoulder. That movement sent her silky hair pooling on my chest and her bare body snuggling closer to mine. "What do you mean?"

Here she was, naked and satisfied in my arms, and even still, I hesitated. But I had to know. I wouldn't have broached the subject if not for the way she looked at me after dinner tonight. As if I'd done wrong by her all those years ago. "We were at that party at Peyton Woodmoore's place and we ended up behind the barn and—and I kissed you."

She forced a laugh. "Yeah. I know."

"But what happened?"

I watched as her brows lowered, eyes slanted to the side. "I still don't know what you mean. I'm sorry."

I should've stopped there, but I never stopped myself when Brooke came around. "You disappeared. You told me to stay there, behind the barn. You said you'd come back. I waited for—for fuck, longer than I should've. What happened?"

She teased a finger over the edge of the quilt, not meeting my eyes. "I don't know. I don't remember it well. There was a lot of beer and shots involved. *Bad* beer. *Bad* shots. I just remember you were gone a few days after that party."

This conversation was like waiting for a bus in the rain. Even if I leaned away from it, even if I hitched up my collar, I was still getting uncomfortably soaked. And I should've known not to wait for a bus in the rain, but now that I was here and wet, there was no sense turning back. "I decided to leave town after that night. I knew I wanted to go, and I knew that was the right time."

"Are you trying to say that was a product of me— what? Forgetting you behind a barn when I was young and drunk? That's why you went to Boston and you're still recovering from your Freedom Trail nightmares?"

"No," I replied. "I'd wanted to go. I'd wanted to go as much as you wanted the same thing."

A fast, breathy laugh shook her shoulders. "You're saying that me forgetting you behind the Woodmoores' barn gave you the push you needed to get the hell out of this town?"

I was quick to reply, "No." Then, "Maybe. I don't know."

Brooke turned over to face me, a gently smug smile pulling at her lips. "You're saying I wounded your tender teenage heart."

I stared at her, torn between coming in from the downpour and staying out here until I caught my death. "You did," I agreed. "I'd thought it meant something to you. I thought that one counted."

"Why? Because it took place behind a barn? After the official end of high school?" She wrapped her arms around my torso, pressed her nipples to my chest. "Or was there some other reason you wanted it to matter, Jed?"

I seized her waist, bringing us as close as we could get without a condom. "I was eighteen. My only reasons were 'because I want to' and 'because someone told me not to do that.'"

"Those are the same reasons anyone kissed me in high school, regardless of whether I was *performing*." She dropped her head to my shoulder. "And then you took off on a journey around the world with your wounded heart in tow."

"Did it mean anything to you?"

She smiled down at my chest, brushed her hand over the ink on my arm and shoulder. I didn't expect her to respond. I figured she'd change the topic or deflect the question back on me, pick at my desire for youthful validation. But then, "You know what's really interesting? You thought I blew you off. You've spent all these years being bitter—"

"I haven't spent any years on bitterness. I left town. I got over it."

She pressed her lips to my sternum, humming. "Yeah, that's why you brought it up now."

"I brought it up," I replied, my tone growing impatient, "because your hair is everywhere and your bare ass is in my bed and I get to bring up whatever the hell I want under those conditions."

"Like I said, bitter." For that, I gave her backside a squeeze. "You thought I abandoned you behind a barn and—for a period of time—you had all these feelings about it. Feelings for which you blamed me." She burrowed against me, her head on my chest, her arms tight around my body, her face angled away from me. "And I thought we'd started something that night, but then you were gone."

I was wet from head to toe now, rainwater filling my shoes and blurring my vision. But it was possible I wasn't the only one waiting for this bus. "What do you mean?"

"I thought it meant something to you," Brooke said to my skin. "For the life of me, I can't remember what happened after I left you behind that barn but I thought... I thought it was real. You said you'd wanted to kiss me all night but had no intention of doing it in front of any of those assholes from our class. That was some advanced seduction technique, as far as high school went. I remember thinking I was going to have one of those glowy summer romances filled with beach blankets and ice cream cones and sunburned shoulders. I thought you were different, Jed, and then you were gone without a word."

I didn't know how we wandered into the land where all the bullshit fell away to reveal pure vulnerability, but I wasn't turning back yet. "I wounded *your* tender teenage heart."

When I brushed her hair away from her forehead, she glanced up at me. There was no smug smile, no contemptuous glare. It was Brooke, eyes wide and lips parted, free from all the space and show she put between herself and the world.

"Is that what I did, Bam?"

"A bit, yeah." She blinked away, pulled a small smile. "But what did we know back then? What did we know about anything?"

I chuckled. "We knew nothing."

"Not sure about that," she replied. "You knew you wanted to kiss me and you knew you wanted it to count."

"Still do." I traced the line of her lips, her jaw. "Do you still want a movie montage summer? It sounds like I owe you one."

"I'm more careful about sunburns now, but there's room on my beach blanket."

"Are you going to forget me behind a barn?"

"I will not," she replied. "Are you going to flee the state?"

"Only if you're coming with me," I said.

"Please," she scoffed. "You don't want to take me anywhere. You can't wait to get rid of me."

"That's not—no. No, I—" I knew what she was doing, but I had to stop myself. "No, I don't want to get rid of you, Bam."

She cocked her head, smiling up at me as she batted

her lashes. "I'd ask if you intend to keep me, but I'm not a woman who can be kept."

And that was why I had to stop myself. It wasn't simple with Brooke. I couldn't tell her I was falling for her —no, fuck that. I'd fallen and I was long past the point of saving myself from her. It wasn't a matter of putting emotions into words, not for Brooke. She didn't trust either.

"Well, fuck," I muttered. "Here I was, thinking you could keep me."

She laughed, shook her head. "You're too busy redefining the entire tourism industry in Talbott's Cove to be anyone's house husband. It would never work."

I knew better, but I asked anyway. "Is that how you see it? That belonging to someone means giving up all of yourself?"

"I don't know," she said. "I don't know what it's supposed to look like. I don't know how to do it. This has meandered down some strange lanes, Jed. I...I don't even know what we're talking about."

"We don't have to talk about anything," I said, rolling her onto her back. "This is enough."

Basis Point: the smallest measure utilized for quoting interest yields.

Brooke: I hate you right now.

Annette: I cannot imagine why.

Brooke: You held me hostage.

Annette: I served you food and wine.

Brooke: You were a decent captor, I'll grant you that.

Annette: You entered into this captivity willingly.

Brooke: That is not my recollection of the events.

Annette: You need to calm down. We had a great little dinner party.

Brooke: Again, not my recollection.

Annette: Then tell me what you recall and I'll tell you why you're wrong.

Brooke: I'm going to ignore that condescending statement for a second while I enumerate the many issues with last night's events.

Annette: I'd expect nothing less.

Brooke: First, I agreed to this gathering under duress.

Annette: If inviting you over in a group text is the duress you're referencing, I'm calling bullshit.

Annette: Didn't you tell me about a time when you convinced a guy to change his name?

Brooke: His name was terrible. I was doing him a favor.

Annette: You're making my argument for me.

Brooke: I didn't want JJ to think I was embarrassed or didn't want to be seen in public with him. Or whatever lame shit guys come up with these days.

Annette: So, you admit you're concerned for his feelings?

Brooke: I admit I'm going to slap you in the boob the next time I see you.

Annette: That might sound like a threat to you, but my boobs are nice and fatty. That would be like slapping a loaf of pumpkin bread.

Brooke: Even if I set the circumstances of the invitation aside, I'd like to point out that the whole night was awkward as fuck.

Annette: It was not.

Brooke: The only way it could've been more awkward would be if you'd spoken through a hand puppet or if I'd revealed to Jackson that you do, in fact, poop.

Annette: Now you're just being ridiculous.

Brooke: Perhaps if you'd massaged Jackson's balls under the table, but did it without trying to be covert. That would've knocked up the awkward factor.

Annette: Considering I did that for no less than 15 minutes, I must've been too covert.

Annette: Or, maybe—and hear me out—you're seeing this through hot pink, heart-shaped, self-centered lenses.

Brooke: Of course I'm being self-centered. It's what I do best. I'm a princess, apparently.

Annette: What I'm saying is you're seeing this from a perspective that doesn't match up with reality.

Brooke: Pardon you and your suggestions of my looming insanity.

Annette: I'm trying to figure out where you diverged from that reality. Was it the high school conversation?

Brooke: Fucking high school. Reason #841 why coming home isn't nearly as good as the movies make it seem.

Annette: I'm taking that as a yes.

Brooke: I never realized people regarded me that way.

Annette: I think you're hearing it differently than we're saying it.

Brooke: We're talking about six of one and a half dozen of another, my dear.

Annette: What about JJ's world travels? Did that push you into the hot pink zone?

Brooke: Why the fucking fuck didn't you tell me any of that? I thought you were my wingwoman. You sent me in blind!

Annette: If you'd given me any notice that you planned on going in, I would've provided you with the most current details.

Annette: But as it turned out, you went in without your wingwoman and decided to fly solo for months.

Brooke: You could've mentioned it during any of our conversations we've had in the past two years about the people in this town.

Annette: Is that how long you've been yearning for him?

Brooke: Oh my prickly pussy, Annette, I don't yearn for anyone.

Annette: You know exactly what I mean and I'm pretty sure you confirmed my suspicions.

Brooke: That I've had a burning desire for JJ Harniczek since I returned to this pastoral hamlet? On the contrary, that burning was from a bladder infection. Some cranberry juice and antibiotics, and I'm good as new. Nothing on fire here.

Annette: Mmhmm.

Brooke: Don't do that.

Annette: Sure. Okay.

Brooke: Do not do that.

Annette: Yep. I got it.

Brooke: I will walk into your bookstore and slap your boob if you don't stop it right now.

Annette: Stop what? I'm just thinking back to all those times we had drinks at the Galley and how you'd push JJ's buttons and how I thought it was just you getting some of your puppy energy out, but now I know you were pulling his pigtails.

Brooke: Allow me to repeat my original statement—I hate you right now.

Annette: Promise me you won't be a bridezilla. Swear to me that you won't scream at a florist over a precise shade of blush-pink peonies.

Brooke: Can't. Putting shoes on. Leaving the house. Coming to slap your boob so hard it slaps the other one for me.

CHAPTER TWENTY-EIGHT

JJ

Insolvency Risk: the risk that an organization will be unable to satisfy its debts.

EXACTLY FIFTEEN MINUTES after the midday rush wrapped up, Sheriff Lau marched into the tavern. If I had to guess, I'd say the man had a deputy keeping track of my patrons and notifying him when it was all clear. As much as it irritated me, I had to give him credit for respecting my terms.

"Sheriff. What brings you in today?"

He stopped, rested his arms on the backs of a pair of barstools. He glanced at me, then Nate. "If you have a moment to spare, I'd like to speak with you privately."

"You're in charge, kid." I passed a bag of limes to Nate. "These need to be washed and sliced." As I dried my hands with a dish towel, I caught the sheriff's raised eyebrow. There was no way in hell Nate missed that eyebrow or the meaning behind it. "When you're done with that," I continued, shaking my head at Jackson, "restock the oranges and olives. That should keep you busy for at least—"

"Nine, maybe ten minutes," Nate said. "I'll refill the ketchup bottles if I feel like getting really rowdy."

"Smart plan." Despite this situation being a pain in my ass, I liked the kid. I enjoyed his permanently dark, surly mood and I appreciated the way he was determined to prove everyone wrong. Add to that he'd taken it upon himself to plant the pollinator garden at the cider house in his free time and I was damn well ready to adopt him. At the minimum, I was getting between him and every shitty eyebrow the sheriff and anyone else in this town sent his way.

I led Jackson to my office and shut the door behind us. Immediately, he remarked, "He seems to be doing well."

I dropped into my chair, glared across the desk. "It's been months. Many months. You're not helping anyone with this."

Jackson, ever the Boy Scout, gave a chastened nod. "You're right. It seems like he's"—the sheriff paused, visibly sorting through his words—"he's back on his feet."

"You're fuckin' right he is," I yelled. "But if you come in here one more time and give him a visual pat-down, I won't be as pleasant when I say 'I told you so.'"

Holding up both hands, Jackson said, "Understood."

"Thank you," I replied. "Now, what the hell do you want?"

Jackson clasped his hands in his lap, inclined his head. "I don't have to tell you our women are best friends."

"Jesus Christ," I muttered to myself. "No, sheriff, you don't have to tell me they're best friends, but it would be good if you found a way to speak of them as something more respectful than 'our women.'"

"What's disrespectful about that?" he asked, his brows bent together and confusion rippling his features.

"Do I actually have to explain to you that they don't belong to us? I recognize there are shades of meaning here and the notion might give you some warm fuzzies, but I'd rather not reduce Brooke or Annette to possessions. In case it's not obvious to you, neither of them need us."

"No, that's plain to see." He bobbed his head in agreement, but he was busy deciding whether he understood my point.

"Listen, I'm not trying to bring down your worldview. I'm just trying to tell you there's a big difference between the things you say to Annette privately, when you're at home, when you're in your bedroom, and what you say to other people. It matters how you talk about women."

He ran his hand up the back of his neck, around the inside of his collar. "I thought I was good at this. The feminist stuff."

"You can be good at it while also accepting some feedback to get better," I argued. "I'm not saying you're a misogynistic piece of shit. I'm saying there's a better way to start a conversation about Brooke and Annette than minimizing them as 'our women.'"

"All right, let's try this again. Annette and Brooke are best friends. That's not about to change. I thought it might be different after we'd moved in together, after we got engaged. Don't know why I thought that," he added, laughing. "I think we have the privilege of taking part in their world. We need to find a way to deal with each other because they wouldn't blink an eye at dropping one or both of us if we ever tried to make them choose."

"That's the straight truth," I replied.

"They've made a family of each other and it's the only family they truly have," he continued. "You and I, we have a number of differences. We don't agree on many things. Hell, half the time I don't think we speak the same language. But it's in our best interest to get this right."

Pressing my fist to my lips, I stared at the sheriff. I didn't relish him being right, if for no reason other than my longstanding disdain for people telling me what to do. Authority figures had been grating on me as far back as my memories went. There was no clean genesis to my anarchist bent; I preferred to command myself, regardless of the outcome.

But Jackson wasn't the real authority figure here. It was Brooke. She was as much of an authority as anyone. I couldn't refuse his peace offering because—for the first time in my life—anarchy wasn't my answer.

"You're right about them making a family," I conceded. "I'm not about to take that away from Brooke."

"And you're not about to let her go," Jackson added. "Or did I misread things over dinner last night?"

Rolling my eyes, I leaned forward, folded my arms on the desktop. "Let's establish some ground rules, *friend*. Number one, you don't read shit into my relationship and I'll offer you the same courtesy."

Fighting a smile, Jackson said, "I can agree to that."

"Second, you're not the sheriff in social settings. You want to argue about drunks stumbling out of my distillery and raising hell on your streets, you save that for a conversation like this one."

"The badge doesn't come off because I sit down for a meal," he replied.

"You don't have to take the badge off, but I'd prefer if you kept a lid on your law enforcement crusades when we're gathered for a damn dinner party."

"Watch it. Annette spent hours making everything perfect for that party," Jackson snapped.

"And it was perfect," I replied. "I ate the leftovers for breakfast. But you have to know the proper times and places to pull the sheriff card."

He circled his hand, urging me to continue. "What else? This is your opportunity, Harniczek. Get it all out."

"We need to find something to discuss that isn't Nate Fitzsimmons or local law enforcement efforts because that's all we've ever talked about and I'm maxed out. Football, the last book you read, the weather, whatever the hell you want."

He stared at me for a long beat before saying, "I'll give it some thought." He continued staring because it wouldn't be a valuable conversation without slapping me with his power penis.

"Are we done here, sheriff? Or shall we play this game until someone comes looking for us? Nate can entertain himself with citrus fruit and ketchup all afternoon, but I'm sure your absence won't go unnoticed."

I expected him to leave without a word or make an ominous remark about keeping an eye on me, but he asked, "What have you heard about the kids hanging out near the old Walker farmstead?" He rattled off a few names. No surprises in that crew. "Every time one of my deputies swing by, they say the kids are being kids and there's no trouble beyond some minors in possession of alcohol. What do you think?"

It was good to slip back into the comfort of our long-established dynamic of sheriff and barkeep, where I kept a handle on under-the-table affairs in these parts and Jackson was the heavy when needed. We knew and enjoyed these roles and they were far less complicated than the ones we found ourselves in now, as the men in Brooke's and Annette's lives.

"I think it's probably a nonissue," I said. "If it's not one abandoned farm, it's another."

"Isn't that the truth," he replied. "So, how about those Rangers? Think they'll make it to the Stanley Cup?"

"That's enough." I pointed toward the door. "We've covered plenty of ground today, sheriff. We have to save something for tomorrow."

"Right," he agreed, pushing to his feet. "We should ask Annette to recommend some books for us. To keep the conversation going."

"We're not starting a book club, sheriff." I jabbed my finger toward the door again. "Not until I know we have compatible taste in reading material."

CHAPTER TWENTY-NINE

BROOKE

Arbitrage: any strategy that invests for the long-term in one asset and short-term in a related asset.

JUNE

I WAS angry about everything today. Everything, but also nothing.

There wasn't a singular source of my issues and that was also bothersome. I wanted to collect all these pebbles of fury and resentment, roll them into a big, craggy rock, and shove it out my front door. If I could push it away— or throw it at someone—I wouldn't have to lug this weight around anymore. I wouldn't have to be angry.

Instead of staying home and marinating in my mood like any normal person would, I filled my pockets with those pebbles and marched down to the Galley. The mermaid with her wheat and berries on the tavern's sign earned an apologetic frown from me on the way in. That poor girl deserved better.

I found the dining room and bar packed with customers, but my usual spot at the bar was open. *Small miracles*. Watching as Nate and Jed worked together pouring drinks, their backs to me, I slipped onto my stool with a contented sigh. Finding a new seat at the bar would've been the last straw in a day filled with last straws.

After sending a tray full of beverages off with a server, Jed made his way toward me. I didn't intend to stare at his bare forearms or the black shirtsleeves cuffed to his elbows or the way his belt buckle sat impossibly low on his waist, but I couldn't stop myself. Couldn't stop myself from noticing the heartbeat between my legs either.

Pointing at his watch, he asked, "What are you doing here at this hour? You don't come looking for attention until after the sun sets."

"That's the problem with the days getting longer. It fucks up my attention-seeking rhythms."

He stepped closer, folded his arms on the bar, leaned toward me. "What do you need, sweetheart? What can I get you?"

"I'd like to make a reservation with your dick," I said, edging closer. The freckles dotting his face caught my eye. I curled my hands around my biceps to keep from tapping my index finger to each one of them. "Later this evening, a seating for one."

Jed ducked his head, laughed. "No request required. You have a standing reservation."

"To think, I dressed, brushed my hair, and put on makeup," I mused, dragging a finger along the neck of my shirt. His tight-lipped gaze followed that finger and dipped to my breasts for a beat. He was still tight-lipped, but that gaze was hot enough to warm me all the way through. "Now, I find out I don't need to do any of it."

He ran his knuckles over the back of my hand. "Need to? No. Never. But you look good enough to eat, Bam."

"I might let you," I replied.

We stared at each other, the noises and people around us fading away. He closed his hand over my wrist. "Talk to me. What's going on with you?"

I glanced around him to watch Nate filling another tray of drinks. I shook my head. "You're busy."

"Shut the hell up and talk to me," he snapped.

"Think about that statement for a second, Jed. Just take a second with it and maybe you'll see why you're asking for the impossible."

Releasing my wrist, he stepped back, pointed a finger at me. "Your head is full of something." He reached for a glass and plucked a wine bottle from the chill chest. "Have you eaten? Never mind. I know the answer to that."

"I'd eat if there was something other than bananas at the house," I replied, grabbing hold of those pebbles again. "But Dad is back on his banana bullshit. This week, it's banana pancakes. It's the only thing he wants. The whole damn house smells like banana and I hate banana." I glanced at the wine he set in front of me. "What is this?"

He deposited a glass of water beside the wine. "It's the Sauvignon Blanc you like."

"I didn't ask for wine." I lifted the glass to my lips. "You're becoming rather presumptuous, Jedediah."

"Because bananas," he replied as he shifted toward the point of sale system. "Chicken Caesar salad, right? Extra croutons?"

I watched as he tapped the screen. "Yeah, sure," I agreed cautiously. "But since when do you know which wines I like and how I prefer my salad?"

Not looking up from the screen, he said, "I don't think I've ever seen you eat anything other than a chicken Caesar. It's the only thing you order here."

Raising the glass to my lips, I studied the way his shirt stretched across his broad shoulders and how it nipped in at his waist. Giving his jeans a thorough review was safer than articulating any of the thoughts in my head or my heart. It made better sense to objectify him than admit it mattered that he remembered the croutons.

Hell, I didn't know how I'd put that into words without sounding like a moron. "Thanks for remembering I like croutons."

Eyes narrowed and forehead wrinkled, Jed returned to my corner of the bar. "You have to stop with that face, Bam."

"Which face?"

"The one that's a cross between wanting to suck a dick and snatch a soul," he replied, his tone dark enough to bring goose bumps to my skin. "I can't get out of here for a couple of hours and there's no way in hell I'm letting you sit there and make that face at me until then. Fix it now or you can eat your salad at home with Butterscotch."

I propped an arm on the bar as I pointed at him. "First of all—"

"Brooke-Ashley! Oh my goodness, I haven't seen you in months! How *are* you and where have you been hiding?"

Jed held my gaze for a long moment, his brows pinched and his lips falling flat as if apologizing for leaving me with Denise Primiani. The woman was old-school Talbott's Cove, through and through. She grew up here, taught in the town's public schools, gossiped like it was her job, and worked her ass off to look like a page out of an L.L. Bean catalog. The turtleneck and Bermuda shorts paired with duck shoes and the type of raincoat folks around here referred to as a "slicker" was fully on-brand. To be fair, Denise had been the first person to turn up at my father's house after his accident, a wagon of casseroles in tow. She'd talk about you behind your back, but she'd make sure you had enough beef stroganoff to get through a difficult time.

With a shrug meant to forgive his abandonment, I shifted to face her. "Denise, it's great to see you. As for me, I'm doing well. I've been here"—I shot a glance in Jed's direction and got a chuckle in return—"and there."

She touched her fingers to my wrist and gave me that close-mouthed smile that women used on each other to make it clear only one of them was capital-S Struggling. "But, how *are* you?"

Since I wasn't plugged into the local rumor mill, I didn't know why I was Struggling today. There was never any shortage of reasons—the unwell father often topped that chart—but there was also the matter of me moving back home. They understood my presence immediately after Dad's car accident, but they wanted to know why I was still here.

My neighbors took it upon themselves to fill in those blanks and that yielded some truly remarkable fiction. I'd lost everything—job, money, will to live, you name it. I'd been disbarred by the SEC, which wasn't a real thing that occurred, but that didn't stop anyone from saying it. I'd been the victim of a terrible crime—rape, attempted murder, kidnapping—and couldn't bear to live in New York any longer.

The ugly, horrible stories always beat out the obvious explanation.

"I'm great. Things are good. It's finally warming up around here ," I replied with as much breezy joy as a tampon commercial. "Every year, it seems like the winter is worse than the one before."

Still pity-smiling, Denise said, "And what about your father? How is he getting around? Is the leg improving at all?"

Jed cleared his throat as he set the salad in front of me. "What else do you need?" he asked, making no attempt to cut the familiarity from his tone. He shook out a cloth napkin and fussed with the silverware, setting each piece in its proper location while Denise watched. "More croutons?"

I laughed at the mountain of croutons rising up from a base of romaine lettuce, chicken, parmesan cheese. I laughed because it was ridiculous, but also because it stopped me from climbing over this bar and into his arms. I wouldn't have the right words, but I could put the pulse in my pussy to good use. "This seems like enough."

Under his breath, he said, "Fix your face." Then, to Denise, "What can I get you, Mrs. Primiani?"

She launched into a detailed story about eliminating sugar for a cruise, but then the cruise being canceled on account of an outbreak of some communicable disease on the ship, and now it was rescheduled for next year, and oh yes, she was still off sugar, so she'd like a dry red wine.

I figured she'd lost track of the unanswered questions in this time, but that wasn't the case. "What were you saying about your father, dear? I haven't seen him in ages, not even puttering around the garden. This time of year, I would've thought he'd be out." Before I could open my mouth to reply, she continued. "I can't tell you how much I miss talking through community issues with him. He'd sit right here, in this very spot"—she slapped her hand on the bar twice while Jed shook his head because no, Dad never sat at the bar—"and discuss the problems. He always knew how to get things done. It's such a shame he never ran for office. If we'd had him on the town council instead of Owen Bartlett with his liberal agenda, we wouldn't be in this mess."

"Which mess is that?" I caught Jed's eye on the other side of the bar and he shrugged, gave a quick shake of his head.

"Too many to count," Denise replied. "The taxes are outrageous while the schools are falling apart and packed to the gills. These children are leaving the cities in droves and overwhelming our classrooms. Do you see any road-work being done? Not a bit. It's nothing like it used to be.

It's not like that at all. They call it progress, but I call it a mistake." She leaned in close, lowered her voice. "And don't get me started on the drug and juvenile delinquency issues. We didn't have those problems in my day." Her eyes as wide as they could stretch without injury, she tipped her head toward Nate. "I hope you're keeping Judge Markham informed about these issues. I'm certain he'd want to know and make his opinion known."

I shoved a crouton in my mouth. "Mmhmm."

"You know what I should do? I should pay him a visit."

I shook my head. "No. No, not right now," I said around the crouton. This conversation needed to end by any means necessary. "Maybe a few months from now. We'll see how he's feeling, all right?"

"Oh, well—"

"Thank you for understanding," I continued. Still gnawing that chunk of crunchy bread. "I'm sure you can imagine the recuperation has been difficult and unpre-dictable."

"My sister-in-law fractured her hip two years ago and—"

"Please don't let me keep you," I said through a bold, brassy smile. "I know we could chat all night, but I'm sure you're meeting people and I'd hate to make them wait."

She wiggled her fingers at a group of women seated at a round table in the dining room. "How did you know it's my night out with the school girls?" she cooed. "We try to get together once a month, but we're lucky if we manage every other month."

Nodding, I went for another crouton.

"It was wonderful to see you, dear." Denise returned her hand to my wrist and resurrected the sad smile. "I'm so pleased you're getting on all right. Give me a ring if there's anything I can do for you and don't forget to pass my thoughts on to Judge Markham. See if you can't convince him to attend some of the town council meetings. We need him on our side!"

I went on grinning as she slipped off the barstool, but I wanted to gather those rocks in my hands, close my eyes, and throw them in every direction.

———

"HOW DO YOU DO IT?" I glanced at Jed as we walked toward his house later that night. "How do you, I don't know"—I shook my hands in front of me as if I intended to strangle something—"put up with this town?"

"Narrow it down for me, sweetheart. We could be talking about anything. What am I putting up with?"

"This entire town," I cried, a manic laugh winding through my words. "This small, insular, homogenous town where everyone is convinced the best days are behind them and the only solution is going backward. And these people who believe the old ways were best and refuse to acknowledge that progress might be a good thing." I stared at him in the darkness. "How do you do it? Because I can't deal."

Jed reached for my hand, layered it between both of his as we walked. "You had a shitty conversation with Denise Primiani. Who hasn't?"

"It's not one person with one shitty outlook," I replied.

"It's the fact that many people share that outlook and feel comfortable announcing it."

"I understand what you're saying, Bam, but that's not a Talbott's Cove problem. That's everywhere and you know it." He shifted my hand to his waist while he unlocked the front door. "What's the Cove ever done to you?"

He pushed the door open and I stepped inside, kicked off my shoes. Butterscotch was quick to run up. "Look around, Jed. The Cove doesn't resemble the rest of the world. It's about as diverse as pasta salad. Noodles and mayonnaise and, if you're lucky, a few bits of color and spice."

"Pasta salad. Okay." His lips twitched as if he wanted to laugh, but he knew enough to hold back. "Owen Bartlett, the chair of the town council, is a gay man. That has to count for something."

"Sure, it counts, but the fact we're handing out brownie points for accepting a native son's sexuality is kind of ridiculous," I replied, pacing the length of the living room. "Not to mention, being able to name one gay man in the whole of this town and trying to pass that off as proof of Talbott's Cove forward evolution is absurd."

"Technically, we can name two because his boyfriend Cole lives with him now."

I held my arms up in celebration. "There we go. Two gay men equals a diverse, inclusive town. Check. Done. Problem solved."

"Perhaps I've mentioned once or twice how I'm working on bringing something new to this town." He perched his hands on his hips. "Jobs, tourists, money.

Those things won't wave a magic wand over the town, but they'll get the tide turning."

"And you know I think it's an incredible plan," I replied. "Perhaps I've mentioned how I have money to invest."

"You know I can't do that, sweetheart. Keep your money."

I stopped pacing, stared at him. "Let me see if I have this straight. I can't complain about people with shitty opinions because they're everywhere. I can't complain about the pasta salad because you're solving that. And I can't invest in the distillery because you need a separation between cocks and stocks. Does that sum it up?"

Jed studied me for a moment, his gaze raking up from my bare feet, over my slim black pants and blousy top, stopping at my lips. He tilted his head to the side as if he'd settled a disagreement with himself and brought his hand to my back, resting between my shoulder blades. He nudged me forward, toward the hallway. Toward the bedroom. "You forgot to add in the piece about you rejecting all the local authority you possess by virtue of birthright."

"That's where your calculations are incorrect." I reached for his belt. "Just because my father leaned into the whole Markhams of Maine thing doesn't mean I can or should."

Growling, Jed yanked the shirt over my head. "You backed away from Denise's bullshit tonight. You didn't call her on any of it and you could have."

I scowled up at him as I unbuttoned his shirt. "Because I didn't want to start a brawl."

"A few well-chosen words and Denise would have a fresh perspective on so-called juvenile delinquents." He pushed my pants down to my knees and held my elbows as I wiggled out of them. "If we don't stick around and call out the bullshit when we hear it, this place will always be the same soggy pasta salad it's always been. It wouldn't be the worst thing in the world for you to put some of your family's leverage to good use."

"You're assigning me more power than I have on reserve, aside from the fact this isn't about me. This town hasn't seen a boom year in my lifetime but everyone is holding out hope we can find our way back to those good old days. If only we could slow down, back track over everything we've gained, and return to a time when the world was a simpler, more oppressive, more restrictive place, and then we'd be on the right track. You make it sound like I should—" I went flying through the air, landing on the bed with a shout. "What the hell was that for?"

Jed climbed onto the bed and settled over me, his knees tucked under my arms and his cock hard between my breasts. "That was for the look you've been giving me for the past few hours." He brushed my hair from my face and cupped my jaw. "It's time for you to suck some dick, sweetheart."

"What about snatching a soul?"

He took my hand, curled it around his erection. "You already did."

"I don't suck dicks," I replied as my hand shuttled over him.

He growled, low and guttural, just the way I loved. "You do now."

I shook my head, the movement causing me to brush my lips over his crown. "Probably not."

"Bam, you can't convince me you don't want this." His hips jerked as I stroked him harder. "I've watched you all night. I saw it in your eyes. Saw how you want to be completely merciless."

"You're selling this rather aggressively."

I shot him an indignant glare as I considered all the creative ways I could explain I wasn't meeting his dick-sucking needs. Instead of offering any of them, I opened my mouth, rubbed him against my lips. He was hot and thick, and throbbing in my palm, on my tongue.

His hand shot behind my head, urging me closer, rubbing my scalp. "Brooke. Fuck. *Fuck*."

I wrapped my tongue around his head and tasted the bead of fluid waiting there. It wasn't as unpleasant as I'd remembered. The muscles in his legs flexed, tightening against my torso as his body tensed. He twisted my name into groans, growls, and curses while his body arched and shuddered.

I wanted it this way. I wanted him begging and shaking, pulling my hair and trapping my body under his. I wanted him to want me even when I gagged, when my eyes watered, when I wasn't perfect.

Even when I told myself I didn't, I wanted him.

JJ THREW the car in reverse and hooked his arm over the

back of my seat. I glanced down at my lap, a warm pulse moving through me as he backed out. It wasn't sexual. It wasn't about his body. It was care and competency and it turned me on, just the way it turned me on when I watched him tap a keg and mix a martini.

I didn't understand how something as simple as know-how could start me up, but I couldn't help it. I felt this as profoundly as filthy words whispered into my ear.

"What's wrong?" he asked, pausing at the end of the driveway.

"Nothing."

"Not nothing. Looks like you're annoyed." He considered me. "Or praying."

"Praying and annoyance are interchangeable in your book?"

"No, Bam. When it comes to you, everything comes with a side of annoyance."

"Or prayer?" I countered. I glanced down at the skintight jeans I'd selected for tonight's double date. We were meeting Jackson and Annette for dinner in the big city—as big as it got in Maine—Portland. The guys didn't know it yet, but they were also taking us dancing. "These are not the jeans of a woman who spends much time on prayer."

"Would you just tell me what your problem is? Goddammit, woman. Half the time you invent arguments just to give yourself something to do, I'm sure of it."

"Right," I deadpanned. "Because I have nothing better to do. Makes complete sense."

"You always have something better to do. That's not in question. It's whether you'd rather do that or start fires."

"Now I'm a fire starter?"

"As far as I can tell, that's how you spend the other half of your time."

I could've said something. I could've told him he looked good tonight or that I appreciated him doing this for me. I could've formed those words and sat there, vulnerable as fuck for a minute.

I didn't.

"It's rather cavalier of you to claim I'm inventing problems or starting fires when you were begging me to suck your cock less than"—I shot a pointed glance at the dashboard clock—"eighteen hours ago."

"Bam, sweetheart, if I were to apply that logic, you'd have to keep that pretty mouth of yours shut on a near permanent basis." He reached out, slipped his hand through my hair. "Since I know there's no way in hell to shut you up, why don't you tell me what's wrong."

"Nothing," I insisted as his grip tightened. "It was nothing. I'm fine. Seriously."

"I don't believe you." He loosened his hold on my hair only to gather up the strands again and twist them around my palm. "Would it kill you to be honest with me? Really, is it that hard for you?"

There it was. The quiet genius of JJ Harniczek. I didn't have to say anything for him to know everything or damn close to it.

I licked my lips, glanced away as much as I could given his grip on my hair. "Sometimes."

"What can I do about that?"

"It's not you."

He tipped his head from side to side. "Sure, that's a

handy answer. But, as you mentioned, you're the woman sucking my cock. I'd like to make it better for you if I can."

"That starts with giving me plenty of warning. I'm not a swallower."

He shut his eyes, drew in a breath. He studied me as he exhaled. "I know, sweetheart. I'm sorry. That one got away from me." He leaned closer, bringing our foreheads together. Then, "Tell me you're all right and make me believe it."

"I'm honestly fine," I said, laughing. "I'm, um...I'm happy you're coming with us."

"You're not convincing me of anything," he replied.

"That's not my problem, Jed. Convince yourself."

"Answer me one thing." I murmured in agreement. "Are you coming home with me at the end of the night?"

"That depends," I replied. "Will you complain about me and Annette dragging you guys to some clubs after dinner? Are you going to give me shit about drinking tequila and dancing like it's my job?"

"Not at all," he answered.

"Will you complain if I dance with other guys?"

His lips pulled up at the corners. "That depends on whether you're coming home with me, sweetheart."

"And if I do?"

"Then I have no reason not to trust you."

CHAPTER THIRTY

JJ

Yield: the return on investment.

BROOKE WORE second-skin jeans and a satin bustier she'd hidden under a blazer during the drive and dinner. She made me watch from the sidelines while she and Annette knocked back shots and shook their asses all over the club's dance floor. That part was tough for Jackson. He couldn't handle the sight of men circling Annette and Brooke without snarling like a junkyard dog.

I did some snarling of my own, but it had nothing to do with the men she cast off with little more than a shake of her head. No, those snarls came from the expanding pressure inside my chest. Brooke-Ashley Markham ruined my life, but she also patched it up and put it back together. Nothing was the same, nothing sat in the proper order, but none of that mattered because I loved her. It was a long time coming, but here, tonight, I saw it up close and I felt the blunt force of it as she moved with the music.

"I'm going out there," rumbled Jackson.

I slapped an arm across his chest to hold him back but never took my eyes off Brooke. "You're not," I replied. "They have this under control."

He jutted a finger toward Annette and Brooke. "That's not under control."

I watched while a random dude pushed himself between them and made an attempt at grabbing Brooke's ass. My hands curled into fists and the pressure in my chest expanded with sharp points, but I waved Jackson off.

"Just wait," I murmured. "Give her a minute. Let her do this."

Brooke looped her arm through Annette's elbow as she rounded on the man. Her hair floated down her back and over her bare shoulders in loose waves, but that didn't soften the stare she sent in his direction. I couldn't hear the words she spoke to him but as I'd expected, they worked. He lifted his hands in surrender as she ticked off a list on her fingers. She mimed him stepping back, staying out of their circle. She wagged a finger at him and I was certain I saw the word *sorry* form on his lips. Then, she flicked her wrist and he bolted from the dance floor.

"Shit," Jackson muttered.

That woman is a motherfucking force to be reckoned with and I love her.

"I told you she'd handle it," I said, as smug as I fucking pleased.

"As impressive as that was, can we get out of here

now?" Jackson asked miserably. "At this rate, I'm going to start making arrests or grow an ulcer. Maybe both."

"Soon," I replied. "Wait until they take their shoes off. That's when you know they're close."

After several minutes of silence between us, Jackson said, "We should've started that book club."

"The first rule of book club is you don't talk about the book club," I said, mostly to myself.

"That's interesting because the second rule of book club is you don't talk about the book club," Jackson added. "But there's no book club, so the other rules are irrelevant."

I shifted to face him, a laugh shaking my shoulders. "That wasn't bad, sheriff."

"High praise coming from you, Harniczek."

It wasn't long before Brooke and Annette left us in possession of their shoes, but they went a barefoot hour before calling it a night. They hugged for ten solid minutes before parting.

I drove her home, carried her tipsy ass inside, and led her to the bed I'd stopped calling *mine* in favor of *ours*. We found each other with unhurried touches and kisses, nothing like the first nights we'd shared together, when everything was over before it started.

"Thank you for coming along tonight," Brooke said.

"There was nowhere else I wanted to be," I replied.

"And thank you for keeping Jackson under control. He wanted to pull the sheriff routine all over the dance floor, I could tell."

"You're right about that," I said, laughing.

"I know group dates and dance clubs aren't your ideal

evening out." She dipped her head, pressed a kiss to my neck. "Thank you for letting me and Annette have this."

"And thank you for letting me watch," I replied. "Do you know how much I loved seeing you kick ass out there? Fuck, you were amazing. Do you know? How much I love seeing you kick ass all the time? How much I love—I love you?" I heard a sudden inhale of breath from her, but now that I'd started, I couldn't stop. "You might not want me saying that. You might have reasons and arguments, but—"

"I love you too." She propped herself up on an elbow, lifted her hand to my cheek. Blinked down at me with those bright blue eyes and hair like heaven. "You're right. I didn't want those words because I don't know how. *I don't know how*, Jed, and I'm terrified I'll do it wrong."

I rolled her onto her back, settled between her legs. "You can't do it wrong, Bam."

"But you can," she argued, her hands warm on my chest. "You can. I've seen it, I've lived through it. My parents, they—"

"They're not us," I interrupted gently. "And we won't be them."

She reached up, loosened my hair from its tie. As strands fell to my shoulders, she raked her fingers over my scalp. "I don't know what I'm doing and it scares the hell out of me, but I know I love you."

Raw, fragile honesty from this woman was like a shooting star. I kissed her then because come the fuck on, how could I not? "That's all you need to know, Bam."

CHAPTER THIRTY-ONE

BROOKE

Discounting: calculating the present value of a future amount.

"WHAT IS THAT?" I grumbled to Jed's chest.

"What's what?"

I pushed up on an elbow, glanced around his bedroom with bleary eyes. Gentle rays of morning sun streamed in through gaps between the curtains. I blinked at the clock in an attempt to clear the sleep and lingering alcohol. As I blinked, the muffled sound echoed through the room again.

"That," I insisted. "Do you hear it?"

"Go back to sleep, Bam." He tugged me down, folded me into his arms so that I heard only his heartbeat.

I dozed for a bit—a few minutes, maybe more. But then there was a heavy knock on the front door.

Jed sat up, murmuring, "Who the hell is at my door

first thing in the damn morning?" Not wasting time on boxers, he stepped into his jeans and zipped the fly. He left the top button and belt open. It read like a promise: he didn't intend to be clothed for long. I admired that promise. "I'll see what this is all about and be back. Stay here with the dog."

He nodded at Butterscotch, who was curled up in her bed and hadn't heard anything. "Yeah, I'm counting on her for guidance."

"It's too early for you to start with the comments, Bam." He snapped his fingers. "Come on, girl," he said to the dog. "You need to earn your keep."

For her part, she jumped up from her bed, galloped toward me, and rubbed her head against my outstretched hand.

"Good girl." With a smirk, he added. "Both of you." He disappeared into the hall only to return a moment later with my purse. "This is vibrating." When the pounding on the door continued, Jed called, "Calm the fuck down, we're coming." He tossed the bag onto the bed. "Turn off your alarm or whatever you have going. It sounds like a time bomb."

I swiped my phone to life, finding seventeen missed calls from Annette, a long line of texts asking me to answer her calls, and five voicemails. There were other texts, other calls. The first ones came in two hours ago and they came from my father's house.

I gazed down at the screen as a ridge of icicles formed along my shoulder blades. My head swam. Goose bumps rippled over my skin. I knew I was clutching the device, but I couldn't feel it. I wasn't certain

I felt anything more than cold. "Jed. Jed, can you come here?"

When the shape of him filled the doorway, I hadn't managed to glance away from the screen. He gathered a few things from the floor as he rounded the bed and settled on the edge. "Give me that," he murmured, snatching the device away and slipping it in his back pocket. "We need to put some clothes on you, okay? Jackson's here. He wants to talk to you for a minute."

Still silent, still staring down at my hand, I didn't react when Jed pulled one of his shirts over my head. Didn't ask why Jackson was here. Didn't complain when it took him several attempts to help me into leggings. Didn't argue when he lashed his arm around my waist and guided me toward the front of the house as if we were practicing for a three-legged race.

Jackson removed his Talbott's Cove Sheriff's Office ball cap, stepped toward me. "Brooke. I'm so sorry."

I didn't do any of those things because I knew my father was dead.

He was gone and my first reaction was relief and I *hated* myself for it.

CHAPTER THIRTY-TWO

JJ

Useful Life: the estimate of the period of time an asset will be in use.

"THERE'S a shipment coming in from Trillium on Friday," I called over my shoulder as I moved through the storeroom.

"Tomorrow," Nate replied from behind me. "I talked to our rep yesterday morning because I noticed we're going through the summer brew faster than expected. He added a few units and bumped us to tomorrow's delivery."

"Even better," I said, pushing through the door to the bar. I tested the taps, checked the ice box, glanced at the garnishes. "Everything is in order."

"What did you expect?" he murmured as he made a note on his clipboard.

I lifted a whiskey bottle to the light, then another. "Did anyone give you trouble last night? Did Lincoln come in?"

"No trouble," he replied, still busy with his clipboard. "Lincoln pounded seven ginger ales and complained about the Sox for a couple of innings."

"Some things never change," I said. "When you get a chance, would you follow up with the beef supplier? We've been running low and—"

"Already done," he interrupted, looking up from his clipboard. "I know you're being thorough but what the hell did you think would happen when you left me to manage this place for a few days? Did you think I'd let us run out of burgers or beer?"

I turned in a circle, my hands on my hips and my mind racing. I needed to get back to the Markham house. I hated leaving Brooke this morning, but I had to run payroll and pick up my suit from the dry cleaner. Annette promised she'd stay with Brooke and assist with the funeral arrangements. Not that Brooke had allowed anyone to help her with anything in the four days since her father's death. She insisted on doing everything herself and I stood by, watching while she did it—and went on working her finance job as if nothing had happened.

"I expected you'd have it under control and you do," I said. "Thank you for handling things."

"No, man, don't start with that. Save your thanks." He pressed the clipboard to his chest, his arms banded over it. "There's no need." He jerked his chin toward the door. "You should get out of here while you can. I've got this."

"Call me if anything comes up. I don't care what it is or when it is."

"Go," he hollered.

"Going." My phone vibrated in my back pocket as I stepped out from behind the bar. I yanked it out, expecting to find Brooke or Annette calling, but it was Barry O'Connor. Of all the times for him to reappear. I waited until I stepped outside to tap the screen. "Barry. Hi."

"Hey, JJ. Is this a good time?" he asked. "I want to run a few things by you."

I paced away from the Galley and toward the harbor. "Ordinarily, this is a good time, but today is difficult. Can I call you next week?"

"Just five minutes," he said. "I'll make it quick."

I lifted my hand to my forehead, shielding my eyes from the day's intense sun. "All right. Go ahead. What's up?"

"Here's the thing, JJ, I'm trying to make a mark. I'm looking for the next great thing."

A seagull squawked overhead. "I'm aware of your aspirations."

"You're all systems go with this gin thing and it's so great, JJ. It's such a brilliant move. It's cool and hip, and going to take off like crazy in your neck of the woods." He drew in a breath, made a whiny noise in his throat. "But it's not for me."

"What?" I barked, confused.

"It's not for me. Small-batch liquor isn't my passion. It doesn't wake me up in the morning and keep me going at night. I want to steer my investments toward my passions, as I'm sure you can understand."

"What?" I repeated. Now I was annoyed.

"My attorney is drawing up dissolution papers today.

He'll have them out to you tomorrow. Friday at the latest."

Again— "What?"

"As I'm sure you recall from the original agreement, the terms are generous," he continued. "There's a five-year grace period before repayment of the initial investment is required." He paused. Another seagull swooped by. "You have to know I labored over this decision for several months, JJ."

A dry laugh rumbled up from my chest. "It would've been nice of you to mention it sooner." A rough estimate of the upcoming construction and production expenses flashed through my mind. "You're not leaving me in the best position here."

"It's just business," he replied. "Look, JJ. I have another call coming in. Look for those papers from my attorney and—"

I ended the call and turned back toward the village. I swept my gaze over the place I'd hoped to redefine as the impact of losing Barry's investment landed in my gut like a brick. Lacing my hands behind my neck, I glanced up the hill to the ancestral estate where Brooke was undoubtedly approving the funeral reception menu while also moving money around the globe at the same time.

She could help. She could get me out of this mess.

But there was no way I could ask her for help. I wasn't going to add that dynamic to our relationship and I wasn't going to be another in a long line of people who expected something from her. If I intended to open this distillery, I was doing it without her saving the day.

CHAPTER THIRTY-THREE

JJ

Current Liabilities: the sum of salaries, interest, accounts payable, and other debt service requirements due within one year.

LAYING Judge Markham to rest was a major event in Talbott's Cove. The flags were lowered and the local court closed. The entire town attended the funeral mass, many spilling out the congregation doors and onto the steps despite torrential rain. The firefighters and sheriff's deputies led a procession from the church to the family cemetery on the Markham estate, where he was to be buried alongside Brooke's mother and hundreds of years of ancestors.

Brooke put on an excellent show. She was gracious and genuine as she stood in the foyer of her father's house, accepting condolences from the hundreds, maybe thousands, of townspeople in attendance. She listened to an endless stream of stories, her hands clasped in front of her, and conjured the appropriate expressions and responses. But I knew it was a performance, and I knew she was heading for a crash.

Despite the best efforts of Annette, Jackson, and I, Brooke continued to refuse all assistance. She'd held us off since her father's death and we were running low on solutions. None of us wanted to force a confrontation or push her into a test of wills, but she couldn't keep going at this pace. She worked around the clock, rarely stopped to eat or sleep, and she hadn't shed a tear. I knew grief took many forms but I also knew this show couldn't go on forever.

When the line of visitors dwindled, Brooke stepped away from her post in the foyer. She joined us on the far end of the front porch, her sky-high heels clacking against the weathered wood in time with distant rolls of thunder. She looked regal in her sleeveless black dress, her hair twisted into a conservative knot and a string of pearls draped around her neck. She also looked exhausted and frail and painfully lonely.

Annette pushed a plate toward her, but she waved it off.

"No, I don't want anything." She ran a finger over her brow and closed her eyes for a moment. I rested my hand on the small of her back. "That's not true. The house smells like ham and wet hair, and I've heard the same six stories about five hundred times apiece. My feet hurt, my hair is frizzing around the back of my neck, and"—she tucked a finger under the belt cinching the dress at her waist—"this thing was a terrible choice."

"Okay, so," Annette started, "ham, shoes, people, and that belt. Anything else bothering you?"

"Many, many things are bothering me," she said, glancing out at the rain. "Very few of them can be improved."

"Let's start small," Annette said. "I can get you a pair of flats and some bobby pins for the frizz."

"There's nothing you need to do," Brooke replied. "No, that's not true. I want you to send everyone home."

"We can do that," Jackson replied. "Give me ten minutes, I'll shut this thing down."

"Ask the caterers to box up the leftover food," Brooke said, rubbing her forehead again. "Get rid of the ham, the roast, the lemon squares. All of it, I want it gone and I want everyone out. Tell the people whatever you want. It doesn't matter anyway." She cast another glance toward the heavy storm clouds overhead. "I'm going upstairs."

"I'll go with you," Annette offered.

"No." Brooke held up a hand, warning her off. "Thank you, but I want to be alone right now and I need you to handle the caterers."

We watched as Brooke marched away. When she stepped into the house, Annette said, "I'm going with her."

"The hell you are," I replied. "You're on catering duty. *I'm* going with her."

"She needs me right now," Annette argued. "You're great and all, but I'm the one who will get her through this."

"Not by yourself, no, you're not." When her eyes flamed with fury, I continued, "Look, I know it's been the two of you against the world for a time. It's not just the two of you anymore."

Jackson held up a hand in warning, but Annette brushed him off. "Okay. That's acceptable. But you need to know I will grind your bones to dust if you hurt her in the slightest way."

"Annie," Jackson grumbled.

"Understood." I gestured to the house. "Now, you fix the ham situation while I get her out of those shoes."

"Sex is not the answer," Annette called. "It's one of the answers, but not *the* answer. Not until after she gets something to eat and a good night's sleep."

I didn't respond, instead jogging inside and up the stairs. It took longer than it should have since the terrible weather meant the entire town was packed into this house rather than overflowing into the outdoor spaces. When I reached the landing, I yanked my tie loose and shrugged out of my suit coat, dropping both on the banister.

Brooke's door was shut but unlocked. The bedroom was as we'd left it that morning and it was vacant. I ducked my head into the bathroom and walk-in closet before noticing the deck door standing ajar. As I approached, I spotted Brooke on the far corner of the deck, staring out at the ocean while the rain washed over her.

"What are you doing out here?" I called, edging onto the deck. "You're soaked, sweetheart. Come inside."

She didn't respond, didn't react.

I crossed the deck and wrapped my arms around her shoulders. "Come on, Bam. You can't stay out here."

She didn't budge, didn't tear her gaze away from the water.

"I know, sweetheart. *I know*. This is fucking awful. It's one gut punch after another. Please, let me bring you inside. You're wet and shivering, and I can't watch you do this. It hurts too much."

I pulled her close, my arms around her torso as she swayed toward me. Then, she did it. She destroyed me all over again.

"I'm pregnant."

CHAPTER THIRTY-FOUR

BROOKE

Equity: the degree of ownership after all liabilities and debts have been satisfied.

THERE WAS a reaction to telling Jed I was pregnant. I was sure of it, though I couldn't make out the words. I couldn't hear anything beyond the whirling in my head, the incessant buzzing that came from realizing how much I resented my parents for expecting me to fix them, how much I hated every minute of caring for my father and rearranging my life to hold the shreds of his together, and how angry I was that he died alone too. No one ever let me say goodbye.

They all died, they all left me, but not before I stole the opportunity to leave them. And the staticky hum in my head was the sound of regret.

Jed gathered me up and brought me in from the rain. He stripped off my wet clothes and swaddled me in towels. I wanted my robe, the one I'd nabbed from that obnoxious roommate years ago, but I couldn't climb past the roar in my head to form words.

He tucked me into bed and climbed in beside me, his body warm and his grip certain. His hand raised to my face, he brushed tears from my cheeks. I hadn't realized I was crying.

"Brooke, are you sure about this?" he asked. "You've had a stressful week. That can throw things off, right? It could be that, sweetheart."

"I took a test this morning." I didn't recognize the watery sobs in my voice. "Then I made an appointment with a doctor."

"Why did you do that alone?" he whispered, his lips pressed to my temple. "Why-why didn't you tell me, Bam?"

"The appointment is on Tuesday. In Bangor." My body shook, quaking as the tears fell faster. "There's no such thing as privacy in this town."

"You're not doing that alone," he said. "You're not doing anything else alone. Do you hear me, Brooke? I'm going with you. I am *staying* with you."

I didn't say anything. I didn't think I could—and it didn't matter. Jed would leave me too. He'd leave and I'd have something new to regret.

CHAPTER THIRTY-FIVE

JJ

Leveraged Buyout: the purchase of a controlling share in an organization by its management using capital provided from outside the organization.

BROOKE DIDN'T WANT to talk to me in the waiting room at the doctor's office. She flipped through a magazine, the pages moving at a pace incompatible with reading. If there was anything to gather from this morning—and every morning since the funeral—it was that I could stay close if I didn't require anything from her.

It wasn't until that fire of hers cooled to embers that I realized how much I needed it, thrived on it, savored it. *Loved* it. I missed her yelling and cursing about every little thing. Missed her silver-tongued demands and her piercing glares. Missed her fight most of all. This chilly silence almost drove me to shake her out of it, to bait her the way she'd always baited me. But antagonizing the woman I loved days after her father died and she found herself unexpectedly pregnant struck me as profoundly wrong, even if that was our first and finest mode of expression.

I followed her into an exam room, staring at a wall of baby photos while the nursing assistant ran through a list of questions. I listened as I studied the round faces, desperate to glean some information, but I didn't know how to use any of it in a meaningful way. The first day of her last period sounded like a riddle no one saw neces-sary to solve for me.

So many little faces on this wall. Some bald, some with as much hair as I had today. Some smiling, some mad as fuck. *What will our baby look like?* I turned, stared at Brooke as that thought simmered in my mind. She sat on the exam table with her ankles crossed and hands balled in her lap. She glanced up at me for a fleeting moment, tipped her head to the side, and held her hand out.

Moving away from the wall, I stepped around the nursing assistant and stationed myself beside Brooke.

"It's fine. I'm fine," she said, her gaze glued to the floor as the nurse wrapped a blood pressure cuff around her arm. "You don't need to do this."

"I'm going to do it anyway," I replied.

The nursing assistant left parting instructions about changing into a gown and a promise the doctor would visit shortly. When the door closed, Brooke hopped off the table and turned her back to me as she undressed. She pushed her arms into the gown and shuffled back to the table, one hand fisted around the cloth to keep it closed.

"I've seen you naked. Don't hide your ass for my benefit."

"I know what comes next with these appointments," she said. "Covering my ass is all I can do to make this bearable."

"Is there anything I can do to make this better than bearable?"

"Do you want a baby right now?" she fired back.

"Do you?"

She was silent long enough that it seemed she didn't intend to respond. But then, she said, "I don't know."

The doctor bustled in, full of smiles and enthusiasm Brooke couldn't match. She dimmed the lights and dropped onto a short stool after instructing Brooke to lie back on the table. The sonogram screen flickered to life. Brooke grabbed my hand.

"There's your baby," the doctor chirped, circling a black and white area on the screen. "See that little strobe light? That's the heart. And this string of pearls? That's the spine. Based on these measurements and the dates you provided, you're about nine weeks along. Here, let's print out some pictures."

Brooke's grip on my hand tightened. There was no way to interpret the meaning behind that gesture, but I leaned down, kissed the top of her head. We'd figure this out.

THE FIRST HALF of the drive back to Talbott's Cove was

agonizingly quiet until Brooke asked, "What do you want to do, Jed?"

As it turned out, I couldn't stop myself from antagonizing her. "Are you asking what I want to do right now, this morning? Because I need to get some breakfast and then run to a meeting at the cider house." I glanced over at her. "Or are you asking about something else, Brooke?"

"It's good of you to loop me in on your plans," she replied.

"I want to do whatever you want me to do," I said. "But I can't do that if you won't talk to me. I'll tell you this much, Brooke. Whatever you want to do, I'm going to support you. Whatever you want. There's nothing you can say to change my mind on that."

She reached into her purse and retrieved a water bottle. She took several sips before asking, "Who are you meeting at the cider house?"

I didn't want to have this conversation. I wanted the one about our baby and the rest of our fucking lives, but this one had to happen eventually. "I'm showing some potential investors around the site."

She whipped her head toward me. "Why? Is Barry renegotiating the terms?"

"You could say that," I murmured. "Barry decided to step away from this project. I've been reaching out to new funders."

I saw the exact moment she added up the pieces, her expression shifting like an unlocked door blown open by a gust of wind. "Why didn't you tell me? I've told you I am willing to connect you with other investors. Real, serious investors. People who do this every day rather than Barry's weekend hobby approach to business."

A humorless laugh tripped over my lips. "You've had your hands full, don't you think? I wasn't about to bother you with this last week."

"Why don't you trust me enough to let me help you?" she asked, her words losing their edge. "Why is that so terrible? Do you think I'd lead you around by the purse strings? Or that I'd lord it over you? What is so terrible about me? Why can't *I* help you? You're sitting here, saying you'll support me no matter what but I'm not allowed to do the same. I'm not allowed to help in the one way I'm able to because—because why? I can't be trusted because I ditched you behind a barn a long, long time ago? Because I can't react to death and babies and love the right way? Why am I terrible, Jed?"

"There's nothing terrible about you. Don't think that, please," I replied.

"There's nothing terrible about me but you don't want my money when you actually need it. When I could make a difference. Don't you see? You could focus on the things you do best rather than wasting your time on sales pitches and pacifying investors," she said. "Yeah, it makes total sense to keep me out of it."

I wanted to bash my head against the steering wheel. "Can we hold this discussion for later? None of this is about the distillery. Not at all. I want to talk about everything, but the next ten minutes isn't enough time to take it all apart."

She jerked a shoulder up, nodded. "I think it makes sense for me to go home now."

"Not a problem. We can talk more tonight, after I touch base with Nate. I'll drop you at home and then head to my meeting."

"I didn't mean my father's house," she said. "I meant it makes sense for me to go home to New York. I can manage anything that needs to be done from there. There's no reason for me to stay any longer than I already have."

"You're sure about that? Because I can think of several reasons for you to stay," I replied.

"You would say that," she mused. "You believe you belong here. You think this is a fine little pasta salad world. I, on the other hand, am long overdue for my exit. I stayed all these years and I killed myself to keep my father comfortable and honor his wishes, and what am I supposed to do now? Live in the house my family has been in since before electricity and indoor plumbing? Raise a kid with you when you don't trust me around your business? Why would I do that to myself? Why would I keep punishing myself that way? The Cove is a far cry from where I belong. If you can't see that, you haven't been paying attention."

"Brooke, I love you but I think you're angry and over-whelmed about a million other things and I don't know where to start with you when I have *minutes* to talk."

"And now I'm the irrational, emotional woman," she said. "How charming and predictable. I've always enjoyed being the villain in your story. Please be sure to keep that resentment going when I'm gone. The town needs some drama."

"You're being ridiculous," I said flatly. "You're also

discounting all the relationships you've formed in Talbott's Cove. People care about you. *I* care about you."

"As great as that is, I'm the one who is pregnant and alone and living in a town where I don't belong," she argued. "I can't plan my life around you and a business you're hell-bent on launching in spite of the money I can provide."

I pulled into the driveway, killed the engine. "I don't have the time to explain to you the fifty ways you're wrong about all that, but I'll be back later and we're having this conversation."

She reached for the door handle. "No. We're not."

"Brooke—"

"Do the smart thing, Jed. Go to your meeting. Dazzle them with your ideas and your appropriately edgy vibe. Win them over and gain their trust. Take their money and build an empire on a pile of apple cores. Focus on that and I'll focus on myself, just as I always have. I'm going back to my empire, the one where I'm not your princess."

She slammed the door and I was out of the vehicle, chasing after her. I was going to be late and I didn't give a damn. I caught her elbow, yanked her back toward me. "You were never my princess," I roared. "Never once my princess. That girl belonged to everyone else. You"—I lifted my hands to her face, cupped her jaw—"you belonged to me." Her chin wobbled as her eyes filled. "It doesn't matter where you are. You're always mine."

"You don't even trust me enough to—"

"I trust you with everything, Brooke. *Everything.* I trust you with my life, my baby, my whole fucking world. Do you want to take over the finance side of my business? It's yours. But you're not giving me a penny. It doesn't matter whether this money is pocket change for you or I'm a fool for refusing it. You're done saving people, sweetheart. You're done sacrificing and stepping aside to make room for everyone else's needs. You're done resenting people for taking and taking and taking from you. So long as I'm in your life, you're done."

Fat tears rolled down her cheeks as she stared at me. "I'm going. I'm leaving."

I pressed my lips to hers in a hard, biting kiss that refused to say goodbye.

CHAPTER THIRTY-SIX

BROOKE

Bear Market: a steady, self-sustaining reduction in the market value of stocks and other market securities.

Brooke: Who is running the breakup pool?
Annette: What?
Brooke: The pool. I'm sure someone was taking bets on when things would fall apart with me and JJ, and who'd be the one to fuck it all up, and I'd like to congratulate the person who bet on me and today.
Annette: What happened, honey?
Annette: No, forget that. Where are you?
Annette: I'm walking out the door, so tell me where you are unless you want Jackson patrolling the streets for you.
Brooke: I'm at Dad's house. The door is open.
Annette: What can I bring you?
Brooke: Just bring yourself. That's all I need.

THE DOOR banged shut behind Annette as she said, "Tell me everything."

I glanced up at her from my spot on the foyer rug. I'd plopped down here after Jed dropped me off and hadn't found a reason to get up since. I didn't know where to go. Every room of this house was colored with overwhelming memories of the past two weeks, the past two years, and everything before that. The foyer was better.

Annette dropped to her knees, reached for my hands. "Say something, honey."

"I don't want to be here anymore," I said.

She bobbed her head in agreement, her dark curls bouncing with the motion. "Okay, we'll go to my house. There's plenty of room and you can stay as long as you need. I'll get some of your things. Don't move."

When she pulled away from me, I squeezed her hands. Tugged her back. "I meant I don't want to be *here*. I don't want to be in Talbott's Cove anymore."

Her sympathetic smile fell and that response cracked my heart open. She brushed her hands down my cheeks, wiping away tears. Again, I hadn't realized I was crying. "Here's what we're doing, sweetie. I'm going to pack a bag for you and we're going to head over to my place. Is there anything specific you'd like me to pack?"

"You don't have to do this. I'm fine. You have a bookstore to run. I'm just—" I shook my head, glanced away. "We had an argument. Jed sees things one way. I see them differently. Neither of us are willing to adjust our positions, so it ended. It was always going to end and now it has." I blinked at the wall of floral arrangements and suddenly understood the cloyingly thick scent around me to be white lilies. Every breath was soaked with lily until I tasted their perfume in the back of my throat. I scrambled to my feet, charged toward the door. "I have to get out of here."

"Wait," Annette called, but it was too late.

I fell to the grass, braced on my hands and knees, and emptied my stomach. She approached, gathered my hair from my face, stroked my back. She didn't say anything while I gagged and sobbed. When it was over, she wrapped an arm around my shoulders and passed me a wad of tissues. "I'm sorry you had to witness that," I said, accepting the tissues.

"What are sisters for if not holding your hair when you vomit?" She brought my head to her shoulder. *Goddamn. I had to tell her about the baby.* "Sisters are also good for helping you put your life back together when it shatters."

Knowing she was right, I said, "We'll go to your place, but just for tonight." I took her hand in mine. "Thank you."

"Anytime." She smoothed her hand down my spine. "I'm much shorter and rounder than you are, so while I'm happy to share all of my clothes, that won't work out well. I'm going upstairs to get your things. Stay here. Think easy, non-pukey thoughts."

I wanted to laugh at the idea of easy thoughts, but my stomach wasn't having it. "I'm not going anywhere," I promised. "Could you pick up my laptop too? I need to handle a few things in the morning and I don't want to come back here to do it."

She pushed to her feet and brushed blades of grass from her knees. "Of course. I'll be right back."

I stood and wandered down the walkway, away from the house—and the mess I left on the grass. Turning my gaze to the bright sky, I wondered whether I was supposed to know what I was doing yet. If I was supposed to know what to do now.

Annette chattered all the way to her house, recounting some incredible news hitting the book world today. She parked me in the living room while she put together some little nibbles, as she called them. I sat there, my hands flat on the cushions beside me while my head and belly swirled. The only solution that made sense to me was returning to New York.

It was what I'd wanted all along. It was the reason I kept my townhouse in Brooklyn and refused to apply for a Maine driver's license. Why I hadn't changed a single thing in my childhood bedroom, even after more than two years of hating all the mint green and pink. Talbott's Cove wasn't home anymore. Loving a grouchy barkeep couldn't erase that truth.

"We have a bit of brie, some sharp cheddar, those great herby raisin crackers you turned me on to, and some dark chocolate because it's necessary for my health and well-being." She set the tray down on the coffee table along with two wineglasses, and retrieved a bottle and corkscrew from her apron pocket. "But first, wine."

I stared at the glasses as she treated them to generous pours. "So, I'm pregnant."

She clutched the bottle by the neck. "*What* did you say?"

I scooped a handful of crackers off the tray and sagged into the sofa. "Yeah, that was my reaction too."

"Okay." She sat cross-legged on the floor, tucked into the coffee table. "Are you exercising your rights or investing in stretchy pants with a belly pouch?"

"No one boils it down quite like you, my dear," I said, laughing. "I don't know what I'm doing. I haven't decided anything." The video montage in my head played a constant loop of my father's house, Jed, New York, the obstetrician's office. Decisions waited for me at every turn. "I haven't decided anything, but you need to hold off on getting married this year. I love you to pieces, but I doubt my ability to host your bridal shower and bachelorette party without the aid of alcohol. And you know none of the male strippers will give a pregnant woman a lap dance."

She selected a chunk of cheddar from the tray. "How do you know this?"

I held up a hand. "Trust me. I know how it is with male strippers." I ate one cracker and immediately felt better. "And there shall not be a single photograph of me helping you into a dress or fixing your train while pregnant. I was angling for a Pippa Middleton-level maid of honor showing, but that's out of the question now." I rested my hand on my belly, even though I was annoyed at myself for doing it. There was nothing there yet. No kicking, no bump. Just an accident, a souvenir from the night Dad bashed his forehead on the nightstand and Jed threw me into his car like he was kidnapping me. "Assuming that, you know, I do this."

Annette poked at the dark chocolate, taking her time to find the perfect piece. "And JJ? What are his thoughts on *this*?"

I popped another cracker in my mouth. "He did everything right."

She nodded slowly. "But you had a big fight?"

"I don't know what comes next for me, now that I'm not taking care of Dad anymore." I motioned toward the windows looking out onto the village of Talbott's Cove. "When I first came home, I thought it was for a short time. I remember telling the partners in my firm that I'd be gone for three months. Six at the most. I thought I'd be able to handle everything in that time. It made perfect sense to me that I'd merely 'handle' dementia in a quarter or two." I ate another cracker. "It's a couple months shy of three years."

"Aaaaaaand you live here now. You have people here. People who consider themselves your family. In case I'm not being clear, I count JJ among those people."

"Yeah? Maybe?" I shrugged, shook my head. "We've yelled at each other while naked for months. What does that amount to? It's not a solid relationship. It's not the kind of family you bring a kid into and hope everything falls into place. The best thing for me is to go back to New York."

Annette's eyebrow arched up as she sipped her wine. "Brooke, you'd rather leave someone before they have a chance to leave you."

"I object to that generalization. Simply because I'm

contemplating it now doesn't mean it's my primary mode of handling shit," I replied.

"You know I love you and you know I say this from a place of love. I'm not trying to burn you at the stake."

I pushed to my feet and marched into the kitchen for a glass of water. "No, only men who don't understand the first thing about women and believe the uterus is where we hide our witchcraft burn us at stakes," I called over the sink. "It's always them with the torches."

"But JJ isn't holding a torch, honey," Annette said. "And he doesn't think you have witchcraft in your uterus. If I had to bet, I'd say he thinks there's a baby in there and he's wondering whether it will be born with a full beard or just a goatee."

I returned to the living room but couldn't sit. "He thinks Talbott's Cove is a fantastic place to live. He's traveled the world and he *chose* to come back here."

"And I'd agree with him," she replied. "The Cove is not without fault, just like New York City and everywhere else in the world isn't without fault. But I'm happy here. If you'd stop resenting this town for a second, you might realize you're happy too. You might realize you resent it for reasons that have nothing to do with the town at all, but everything to do with your roots."

I stopped pacing, met her gaze. "I found you here—"

"I found *you*," she argued.

"We found each other," I said pointedly. "And I'm so thankful for that. For you. But it doesn't make sense for me to stay here, Annette."

"You'd rather leave than be left," she said. "You push, push, push. You make everyone prove they really want you by pushing so hard that only the most stubborn and defiant of us stick around. You make us prove how much we really want you by forcing us away and waiting to see if we'll return."

I banded an arm across my chest. "You make me sound like a manipulative psycho."

"No, honey. You're just like the rest of us. We're all dented and defective in our own little ways and we hold it together the best we can."

"You say that, but all I hear is 'manipulative psycho.'"

"Because you're not used to anyone wanting to help you hold it together. You don't know what it means to stick around and push through the discomfort of embracing something new and scary. You're not used to anyone seeing past all the barriers you put up and the ends to which you drive people."

"So…I'm just super fucked up. That's it, I'm super fucked up. Considering that, I should definitely leave. I can't live in a small town where everyone knows I'm super fucked up and watch them tiptoeing around me. That would make me even more fucked up."

"We're all fucked up, Brooke. Sometimes, you lean into it. I'm only pointing it out so you don't walk away from something—and someone—good." She paused, sampled more of the chocolate. "You should know that if you leave, he'll follow. He'll abandon his distillery. He'll go to New York, he'll find a job that isn't the one he's poured his life into, and he'll do it because he adores you. But, honey, that's not what you want. I *know* it. I know it and I need you to know it too."

I dropped down on the floor beside her. "Okay—yeah

—so what? I stay here and have a baby and live in my father's house? And we start a baby buggy power walking club for moms where we compare Kegel routines and bitch about our husbands leaving their dishes in the sink or pissing on the toilet seat?"

Laughing, Annette said, "You just married us off and got me pregnant in one little daydream. And opened us up to new friends. That's how deep you're in this, honey. That's how far you've thought this one out. We're talking to *other people*."

"But that's where this is going, isn't it? We'll be pregnant and our kids will be best friends and our husbands will learn to tolerate each other and we'll plan our group vacations to Disney World."

"You're absolutely right, my dear." She grabbed hold of my hands. "I'll wear something Snow White-inspired and I'll work on getting you into something Sleeping Beauty-ish. Jackson will scope out the wait time for each ride and formulate a plan around snacks and naps. JJ will wear the diaper backpack and insist on pushing the stroller too. That's his way, even though you won't let your youngest out of the Baby Bjorn."

"I won't let my youngest out of the fucking what?"

"The Bjorn. You know, it's the mommy-and-me equivalent of a wrap dress." Annette motioned as if I should know what she meant. I shook my head. "The fabric thing you use to wear the baby."

"That sounds like a terrible idea," I said. "While this Ghost of Uteruses Future moment is really fun and all, I am still processing the notion of—of any of this. I can't live here and get married and have a baby and dress up like Sleeping Beauty."

Still laughing, Annette asked, "Has JJ even asked you to marry him?"

"In which universe do I strike you as someone who waits for a man to propose? It sure as hell isn't this one. If I want to get married, I'll tell him. It's a conversation, not a surprise attack." I glanced at her and tried to swallow around the foot in my mouth. "I don't mean—"

She held up her hands. "Nope. It's fine. The surprise attack worked well in my situation, and to be fair, there was a conversation beforehand. Several of them. I didn't expect he'd be in such a hurry to go forward after those conversations, but you know Jackson. He likes efficiency. It's too bad we haven't been able to apply that same efficiency to wedding planning."

"Okay," I replied, unconvinced that I hadn't kicked the puppy of our friendship. "I'm not trying to—"

"I said it was fine and I meant that. We don't get bent out of shape over things like this, Brooke. We don't let little nonsense divide us. You're spinning too fast to see that right now, but believe me, we're okay."

I bobbed my head. "Thank you."

"Don't thank me," she replied. "And don't leave because you're scared. If you really, truly want to go, I'm not going to stop you. I won't ask Jackson to chase you down the interstate or close the airports. If this is what you want, I won't try to change your mind. But I'll miss the hell out of you. I'll miss having you down the street. I'll be sad I don't have the same relationship with you, but

I'll be happy you're getting what you want. You deserve that."

I layered my hands over my belly over the little blob of cells inside me. "I don't—I don't know what I want."

Annette's eyes softened as she smiled. "Then stay here and figure it out." She lifted her hands. "Or leave and figure it out in New York. I'll be here for you either way. I can think of someone else who will be here—anywhere—for you too."

I wanted to believe that. I wanted to believe I hadn't killed the possibility of us with fire.

But I couldn't.

CHAPTER THIRTY-SEVEN

JJ

Liquidity: the ease and speed with which a purchase or sale can be completed.

IT WAS one of those unusually quiet nights at the tavern, the sort where I checked the town calendar for big events and stepped outside several times to confirm the lights were on. As far as I could tell, the golden combination of glorious July weather, late sunsets, and minimal responsibilities meant everyone was cooking out, going on evening walks, or coming up with reasons to avoid the indoors.

I couldn't comment on the weather or the sunset. I hadn't noticed either today. The only thing I knew was Brooke left town first thing this morning after turning off her phone and spending the night with Annette. Jackson was kind enough to pass that information along to me. Brooke, not as much.

But I knew it was coming when she wouldn't see me last night. Annette swore Brooke needed time to process the recent events and she'd take care of my girl, but I knew she was as good as gone. She needed to do this and I needed to let her. *Letting her* had its limits, however, and there were approximately twelve hours left on this experience before I hit mine. As much as she inspired me to club her over the head and drag her home, I wasn't letting it go down that way. I didn't want her to be alone right now and I wasn't letting her do this alone for one more day. If that meant following her around New York City, I'd be hot on her heels.

I checked my phone at the off chance I'd missed a call or message. Nothing new.

The door creaked open, and for a split second my heart pulsed into my throat thinking it was Brooke. God, it would be so good to see her. Hold her. Instead, it was Cole McClish, the better half of lobsterman and town council chairman Owen Bartlett. I kept watch on the door, expecting to find Owen close behind.

"It's just me tonight," Cole said, following my gaze. He gripped the back of a stool and cast wary glances at the stragglers seated around the bar. "Is this okay? Should I—"

"Sit your ass down," I barked. I flung a coaster across the bar top, dropped a menu beside it.

"Yes, sorry," he murmured as he settled into the seat. "What do you recommend?"

I stared at him. Blinked. Exhaled like a motherfucker. "Narrow that down, would you? I'm not going to sit here and recommend appetizers when you're only interested in red wines. I got better things to do with my time."

Cole glanced at the menu, a deep frown etched into his face. He was the newest Talbott's Cove import, all the way from sunny California. He was one of those tech sensations who'd earned his first billion before he was old enough to drink to his success. Somehow he'd found his way to our corner of the world and into Owen's heart. The two of them were damn near inseparable, which made Cole's appearance here even more unusual than the empty dining room.

He pushed the menu aside. "I could use a drink. How about a bartender's special? I don't have any strong preferences or aversions."

For a second, I thought about blasting him with some noise about having a drink menu for a reason, but I couldn't do it. I was tired as hell. I missed Brooke like I didn't think possible. If I stopped long enough to get my arms around the idea of Brooke being pregnant—and *gone*—and the distillery's uncertain future, my brain short-circuited.

"All right. Let's shake something up." I reached into a low cabinet for one of my small-batch gins and set to mixing the distillery's proposed signature martini.

Surprising the shit out of me, Cole scooped a handful of pretzels out of a communal bowl and shoveled them in his mouth. Then, he propped his arm on the bar, rested his cheek on his hand, and dragged the bowl in front of him. He selected individual pretzels, eating them one at a time as he said, "I stepped on Owen's overgrown toes tonight. That's why I'm here."

Not taking my eyes off him, I reached for a martini glass. "I'm gonna need you to be clear. Is this a metaphor or did you actually step on his toes?"

"It started when we were changing the sheets this morning," Cole said. "I told Owen he was doing it wrong —and he was. The fitted sheet was inside out and I merely told him this."

"Metaphorical, then," I said to myself as I filled the glass.

"We weren't finished with the sheets even ten minutes when Owen decides he wants to revisit a mistake I made last weekend," he continued. "I'd picked some berries in the woods near the house, but it turned out they weren't edible. They looked like wild blueberries. Like I said, it was an honest mistake. He didn't have to keep bringing it up as if I was an incompetent child who couldn't be trusted to play in the backyard without supervision."

I set the glass in front of him. "Not edible or poisonous?"

He closed his fingers around the stem, shook his head. "I'm not sure. Owen prefers an abundance of caution in all things."

I leaned back against the opposite countertop, crossed my ankles and peered at Cole. "Did he mention which kind of berry it was?"

"Pokeberry? I'm not sure. Something like that." He sipped his drink. "Oh. This is fabulous."

I warmed at the compliment. "Good to hear it, but those pokeberries are poisonous. A handful will kill a child. Two handfuls would take down either one of us."

Cole jerked a shoulder up and pulled a defiant frown.

"Even so, it doesn't benefit anyone to treat your partner like a helpless fool and there's no sense bringing it up days later."

"Yeah, Owen should've gotten over the poisonous fruit you touched and brought home to eat much sooner," I replied. "It's outrageous to think he's ruminating over this incident."

"How do you know this?" Cole asked. "How do you know when it's a blueberry and when it's a poison berry? Owen said I should've noticed the color of the stalk."

"The pokeberry has a pink-purple stalk. Blueberries have a green stalk."

Cole shook his hands at me. "How do you know this? I don't think most people carry this kind of information with them. If I went back to Silicon Valley and asked around, I doubt I'd find anyone who knew these distinguishing characteristics."

"It's the sort of thing you learn when you grow up with Talbott's Cove as your backyard." I crossed my arms over my torso. It was all I could do to keep myself right here, rooted in this spot, rather than running and not stopping until I laid eyes on Brooke and convinced her we were in this together. "But, also, didn't you invent something where you can take a photo and the internet tells you what you're looking at?"

He set the martini glass down and leveled me with a glare. "Do not weaponize my tech against me." When he was satisfied that point landed, he continued, "Anyway, as I was saying, I must've stepped on all of his toes because it didn't end with the allegedly toxic berries. We had to dredge up the bad experience we had with the dog groomer and how Owen knew that person wasn't right for the job and I never listen to him and now we've traumatized the dog."

When he drained his glass, I picked it up, asking, "Another of the same or something different?"

"Surprise me," he replied. "I agree, Sasha was horribly groomed and we'll never go back to that shop. I understand that he's putting all his stress and anxiety about our poor girl's bad haircut—plus a dozen other things that have nothing to do with the dog—on me and I know he's doing that because he trusts me with that stress and anxiety, but sometimes, it's tough to absorb it all."

On any other night, I would've tuned out this story the same way I tuned out all the others, picking up enough to chime in at the appropriate time with nods and murmurs of agreement. But listening to Cole only pressed the sharp edge of Brooke's absence deeper. It made me realize I wanted to argue with her about sheets and poisonous berries and dog grooming. Or, some version of that. I wanted to fight with her about everything, every day, and I wanted to do it until I ran out of days.

Goddamn, I should've told her that. I should've stopped and said that before I said anything else. I should've said nothing but that. As I shook Cole's next beverage, I shot a glance at the wall clock. It was too late to catch a flight to New York. The best I could do tonight was call or text.

Setting a fresh drink in front of him, I said, "This one is a little floral. The gin is steeped with beach rose. If it's too strong for you, I'll make something different."

He sipped, glanced at me over the rim of the glass,

and sipped again. Then, "How is it I've lived here almost a year and I'm just now having a beach rose gin martini?"

I wiped my hands on a towel and busied myself with rinsing out the shaker. "I don't know your life, man. Maybe you should come in here more often. Get that boyfriend of yours to socialize a bit."

"That will be my next order of business after fixing his bruised toes," Cole replied. "I can't believe this drink. It's amazing. When you said floral, I thought I'd be choking down some hand soap, but this is the right kind of rose martini." He took another sip. "My original CFO from back in our startup days loves gin. He kept a trophy case of gin in his office. It was very strange. He lives on a chain of islands he bought in the South Pacific now. Rumor has it, he's building an end-of-days bunker. Not sure the South Pacific is the right place for that sort of thing, considering how oceanic it is." He lifted the glass up, studied it in the light. "I've missed the days of drinking good gin martinis with him."

I glanced at the clock again. "No hand soap served here."

Cole swirled the liquid in his glass. "Which brand is this? I'd love to send him some. He'd get a kick out of my tastes evolving for the better."

Against all my better judgment, I replied, "It's my brand. I distill small batches of gin and vodka in-house."

Not missing a damn beat, Cole said, "You need to develop a national distribution strategy."

Laughing, I said, "I've explored several expansion opportunities. They haven't panned out as of yet."

Giving me his best *that doesn't sound right* face, he

asked, "What kind of opportunities and why didn't they pan out? Was it a licensing issue? Distribution? I know certain states have blue laws that go back to the Puritan days and those can create headaches, but it's a simple matter of locating your warehouse in a more legally friendly state."

"It's not that."

"Then...what is it? This is phenomenal liquor and there's no reason to keep it a secret. Why isn't it flying off the shelves?"

I wasn't one for sharing. Not my stories and not those of others. But tonight, with a near empty tavern and every vital organ aching for Brooke, I didn't have the strength to hold back. "It's not going anywhere because my financial backer bailed on an initiative to convert the local apple cider house into a distillery and gathering place with dining and event options."

Cole stared at me, bobbing his head slightly. "Who owns the property? The apple juice place, I mean."

"I do. It was cheap enough to grab on my own," I replied. "Rather, the *cider house* is owned by the tavern."

"One of these days, you can explain the difference between apple juice and apple cider to me, but not tonight," he said. "What's it going to cost to turn the apple juice place into the type of location that will yield the kind of traffic you want?"

A dish towel clenched in my fists, I gazed at him for a long moment. "It's great that you like my gin, but I don't want to talk about money with you."

"Why not?"

Because I hate talking about money with people who have more of it than I do. "Because this isn't the time."

He held up his hands, glanced around. "What better time than now? I'm enjoying your product and I want it to be widely available so I can enjoy more of it and brag to my friends about finding a hot new label before they did. This is the perfect time." When I didn't respond, he continued, "All I want is a loose estimate. I'm wondering what this sort of project costs. Consider it pure curiosity on my part. I could guess, but I shouldn't. Guessing gets me into trouble because I meander down long mental paths until five days have passed without me noticing it."

"You're not leaving until I tell you."

"No, definitely not," he replied with a laugh. "Owen needs more time to cool down and I want to know everything about this distillery."

With a sigh, I grabbed a cocktail napkin and scribbled a figure on it. I pushed it across the bar. "Consider your curiosity quenched."

Blinking rapidly, Cole stared at the napkin. "Characterize this amount for me. Is it bare bones, middle of the road, bells and whistles?"

I dumped several jiggers, stirrers, and mixing spoons into the sink, unconcerned with the bracing clatter of those items hitting the stainless steel basin. "Somewhere between middle of the road and bare bones."

He pushed the napkin back across the bar. "Write down the bells and whistles number. For my curiosity."

I pointed my pen at him. "You know something, McClish? Most people come in here, get a drink, watch the game. They don't tell me about the poison berries they brought home and they don't expect a business plan to garnish their martini."

"I've never once succeeded at doing the things most people do," he replied. "Everything that's ever gone right in my life is the result of following my own path, fucking it up along the way, and acknowledging that conventional wisdom doesn't work for me." He pointed at the napkin. "Since I'm not going to watch the game and you've already heard about my berries, why don't you write down that number and see what happens?"

"Fuck it," I mumbled, snaring the pen's cap between my teeth.

Cole didn't look at the napkin when I pushed it toward him. "What happened with the investment partner?"

"He liked the idea of building a food and beverage destination here, but he wanted to exploit every trend in the market. Ciders, seltzers, pirates." I ran the dish towel over the lip of the bar. "For better or worse, this place is about craft gin and vodka, and that didn't excite him enough. I'd rather see the distillery fail before getting off the ground than die a miserable, trend-chasing death."

Cole finished his drink and then reached into his back pocket, pulled out his phone. He tapped out a message, nodded at the screen, and tapped another message. "Expect a call from my aide-de-camp. Her name is Neera Malik and she'll need your bank information. She'll send some legal paperwork for you to sign. All boilerplate. Your basic covenants and restrictions and such. If you get it back to her tomorrow, you'll have the full amount"—he tapped his finger against the second figure, the bells and whistles—"by the weekend."

"What the hell did you just say?"

"Neera Malik," he repeated. "She'll call you—"

"No, I caught that much," I interrupted. "Why are you doing this? What are you getting out of backing my distillery?"

Cole scratched his jaw. "Why? Because Owen loves it here and I love Owen. This town desperately needs new ideas. Small places like Talbott's Cove are struggling because there's a painful absence of innovation. Nothing new has come to town in fifty years, maybe one hundred, and those things aren't new anymore. Hell, people have no real options beyond leaving. Change is fucking scary, but without it Talbott's Cove won't survive another twenty or thirty years." He glanced to his phone and typed out another message. "And what do I want? For starters, a case of gin each month. Beyond that, I want to connect you with branding and marketing people who know their shit. I'd like a seat on your board of directors, but I know fuck all about running a business so I'll keep quiet."

"That's it?" I twisted the towel around my hand. Untwisted it. "You drop some cash because you believe in Small Town, USA, sprinkle some marketing on top, and cross your fingers?"

He placed his phone on the bar, clasped his hands. "It seems like you want this to be more complicated. I can ask Neera to do that for you, but I have no desire to do that myself. I'm offering you a clean deal. Take it." He glanced at the clock, nodding. "I think Owen has had enough time to cool off."

"How do you know that? How do you determine the right amount of time?"

"I won't call myself an expert, but I think it depends on the size of the fight. We weren't yelling at each other about berries or sheets or dog grooming. We were yelling about time. I'm pushing a new product through beta testing and I've been spending unconscionable hours at my computer. The summer season is kicking Owen in the ass and he's exhausted. We had to get our frustrations out, even if that meant going hardest on the person we care about most." He slipped his phone in his pocket. "Owen needed a couple of hours to be angry, but once he works his way through it, he's done with it."

"And what if you go to him before he's done with it?" I asked for entirely selfish reasons.

"Then I give him the space he wants," he replied. "I've learned to accept that Owen works through things differently than I do and I can't expect him to hurry up because I'm ready to move on."

Cole tried to drop some cash on the bar, but I waved him off. "Don't drink this on the walk home," I cautioned, setting a fresh bottle of beach rose gin on the bar. "Thank you. I can't explain how much I appreciate this."

"No need for pleasantries. We'll thank each other when we've grown a new economic base for this town and my Silicon Valley friends call me the craft gin evangelist."

The door thunked shut and I caught sight of Owen

Bartlett. "There you are." He charged across the room. "I've been looking all over for you."

"Found me," Cole chirped. "Look at this, it's gin flavored with beach roses. Do you know what those are? I'm sure you do. Maybe you can show me tomorrow because I have no idea. Also, it's amazing and I worked out a deal so we're getting a case of gin every month. Isn't that awesome?"

Owen smiled at me over Cole's head. "If that makes you happy, baby, then I'm happy."

"Can we go home now?" Cole asked.

"That's why I'm here. I came to get you," Owen replied.

"Good night," I called as they shuffled out, their arms tangled around each other. Watching them together hurt like I couldn't believe, but I had my phone out before the door rattled shut behind them.

This was the only thing for me to do—wrap my arms around her as best I could from hundreds of miles away and ask if she was ready to come home.

JJ: There are a lot of things I want to say. I've been trying to figure out the right place to start all day, but I don't think I know where it is.

JJ: Since there's no good place, I'll start with the thing I wish I'd said the yesterday.

JJ: I don't want you to leave, but I'm not talking about Talbott's Cove. You can go anywhere in the world. I want you to be where you're happy. But please don't leave.

JJ: I didn't tell you about losing Barry and his investment

because I didn't want to bother you with it. I know it wouldn't have bothered you. Hell, it might've been a good distraction. But then everything happened with the baby, and the distillery was the last thing on my mind. I can't convince myself I should've added that to your plate, sweetheart. Not right then. I'm sorry it came out the way it did, but I'm not sorry for protecting you.

JJ: I'm going to keep doing that, you know. You'll hate it and you'll throw fire at me, but if I'm extremely lucky, you'll put up with it.

JJ: I think I'm extremely lucky, Brooke.

CHAPTER THIRTY-EIGHT

BROOKE

Hedge Fund: a pooled, collective investment vehicle used to yield aggressive returns.

I KNOCKED on Jed's door. At first, it was a polite knock. A light tap of the knuckles against solid wood. When that resulted in nothing, I put some muscle into it. A deep thunk vibrated across the slab and echoed down the street. Damn near bruised my hand in the process.

It was the middle of the night, the summer air heavy on my skin and cicadas hissing in the trees as if I required more recrimination. I did not. I knew where he kept the spare key, but it didn't feel right to let myself in, not when I'd escaped from the Cove before sunrise like a fugitive.

Even if I wanted to climb into his bed and tuck myself up against his body and sleep for the longest time, I couldn't do that. Not until I'd earned the right.

The door swung open to reveal Jed in black boxers,

that delicious line of fuzz running down his belly and the octopus climbing his arm. Butterscotch galloped up, her tail wagging her entire body while her front paws danced. She jostled Jed out of the way and circled me twice, huffing and whining as she went. She nudged me over the threshold and into Jed's house.

"Okay, Scotchie, okay," I sang, my hands sweeping over her coat as she nuzzled my legs.

"My dog has never loved anything or anyone the way she loves you," Jed mused. "If you're not here to tell me something good, I hope you know you're gonna break the old girl's heart."

"I tried to go home today," I said, still dividing my attention between him and the dog. "I have a townhouse in Brooklyn. The Vinegar Hill neighborhood. I don't know if I've ever told you that."

He leaned back against the door. "Probably not."

"But I didn't have a key," I continued. "I'm sure I did at some point, but I couldn't find it today. I couldn't get in."

Jed crossed his arms. "Seems like an important detail."

"Not anymore," I replied. "I sold it. I sold my townhouse."

"Wait—how? In one day? What?"

I ran my hands through my hair, shrugged. "I know people. I know how to get things like this done and I wanted it done."

"You sold your place in Brooklyn," he murmured. "Now what? Buying something new?"

"That would be a smart investment," I said, pacing the length of his living room. "Generally speaking, real estate is the most stable, low-risk investment most people will ever make." I turned back toward him, my hand on my belly as it had been all day. "I'm not a stable, low-risk investment. I'm a high-risk investment."

He stared at my torso for a second. Then, he tipped his chin up. "How do you figure?"

"I'm-I'm not going to pretend my head isn't a mess," I said. "I've been dragging a little red wagon's worth of issues around since forever. I'm still fucked up over losing my mother the way I did plus everything I went through with my father. I don't think any of that is going away right now." I shook my head, willing him to understand. "I am a high-risk investment, the kind of risk on which I'd never gamble. And I'm proof that babies don't make people happy. They don't make anyone fall back in love and they don't solve relationship problems. Babies can't fix their parents."

"I know, Brooke. I know that."

His gaze skated over me from head to toe as he stood silent. Eventually, he reached out, grabbed a handful of my dress, and yanked me up against him. Butterscotch protested with a series of yips and barks, wiggling her body between us.

"She wants to protect you," he whispered against my neck. "Can't say I find any fault there."

"I shouldn't have left the way I did. I shouldn't have said the things I did. I was wrong, although I had to go. Had to drive to Portland in the dark, wait for my flight there, wait on the ground at Teterboro, crawl through traffic in Manhattan and over the bridge, all to find out I couldn't go back to the place I'd thought was my home. I had to figure this out, Jed."

"I could've gone with you," he replied. "You could've figured it out with me right there beside you."

"Maybe that's true," I conceded. "But I don't think you would've let me sit on the grass at John Street Park and cry for an hour. You would've insisted I tell you how to fix it and I would've told you I wanted to fix it myself. We would've argued under the Brooklyn Bridge and solved nothing."

"That's where we don't agree. I want to fight with you. Every damn day of my life. I don't want a day to go by without feeling your fire. But understand this, Brooke. I don't want to fight you. I want to stand on the same side as you."

"I don't know how to do that, Jed. I don't know how to do any of this." I layered both hands over my belly, my eyes wide and pleading as I stood there, the farthest thing in the world from perfect. I was exposed and vulnerable, and terrified he wouldn't understand. "I am telling you I don't have the answers and I don't know what I'm doing, and I don't think I've ever been so—"

He pressed his lips to mine. "Beautiful." Another kiss. "Open." Another. "Real." And another. *"Mine."*

"But Jed, I'm—"

"Are you staying?" he asked. "Or am I going with you?"

"Staying. I'm working on getting used to that idea but I sold my townhouse so I'm running short on options at the moment."

"Are we still in this thing together?" he asked as he steered me down the hall.

I nodded. "Yes."

He tugged the dress up, over my head. "Are we still having a baby together?"

Another nod, a terrified gulp, a hand to my bare belly, and— "Yes."

He wrapped his arms around me, brought my head to his shoulder. "There's nothing to forgive. We'll argue, probably every damn day. We'll walk away, cool off, come back. We're in this."

I tapped my index finger against his sternum. "About the distillery—"

"Handled," he replied.

"Yeah? The meeting went well?"

His body shook as he barked out a laugh. "The meeting was a train wreck," he said. "But Cole McClish came into the tavern tonight and we started talking about gin. He sampled the beach rose batch and funded the entire launch on the spot." He pressed a kiss to the crown of my head, my temple. "You can blame Cole for robbing you of that bargaining chip."

"So, that's it?" I asked, glancing up at him. "Cole saved the day and you've accepted my apologies? It's that…simple?"

He dropped his hands to my ass, squeezing and grinding me against him. "If you really want to make amends and apologize for putting me through hell today, you're welcome to suck my cock."

I sighed. "I'm going to be someone's *mother*, Jedediah. Mothers don't suck cocks."

"And yet the term *motherfucker* exists," he mused as he relieved me of my bra.

"It's only available to those up to the task," I replied.

He dragged my panties down, his eyebrows arched. "Since I'm the one who knocked you up, I believe I'm uniquely qualified for this job."

"Can I make one request?"

His chin bumped my head as he nodded. "Anything you want, Bam."

"Take your fucking boxers off."

"All right. That's what you want? Not a problem." He drove his fingers through my hair and tipped my head back. "Don't think I'm throwing you on the bed. You deserve it, and fuck me, I want it like you wouldn't believe. But you ran off to New York City and you cried in a park and you're carrying my child. Right now, I need to hold you more than I need to give you a good toss."

I eased out of his arms, climbed onto the bed, and settled in the middle. "Come here. Come hold me." I nodded at his boxers. "After you drop the shorts."

His underwear hit the floor and then he was beside me, one knee between my legs and his arm under my shoulders as he skimmed a hand up my torso. He gazed at my belly for a long moment. "You're a real piece of work, Bam. The shit you put me through, my god." He rested his forehead between my breasts and released a jagged exhale. "Promise me you won't stop."

I reached for the knot at the base of his skull, pulled his hair loose. The unruly strands fell to my chest and I lashed my arms and legs around him. "Never."

He brought his hand between my legs. "What am I allowed to do?"

"Everything," I replied, arching into his touch. "Give me everything."

Our lips met as he pushed inside me, a chorus of groans and growls passing between us. To the corner of my mouth, he said, "You will tell me if anything is uncomfortable, Bam."

I hummed, canting my hips up to take more of him. "I will."

"You'll tell me to slow down." His hips rolled gently while he continued gazing at me. "I'm not letting you hurt tomorrow."

"And I'm not letting you give me a weak fuck," I replied. "I don't want you holding back. I know how to speak for myself and you know I will. Give it to me or get off me."

"I love you a whole fucking lot," he said, roping his arms around my torso.

"I love you just as much." Then, I felt a flutter on my foot—and wetness. "Jed, honey, oh my god, she's licking my foot."

He peered at me. "What are you talking about? Who?"

"Butterscotch." I gestured to the side of the bed where she had her front paws perched on the mattress and her tongue trained on my toes. "She's licking me like a popsicle. This seems incredibly strange but I can't move since I'm trapped under a lumberjack."

He glanced behind us as Butterscotch hopped onto the bed and plopped down right beside me, her face tucked into the crook of my elbow. "Oh, fuck." He snapped his fingers, pointed to her bed. "Scotchie, off."

She turned her head in the opposite direction and thumped her tail against his ass.

"What do we do now?" I whisper-screamed.

"I-I don't know." To the dog, he said, "Butterscotch. *Off.* Right now." She huffed out a sigh and nuzzled closer to me. "Looks like you're the boss, Bam."

"Butterscotch," I sang. Her ears perked up. "Go to your nest, pretty girl."

She licked my arm, shot Jed a disgusted glare, and jumped off the bed. She trotted over to her corner, circled her bed twice, and dragged a paw over the fleece surface. Eventually, she flopped down and started snoring.

"And here I thought I could keep you all to myself," Jed mused.

"I told you I can't be kept." I locked my legs around his waist and drove my fingers through his hair. "But that doesn't mean I can't keep you."

EPILOGUE

BROOKE

*Consolidation: the joining of two or more organizations
to form a new organization.*

THE NEXT SUMMER

IT WAS a gorgeous day for a wedding.

With my dress gathered in my hands as gingerly as I
could, I walked a circle around the outdoor ceremony
setup. White chairs curved in a half-moon around the
pergola and thick garlands of white hydrangea led the
way down the aisle. With the ocean as the backdrop and a
bright, shining June sky overhead, it didn't matter that the
peonies filling the pergola were a slightly darker pink
than I'd expected.

Satisfied, I traveled toward the tent constructed for
this evening's reception. I moved between a pair of long,

rectangular tables, each dressed with an assortment of linens, candles, and flowers. The design was simple without being plain, rustic without being rough.

On the far end of the tent, I spotted Owen Bartlett pacing a short route between the six-tier wedding cake and the dessert table. I headed in his direction.

"Are you ready for this?" I called, gesturing to the space around us.

He eyed my dress with a pleasant grin. "Are you?"

"I will feel much better when you tell me you have your portion of the events on lock."

He glanced at his small leather notebook. "This is my eighty-ninth wedding ceremony. I didn't think I knew that many people, but here I am, presiding over all these unions. It's surreal when I think about it." He patted the notebook. "I have this on lock, Brooke."

"I expected nothing less." I peered around him. "Where's Cole?"

"Where do you think? He's back in the distilling room, geeking out over the newest batches JJ has in the works." He shook his head as if he didn't relish his husband's obsession with Down East Distillery's research and development efforts. "Have you given any more thought to the proposals on the table? Mind you, I'm not trying to rush the process. Just curious. I get that from Cole."

As it did whenever the topic of my father's estate surfaced, a sudden pressure filled my chest. In the year since his death, my perspective on the home my lineage had kept for centuries evolved. At first, after collecting my things and moving them to Jed's house, I'd wanted to sell. Be done with the ancestral property and move forward. But it wasn't as simple as hanging a For Sale sign in the yard, not with generations of history packed into every corner.

After the summer ended and the loss wasn't as raw, Annette convened a clean-out party disguised as another one of her double dates of vengeance. We managed to remove much of the recent history—leftover boxes of sterile gloves, dementia-proofed door handles, banana-flavored pudding mix—and that eased some of my tension. I didn't feel the need to avoid the property anymore but I didn't know what to do with it either. Not wanting to deal with that on top of growing a human being and reorganizing my entire life, I set it aside. Until the offers started coming in.

Most were easy to dismiss—the numbers were too low or the buyers weren't qualified—but each one forced me to think about how I wanted this to unfold. As much as I struggled with the truth, I couldn't walk away. I didn't think I could look at the house atop the hill without believing some part of me belonged there and some part of it belonged to me.

"I haven't made any decisions, though I am leaning toward the historic preservation proposal," I admitted. "I like their focus on expanding the gardens, converting the bedrooms into guest suites, and updating the outbuildings."

"And you retain ownership," he said, laughing.

"That always helps," I replied. "That proposal makes the most sense. Turning the house into a museum as other developers have suggested seems—I don't know—wasteful. The only people who will visit are elementary school kids on class field trips and that's not a punishment I'm prepared to administer. I'd rather reimagine it as an inn, a horticultural center, something like that."

"I understand, and I'm confident the town council will approve the zoning changes necessary." Owen jerked his chin toward the main entrance. "You should get back inside. People are going to arrive early. They're all chomping at the bit for a look at the place."

"As they should be," I said, motioning to the lush grounds. "This place is fucking amazing. Did you see that patio area over there? And the gardens? Holy shit. I didn't know gardens could look like that. It's hard to believe we're in Talbott's Cove." I swept an arm out. "A wedding with three hundred guests tonight? No problem. A grand opening next week? Got it covered. Farmers markets and food festivals and five different pop-up events the week after? Business as usual." I tapped an index finger to his suit coat. "Start planning for more stoplights, my friend. This town is never going to be the same."

A rare smile pulled at his lips. "What a remarkable gift it is to get on your good side."

Shaking off his words as I moved toward the doors, I called, "If I see Cole, I'll send him your way."

I slipped inside, careful to keep my steps silent against the concrete floors. It was wild to think this old cider house was ready for its debut after all these months of work and planning, all while welcoming a newborn baby into our lives.

As I ducked down the hall toward the distillery's offices and private rooms, I found Nate marching toward me. His sleeves were rolled to his elbows and his collar was open, a necktie dangling from his back pocket. All he needed was a tweed vest to complete his barkeep chic look.

"Where are you sneaking off to now?" he asked.

"Sneaking? Me?" I asked, feigning all the shock in the world. "Never."

We shared a laugh and I skimmed a glance over the fully grown man we referred to as our foster child. These days, he managed the Galley while also tending to the distillery's gardens. Much like Jackson and Annette, Nate was our family. He was part of us.

"Do you need anything?" he asked.

"You'd know if I did." I reached up, brushed some dust from his short beard. "What is this? Have you been rolling around in an attic? Don't you have better things to do, Nathan?"

"Rolling around on the floor," he replied. "I was fixing one of the refrigerators at the tavern."

"That doesn't sound like any fun."

Shaking his head, he said, "It wasn't, but I got it patched up. That's all I care about."

"The next time you're rolling around on the floor, please try to have fun while you do it." I patted his forearm. "Perhaps you'll meet someone who shares those interests this evening. You know what they say about single women and weddings."

Here I was, thirty-five years old, living in my hometown, and meddling my ass off as mothers have since the dawn of time. Even in my worst nightmares, I'd never imagined this would be my life.

And I wouldn't trade it for anything.

"Don't start with that again, Brooke," Nate warned. "I appreciate your concern, but I can't get involved with anyone. Not yet."

"I know, sweetie. I'm just saying this"—I circled both hands at his tightly bunched shoulders and stiff jaw —"might benefit from a night of rolling around on the floor with someone." Before he could respond, I held up a finger, silencing him. "Do you want me to explain how one-night stands work? I will. I'll give you the overview right now. Better yet, I'll grab Annette. We'll do it together."

"Please don't." Nate shook his head. "None of that is necessary. None of it at all. Not a single word."

"Let me know if you change your mind," I said, backing down the hall.

"I promise you, I won't," he called.

"But if you do," I shouted back.

"But I won't," he replied, his laugh echoing after him.

I stepped into the room designated for wedding preparations. Wrapped bouquets sat in low vases with just enough water to keep them perky. Hairspray and makeup littered the tabletop.

I glanced at my reflection in the mirror, smoothing my hands down the long dress. I never would've selected this style for myself, but Annette convinced me to try it on and the rest was history. I looked different now, my hips wider and my breasts fuller, but I recognized myself. I was my kind of perfect.

From the hallway, I heard, "Where is my wife? No, I've been out there already. This place isn't that big. I should be able to find one tiny woman without—"

The door opened and I met Jed's gaze in the mir_
My lips pulled up in a smile.

"There you are," he said, our son squirming against his chest. "I've been looking everywhere."

My husband's large hand covered the entirety of the baby's back, and if that wasn't enough to arouse me in the strangest ways, the burp cloth over his shoulder sealed the deal. Another bit of strange-but-true sources of arousal: my husband's wedding ring.

The baby, the towel, and the ring. *Fuck me.* It wasn't even fair.

"I heard you," I replied, holding out my hands for Elliott. "Is he hungry again?"

Jed crossed the room and shifted the infant to my arms. Elliott was a sweet, squishy ball of baby with my eyes and his father's hair and coloring.

"Much like everyone else around here, he just wants your attention." He leaned in, kissed my forehead. "This production is nice for Jackson and Annette, but I'm so fucking happy I married you in the backyard last month."

I never would've chosen this place or these people for myself, but now I couldn't imagine choosing anything else. "Me too."

THANK **you for reading** *Far Cry!* **I hope you enjoyed Brooke and JJ. If you did…would you like some more? Click here to signup for an extended epilogue.**

. . .

AFTER A THORNY PAUSE, I asked, "How is your meal?"

He bobbed his head as he savored a bite of dosa. "Excellent. Best I've had in—I don't know—years. And I think that was in Mexico City."

"Mexico City has amazing Indian food." I hummed in agreement. "Whenever I'm traveling, I try to sneak in stops at local Indian restaurants. I have an ongoing samosa study."

I watched a warm, cheerful smile brighten his face and crinkle his eyes. "What's this samosa study involve?"

I pressed the edge of my fork into the uttapam, suddenly and irrationally shy about my multi-continent cataloging of Indian cuisine. "I'm not sure whether it's an atavistic desire or callback to my childhood." I paused, studied my tray. "We didn't eat out when I was a child. We didn't have the money for restaurants and my parents didn't enjoy the local favorites. But on special occasions, my parents loaded us into the car and we'd drive to different cities in the area. Greenville, Spartanburg, Asheville. Athens, once. We'd always go out for Indian and meet the Desi people in that area. And now, well, I just—I tend to judge cities by the quality of their samosas...and other dishes."

He made a sound. A rumbly, growly, throaty sound. Somehow, I knew it was one of approval. "Yeah? Any surprises?"

"I'm not sure about surprises." I sampled the uttapam. I loved these savory pancakes topped with tomatoes and onions. That they constituted a traditional south Indian breakfast mattered little to me. If they were crisp and fresh, I'd eat them any time of day. "There are Desi people all around the world and many of them make superb food." I gave him a pointed nod. "Just as there are French and Brazilian people everywhere and some of them choose to carry on their cultures in most delicious ways."

"Point taken." He drummed my wrist again. This time, he went to the trouble of dragging his fingertips over the back of my hand and staring into my eyes while he did. *So damn arrogant.* "But I still want to know your favorites."

I thought for a moment. "Albuquerque. Egypt, outside of Cairo. Beijing. Then again, there are no bad meals in Beijing."

"Haven't been."

I tipped my chin down. "Now, that's surprising. I figured you'd gone everywhere worth going."

Shaking his head, he said, "South and Central America, sure. Western Europe, yes. Portions of Africa, mostly northern. As far as Asia and much of North America, I have a lot of ground to cover. I don't know much outside the southwest."

I pointed my fork at him. It was rude but I found myself wanting to be rude with him, just a bit. "You don't have much an accent."

He pressed his tongue to the inside of his cheek. "Neither do you."

"I grew up here." I waved at the table. "Not California, but South Carolina. I'm American."

"Doesn't South Carolina saddle its progeny with a loose-tongued twang?"

I thought back to my pre-college self. Before Stanford, the Bay Area, and Silicon Valley stripped the south from me. Not that I missed it. South Carolina was the place my parents lived but it wasn't fundamental to my identity the way some of peers held California or Colorado or Texas fundamental to their identities.

"Some. Doesn't Brazil do something of the same?"

"No twang with the Portuguese, *querida*." He chuckled, drew his index finger over my knuckles. "Whichever accent I had, I lost at boarding school."

I watched as he dragged a bit of naan through the remains of several dishes, blurring all sauces and spices into one savory scoop. "Tell me, Mr. Guillmand." I grinned as the name bristled over him. "How are you finding California?"

He seesawed his hand. "I got *here*, didn't I? I can handle a map."

"That's not what I meant, you unbearable man."

He shrugged, held up his hands, rested his leg between both of mine. His jeans were rough against my unadorned skin, almost overwhelming, but I kept that reaction off my face. He eyed the gulab jamun on my tray, pointed. "What's that? They smell like flowers."

"Rosewater." I tore one in half and offered it to him. He accepted, but not without curling his fingers around my wrist and eating from my hand. "It's similar to a doughnut hole, but for dessert."

He sucked the sweetness right off my fingers and he did it while the VCs gaped at us. More than one Slack channel was blowing up this evening. "Delicious," he murmured, seemingly immune to our audience.

"Mmhmm." I gulped back a groan. "If they weren't boiling hot from the fryer, I'd eat them before anything else."

Gus tilted his head to the side, brought my thumb to his lips. "I'd eat you before anything else, Miz Malik."

AN EXCERPT FROM HARD PRESSED

"You sit here," I ordered, unbuckling my duty belt. "I have to—uh—handle a few things."

First order of business: adjusting the erection hammering away at my trousers. Next up, pulling every curtain shut. That would probably set off alarm bells of its own with the locals, but that was an issue for another day. Once the house was adequately buttoned up and my gear and firearm were stowed in the safe, I poured a glass of water for Annette and snatched a banana from the fruit bowl.

That was when things went pear-shaped.

Annette wasn't in the living room anymore. She was right behind me, standing in the middle of my kitchen, bare-ass naked. My fingers tightened around the banana. "Annette," I warned. "What—what are you doing?"

"I might be fragile," she purred, swaying a bit as she stepped closer to me, "but that doesn't mean I always want to be treated like I am."

I was working hard at keeping my eyes above her chest. I had a peripheral awareness of her nudity but I'd yet to allow myself the kind of long, quenching gaze at her lush curves. Goddamn, I wanted to look. I wanted to drop to my knees and press my face to the soft lines of her belly, drag my fingers up her calves and grab her ass like I meant it. I wanted to feel her spine arch under my hands and her body tighten around me. I wanted to get lost between her legs and never, never find my way out.

Clumps of pulverized banana filled my palm, and I turned away. "I'll get you something to wear," I said over my shoulder. I tossed the fruit in the garbage and then rinsed my hands at the sink, but I knew she was watching me. I felt the intensity of her stare on my skin, and I wanted to give it right back to her. I wanted it more than anything.

Turning, I said, "Annette—"

She wasn't hearing it. She flew into my arms and pressed her lips to mine, and for the second time tonight, I was paralyzed. Dumbstruck and frozen in place. But then my body and brain returned to me in pieces. I sighed into her kiss, forgetting my job, my duty, myself. She tasted of liquor and juice, and something succulent and special all her own. I couldn't help myself. I curled my arms around her torso, backed her against the refrigerator, and rocked myself into the valley of her parted legs.

I stayed right there, trapping her between the hard lines of the refrigerator and my body while I drank in every ounce she offered up. I couldn't even process the glory of her naked skin under my hands. It was one gift too many.

Annette broke away first, turning her head a few degrees and hiccup-giggling against my cheek. Then her hand slithered down my back and she slapped my ass.

At first, I was stunned into silence. That was becoming my default reaction to this woman. But then I remembered she was sloppy drunk, and I wasn't the type of man who capitalized on that condition.

Her palm cracked over my backside again, and another hiccup-giggle rang out. "You're so...hard," she whispered.

I surrendered to her words rather than my judgment and rutted against her core. If she wanted to know something about hard, I was happy to illustrate. "You have no idea," I replied. "Not a clue."

She tipped her head back against the refrigerator and gazed up at me, her lips parted and her eyes unfocused. "Whoa," she murmured. So beautiful and so drunk. *"Whoa."*

Right then, my responsibility came down on me. It was lightning fast and there was no way I was coming back from it this time. Not tonight.

I tossed Annette over my shoulder and blocked out the sensation of her smooth thigh against my cheek. No, that wasn't true. I was keenly aware of her thigh. But I wasn't letting myself enjoy the thigh.

"Please tell me we're going to a bedroom," she called. "That would be fabulous."

"We're going to a bedroom," I replied, "and I'm putting you to bed. Alone."

"That's the story of my life," she whined, dragging her fingertips up and down my flanks. Goddamn, that felt good. I could die happy after nothing more than a night of her hands moving over my skin. "Me, in bed, alone. It's never my turn."

I wanted to argue with her, insist that she'd get more than a turn from me as soon as she sobered up. But it occurred to me that she was offering this information under drunk cover, and chances were good I wouldn't hear the same tune tomorrow. Annette had been pleasant to me since my arrival but hadn't given me much more than passing, platonic glances. She wanted someone right now, and I was that person only because JJ called me in to collect her. If he'd walked her home, he could be receiving the same treatment. He could've been the one getting her hungry kisses and gently demanding touch.

That idea did terrible things to me. *Terrible.* I tightened my grip on her thighs and gritted my teeth as I stomped through the house, barely fighting off the urge to throw her down and make her crave me the way I'd been craving her.

I could do it too. I'd lay her down on my bed. Make her comfortable. Kiss my way from those sexy ankles to her full lips, the ones that looked even more delicious now that I'd tasted her sweet smile. I'd skip the places she wanted me most. I'd make her wait the way I'd waited for her. She'd ache and squirm and beg, and then I'd hike her legs over my shoulders and show her everything I'd held back. And then she'd know. When I was deep enough to steal her words and everything else save for screams, she'd know I'd wanted nothing but her for months.

Instead, I set her on my bed and only allowed myself

an extra moment with my hands on her body before turning away. I couldn't meet her hungry, needy gaze again. Not without tearing my pants off and feeding her my cock. I moved toward the door but couldn't leave. I stood there, my hands gripping either side of the door-frame while I stared unseeing down the hall. I needed this moment to gather myself, pull the loose threads of desire tight and sew them up. Set aside the urge to forget myself and take everything she was offering.

"Where are you going?" she asked. Her voice was small, almost childlike. "I want you to stay with me. You're not leaving. Are you?"

Go ahead and flay me open, woman. Go right ahead and gut me where I stand.

"No," I choked out. There was no way in hell I could walk away now. "Just going to grab some water for you." I shot her a glance over my shoulder. That was a huge fucking mistake. She was tucked back against my pillows, her knees drawn to her chin and her ankles crossed. It was a modest pose, her most private places covered, and I didn't believe there could be anything more intimate. Or anything that could make me want to crawl to her on my hands and knees more. I wouldn't be able to look at those pillows again without wanting her right there, exactly like that. "Put your head down. I'll be right back."

I stood in the kitchen for several minutes, my hands curled around the lip of the countertop while my cock thrummed against my zipper. I had to remind myself I didn't know Annette, not beyond her reputation as the town sweetheart and everyone's favorite book mistress.

But that bright, joyful woman, the woman who had a smile and buckets of patience, wasn't the one begging me to join her in my bed right now. The slightly heartbroken and fully drunk woman was asking, and there was a world of difference between the two.

Hard Pressed is available now!

ALSO BY KATE CANTERBARY

Standalone Novels

Coastal Elite
Before Girl

Talbott's Cove

Fresh Catch
Hard Pressed
Far Cry
Rough Sketch — arriving October 2019

Adventures in Modern Dating

The Magnolia Chronicles
The Ash Affair — arriving June 2020

The Walsh Series

Underneath It All – Matt and Lauren
The Space Between – Patrick and Andy
Necessary Restorations – Sam and Tiel
The Cornerstone – Shannon and Will
Restored — Sam and Tiel
The Spire — Erin and Nick
Preservation — Riley and Alexandra
Thresholds — The Walsh Family

Get exclusive sneak previews of upcoming releases through Kate's newsletter and private reader group, The Canterbary Tales, on Facebook.

ABOUT KATE

USA Today Bestseller Kate Canterbary writes smart, steamy contemporary romances loaded with heat, heart, and happy ever afters. Kate lives on the New England coast with her husband and daughter.

You can find Kate at www.katecanterbary.com

ACKNOWLEDGMENTS

You know who you are. You know what you did. You know I appreciate it more than any write-up in the back of a book can ever say.